Bitter Honey

Honeysuckle Love

"Honey is mighty sweet," Jed said, throwing one arm around Margaret's neck and drawing her down. His kiss was gentle and warm like the day itself, and the smell of what might have been honeysuckle drifted through the air. She lost herself in these sensations, and did not think beyond the moment. The whole day seemed turned to honey as they lay there, languidly embraced. It was something she had never known before.

Jed reached with thumb and forefinger to feel one of her dark curls. She gently rubbed at the flaking mud as it slowly dried on his face. When their lips came together again, it was as though neither willed it. But their lazy feelings warmed. She stroked the hard muscles of his browned back, while he pulled aside her bodice until the milky white breast was revealed under the heavy sun. His mouth sought the nipple. Deeply stirred, she moved her hips toward him.

"Oh, lady," he murmured painfully. "There's all this cloth between you and me." Smiling gently, without a second thought, or any thought at all, she slowly stripped herself of the calico gown until the two of them were as naked as Adam and Eve. . . .

BITTER HONEY

AVIS WORTHINGTON

PINNACLE BOOKS   LOS ANGELES

BITTER HONEY

Copyright © 1980 by Avis Worthington

An original Pinnacle Books edition, published for the first time anywhere.

First printing, March 1980

ISBN: 0-523-40573-1

Cover illustration by Norm Eastman

Printed in the United States of America

PINNACLE BOOKS, INC.
2029 Century Park East
Los Angeles, California 90067

Chapter One

It was a river unlike any she had seen before. Unbroken and oppressive forest, so wild that she might have been the first ever to view it, lined the shore. But the river served as a highway and had done so for years. Keelboats and flatboats drifted down past the *Belvidere* as it steamed upriver. At night a sudden flare from a boatman's torch would reveal a silent traveler.

This night there were no other boats in sight. Moonlight, unearthly in its brightness, shone down upon the steamboat deck. The air was pure here in America, unsullied by the smoke from hundreds of coal and wood fires that greyed the atmosphere at home.

Margaret Havershill loosened the cashmere shawl about her shoulders and watched the wide muddy waters of the Mississippi glide by. She stood out of view, in part of the gallery than ran around the passengers' cabins. She breathed a sigh of relief that the stout man in the checkered suit was well away in some other part of the vessel. He had plagued her journey upriver from the beginning by constantly watching her from different

1

vantage points on the *Belvidere*. Several times he had seemed about to speak, but she always avoided him. Something in his aspect was repugnant to her—not merely his moist, perspiring face, but his attitude, set her teeth on edge. Then, too, she was not yet used to the American way of striking up conversations with strangers.

Except for the fat man, Margaret felt great peace at this stage of her journey. She had left England in the first month of 1828 to sail seven weeks across the stormy Atlantic into the Mexican Gulf. She had seen the ocean waters merge with the muddy waters of the Mississippi where large flights of pelicans soared upwards, then landed on the flat muddy banks and sand bars. They were the only sign of life long before city or forest came into view. A pilot came out to guide them into New Orleans.

Bound now for Memphis, the closest river port to her sister's house, Athena Hall, Margaret had no very clear idea what would greet her at journey's end. This period of suspended time on the river, she suspected, might be one of the few serene interludes of her life. Lazier and more pleasure-loving than her sister Elena, Margaret had enjoyed this adventure so far. Elena would have her involved in worthwhile activity soon enough.

From the deck below, sounds of laughter and loud voices occasionally floated up. There were some hundred or so Kentucky flatboat men down on the lower deck, a rough bunch who drifted downriver, then sold their boats and cargos at New Orleans. The steamboat carried them upriver again. Margaret and the other passengers rested far above any contact with the hard-drinking, hard-gambling men below, but she had had occasional glimpses of them.

Then, out of the corner of her eye, Margaret saw the stout man appear on the gallery and her isolation became threatening rather than a refuge. He was well dressed, though his coat was patterned and loud and his

2

vest looked too tight for his bulk and too warm for his meaty body.

She turned so that the broad brim of her poke bonnet shielded her face and she avoided his eye. Instinctively she had known since her first glimpse of him that she would not like him. His footsteps drew nearer, then halted just behind her. Reluctantly she glanced back to survey him. At once he removed his high hat from his round, balding head and gave a slight bow. His portly body bent none too well.

Margaret automatically pulled back and leaned against the rail, saying nothing in response to his bow. Drunken cries from the men drifted up from below as she waited for him to speak or retire.

"Miss Havershill?"

Margaret felt a little shock. He knew her name. She turned to face him more directly.

"Why, yes. How do you know me?" she asked softly.

He stepped out of the shadows of the cabin into moonlight so bright that he cast a shadow himself. His eyes glistened.

"The resemblance to your sister is remarkable, though of course you are not so dark. For a while I wondered how it could be since I know—or thought—you were in England." He paused for a moment, then took out a large linen handkerchief and blew his nose. "The longer I watched you, the more I realized you could be no one else." The man sighed. "Yes, yes, you bring her plainly back to me. She would stand so straight, looking taller than the little woman she really was. She was so slim and proud with her black curly hair."

A slight breeze ruffled Margaret's brown curls as she stood watching him uneasily. She peered at him in the half light, startled at his choice of words—she *was* so slim? There seemed to be a pause in all the noises of the steamboat before she could bring herself to ask him to speak plainly.

3

"Was, sir? My sister is well, I hope?"

He lowered his voice to a sonorous level.

"I expect we are all well in our graves." He fixed his gleaming eyes upon her. "I'm sorry, but it is my duty to tell you."

Margaret felt her thoughts become confused. The round face before her swam in the strange light. The fat man seemed incorporeal. What on earth could this morbid man be saying? Again Margaret felt that pause in the world as though the *Belvidere* were suspended in time.

"Elena is dead?" she whispered. He could not mean it, not when he stood there so complacently, looking so triumphant. It must be some rustic frontier joke.

"Indeed, yes, though I warned her many a time . . ." The floating face nodded up and down.

"What are you trying to tell me?" Margaret cut in. "That my sister is dead?"

"I am sorry," the stout man said almost primly.

Feeling her vision blur, Margaret held her head in her hands for a moment, then looked up to stare at him with the full attention she had denied him since the beginning of the trip. She must try to see clearly. Elena had been the companion of her life since infancy. Surely she must be waiting upriver at Athena Hall. Not so long ago there had been four of them, the Havershill parents and daughters, with grand plans to make the world better and much laughter at their own grandiosity. Now, was it true that there was only she?

She shook her head slowly to order her thoughts and drive away waves of faintness. Theirs had never been a family that lost its self-possession. She must hear what this man was saying, if indeed Elena was dead.

"Excuse me, Miss Havershill," the stout man said in his flat accents, bowing again. His eyes seemed focused inwards on his own importance. In some way it seemed he had almost forgotten her. His oily voice was almost like an actor's. "My name is Edmund Blair. I conducted

4

the business affairs of your sister and of Athena Hall. I am a man of business, buying land, purchasing and banking for plantations, both in New Orleans and in Memphis—"

"Mr.—Blair. I cannot talk of banking at this moment. You tell me my only sister is dead. How did it happen?" She rubbed her fingers across her eyes. She was astounded that he could go on in such a self-important way when she was in such a state of shock. Shakily she sat down upon a dusty keg.

"Oh, I know Elena was slight, but she was really very strong and not prone to disease."

"No, no. It was not fever." Blair's words halted in a state of confusion. He raised himself on the balls of his feet, his stomach protruding under his waistcoat, then settled back again. He nervously rocked back and forth in this manner several times. "They found her lying on the floor of her bedroom."

Margaret nodded, sickly wishing him to continue.

"She was covered with blood."

"No," Margaret whispered faintly.

Warming to his subject, Mr. Blair ceased to rock.

"There was a dagger—I guess you would call it that. It looked to be old with a gold handle. It was quite small as though meant for a lady to carry. Someone had struck her through the throat."

Margaret was stunned by the picture his words drew—Elena with her dark curly hair disarranged, the folds of her light dress in disarray, blood, a dagger . . .

"Mr. Blair," she whispered, feeling herself tremble. "Who did it?"

Blair stood solid and foursquare on the deck, seeming very satisfied with his tale.

"Well, no one has admitted to it, though I can tell you I have suspicions of my own."

"Suspicions?" Margaret's lips were cold. Despite the warm night she pulled her shawl close about her now.

"The work your sister was doing at Athena Hall was

5

unnatural. I told her so many times. She was educating her own killers, I think. She and Henry Stanley didn't know how to keep their niggers in hand." He spoke rapidly, once again rocking on the balls of his feet. Margaret sensed a rising tide of anger—almost violence—behind his words.

"But you don't know who killed her." His judgment made her horror double, for she was a deep believer in their work at Athena Hall.

He admitted the truth of her opinion by shaking his head.

"Then please don't speak of it. If you'll excuse me. Please understand my shock and that I must be by myself for a while." She began to walk past him. His fat strong hand took her by the wrist. She resisted her impulse to shake herself free.

"We'll be in Memphis tomorrow afternoon, I guess. We'll have to take horses to ride to Athena Hall. It's fortunate we met each other. You are your sister's only heir." He fixed his glistening eyes upon her. "I want you to depend upon me, Miss Havershill."

Margaret nodded quickly, wrenching her arm from his moist, clinging hand. "Yes, yes. We will talk more later." She fled past him, past the men's cabin, to the ladies' cabin. She wanted to be free of all contact with him and to think about the horror he had described—to reconcile herself. It was also important to her that she not burst into tears where he could see. She had always been the weepy one of the family.

The cabin was full of women who were wide awake and anxious to speak to her in the almost overfriendly way Americans had. They took no notice of her breathless agitation.

"Miz Havershill, don't you think it mean of the men to keep us cooped up in the ladies' cabin here when we could be playin' cards or talkin' in the big cabin on a night like this?"

6

For some reason American ladies were not allowed in the men's cabin except at mealtime.

"Oh, pooh!" another lady cried. "All that smokin' and chewin' and spittin' tobacco! It's much nicer in here."

Margaret stood in the doorway looking at them and breathing in short gasps. She flashed a false smile at the three who shared the cabin with her, and then withdrew. She closed the door on the stale, sour smell of the cabin carpet. Carefully she found a section of the gallery out of sight of Edmund Blair and sat down on another keg. She leaned her head on the rail tiredly.

A thousand questions rushed to her mind. Tomorrow she must indeed speak again to Mr. Blair and learn more. She wished she could believe it to be a hideous mistake. But now thoughts and images raced through her mind—a dagger, a bloody dagger—too theatrical an object for the American wilderness—Elena, lying bloody and dead.

In life Elena had been known for her vitality. Now she must be buried near this great river that flowed so many miles from home. Margaret was the last of her family. She felt the tears well up as she looked upon the foreign landscape under the strange light of the moon. Across the river the forest rose up like a wall. Sometimes when they were close enough to shore she could see the white round discs of dogwood floating on branch ends—the beginnings of spring.

What had this foreign country to do with the civilized Havershills? Margaret clearly remembered a late afternoon some years back that had changed their lives. She had been about eighteen or nineteen, Elena about twenty. It was a dull November day. Margaret, full of thoughts and chatter from a visit with friends, hurried towards the family's solid brick house in Manchester. Her large shawl was wrapped tightly over her waist-length jacket. Under that she wore a thin fashionable dress. Vanity had made her leave her warm mantua at home. Her delicate, ribboned slippers, another vanity, did little to keep the chill from her feet.

Margaret burst in upon Elena and her father reading by the library fire. Father, an angular man, lay aside a leather-bound volume to greet her. Margaret felt her cheeks and hands burn as she stood as close to the glowing coals as possible. An old servant brought in the tea.

The room had a few pieces of elegant furniture, though the Havershills tended to be absent-minded about their surroundings. Elena reclined on a window seat with carved arm rests. She dropped her book on her lap and rubbed her eyes, for the light was growing dim. She looked properly classic as young ladies of their circle tended to look. Anything Greek or Roman was the rage, and had been since the time of the French Revolution. Elena wore her curls pulled back in the manner of a sculpted goddess from the Acropolis.

But Elena was far from cold marble. Her dark eyes danced, the corners of her mouth turned up with humor, as she gestured with a slim hand and began to declaim about the book she had been reading. Here was no passive scholar. The printed word spurred Elena to action. But in their own room the two young women often talked of passion and of love—although they were as yet inexperienced in these matters.

Just then Mama came in, plump, cheeks aflame from the cold. She sped to the fireside, discarding her bonnet, and began describing her charitable afternoon. The high-waisted matron's dress accentuated the round contours of her body. Mama's demeanor clashed with the classic pieces of furniture just as her selection of flowered paper on the walls did.

"There was a man there from America." Mama's dark shoe-button eyes turned from one to the other of them. Her black hair was pulled back from a high, round, ivory forehead. "And his descriptions of African slavery there were so dreadful that he made some of the ladies quite faint. It seems the more demand there is for cotton and tobacco, the more brutal the conditions of slavery become."

"Was that the Mr. Rogers that I heard last fall?" Elena asked.

"I believe it was," Mama replied. "He said there must be an end to slavery. I don't understand how one group of human beings can treat another so badly, but I'm not sure what we can do about it." She went then to close the heavy curtain to keep out the drafts. The candle sconces on the walls were already lit as well as an oil lamp on a table next to their father's upholstered chair.

"Thank goodness England has outlawed the slave trade," Margaret put in. "But slavers justify themselves everywhere else in the world by insisting that black Africans are of inferior mentality." She wrapped herself more securely in her big shawl and went to sit stiffly in a corner chair.

"Well, I am glad to see you think of some more serious problems than new dresses or drinking tea with your friends, Margaret," her sister said, "and you are quite right." Elena sprang to her feet and crossed the flowered carpet to stand by the fireside. She fixed a slice of bread on the toasting fork and held it over the fire, deep in thought.

"Indeed, yes, slavery must end. If I thought of a scheme against it, could this family carry it out?" she said at last.

"In cases like this, I generally begin by asking your mother," her father responded in his low and humorous voice.

"Whatever you think, dear," Mama replied vaguely.

The money in the family had come through Mama. Mr. Havershill had been a clergyman and a rather impecunious one at that. He courteously questioned his compliant wife whenever one of his charitable social projects was launched.

"I sense that my eldest daughter is about to urge us to some new venture." Mr. Havershill smiled through a cloud of pipe tobacco smoke. "I almost hesitate to ask what it might be."

Elena stood before them in her white muslin dress, her dark eyes flashing. She seemed not to feel the chill of the room as she tapped one toe impatiently, the hem of her skirts swinging just above her narrow ankle bone, as she lectured. The Grecian style of the day accentuated her slender throat and the gentle curve of her bosom.

"What we need is to provide a group of slaves with a European education. That would soon show the slave owners the arrogance of their ways."

Margaret felt herself caught up in her sister's enthusiasm.

"Yes! How well do they think they would do if the situation were reversed and the slavers kidnapped and set down suddenly in the middle of Africa," she said.

"You're surely not thinking of going to America, are you, my dear?" Mama asked Elena. "Leave a comfortable house for such a long journey? Why, a carriage trip to London exhausts me for a week after." She groped for her copy of Miss Austen's *Pride and Prejudice*, which she had read over and over again and was fond of discussing when the girls stopped talking of their own concerns.

"My dear young ladies." Their father looked at his daughters indulgently. "I am well nigh an old man. Here in England the spinning jenny and the power loom rob our weavers of their independence. Someone has to concern himself with the effect of the new factories on poor people's lives. Why, good craftsmen are become nothing but cogs in the great machine—reduced to pauperism. How can I take up a totally new cause—and in a country so wild and far away as America?

Here they were interrupted as the elderly woman servant came in once more to see how the tea was progressing.

"Does the Reverend Mr. Havershill want toast, then, after all? I do think you take a poor sort of tea."

"No, no, Mrs. Eames. No toast. And no Reverend. I have dropped that form of address for some years now, and I'd like you to remember it."

Mrs. Eames set her lips and departed. She did not approve of a clergyman who kept at such a distance from the church, and so took every opportunity to call him Reverend. But reversing the trend of most men, Mr. Havershill had become increasingly free-thinking with age. He did his current work for poor weavers and others although he had left the church.

Elena took up her idea again.

"Anyway, Mama and Papa, I intend to do something about educating and freeing black slaves if I can. You see, I believe we could apply some of the new theories the Swiss educator Pestalozzi is developing in Europe— a new kind of education entirely. He believes in combining studies and work. That way we could help the slaves buy their freedom."

"My dear, I shall leave all those problems in the capable hands of my progeny," her father replied. "And I pray that you will not have to travel too far from Manchester to accomplish your purpose."

"But do you think it a good purpose, Father?" Elena demanded.

"Of course, my dear. It is an excellent purpose."

Mama looked at them over *Pride and Prejudice* and nodded agreement.

It was not much later that her parents, ministering to a particularly wretched and miserable factory family, caught the disease that was to be their last. Though their two daughters labored through long nights to save them, their parents died on successive days.

11

At this time Margaret had depended upon Phillip, a young friend of hers, for consolation. They had talked listlessly of marriage but, both being free thinkers, they wanted to avoid this rather conventional state. Yet they were too much creatures of their times to become lovers, and so the passionate side of Margaret's nature remained unexpressed.

Henry Stanley, their father's assistant and another former clergyman, visited the young women often to recall with them the considerable good works of their parents and to discuss theories and issues of the day. He became an invaluable aid to them.

When their grief began to pass, Elena began to think more seriously of her American plan. She determined to set out. Henry Stanley, still mourning the loss of her father, his mentor, joined her in this venture.

Shortly upon her arrival in Tennessee, Elena had been able to buy a newly deserted plantation with a wood house built in the Greek style. This she had named Athena Hall, "because the goddess of wisdom was a woman," she wrote to her sister.

Margaret remained in England until she realized that what she and Phillip felt for each other was hardly love. A barrier always remained between them. Finally she had written a letter to Elena saying that she would leave in a month's time.

Perhaps Elena had never seen the letter, she thought wearily. The prospect of never seeing her again filled Margaret with such a feeling of bleak despair that she began to sob silently, conscious of the women in the cabin behind her. She could not bear to discuss it with anyone yet.

Beyond the railing, the river flowed as serenely as ever under the bright moon. The sight calmed her. Mile after mile of forest flowed by as the boat's paddle wheel turned steadily. She wrapped her shawl more tightly

12

about herself and began to study the problems that faced her.

There must be much business to settle at Athena Hall. The most important matter would be to discover how and why Elena had died. If the responsible person were to be found, he must be called to account for it.

Reason had become a sort of god to the Havershill family. Surely, Margaret thought, the scientific processes of reason could be addressed logically to the circumstances surrounding Elena's death and the matter of it understood. The waves of grief that threatened to engulf her might be soothed into some sort of peacefulness if her mind was to be involved with problems concerning Elena.

Elena had been the daring one of the daughters, the most brilliant of the entire family. Margaret, more slothful and passive, must now take on some of her sister's qualities. She sighed, wishing for a moment that Phillip was with her.

Her thoughts returned to Elena's mysterious death. One thing that puzzled her immediately was the dagger. Who in Tennessee would carry such an unusual weapon?

Behind her in the cabin the women's voices gradually faded away as they lay themselves down to sleep. Now and then sounds of the men roistering down below drifted up, as she knew they would far into the night. The moonlight was awesome, its bright light bathing the decks and the wilderness beyond. The more tropical foliage around New Orleans was left far behind. No sign of habitation appeared upon the shores, though occasional blossoms from wild cherry or trees less familiar to her flared out from the darker areas along the banks. How Elena must have loved the sight!

What was it the repulsive Mr. Blair had said? "She was educating her own killers." Oh, surely not. With great sorrow Margaret determined that if at all possible

13

the experiment must be saved and protected from slander. Elena could not have her life snuffed out without some monument left to her.

Rising to her feet with a jagged sigh, Margaret went inside to lay herself down for the night.

Chapter Two

In the morning Margaret and the other ladies went into the men's cabin for breakfast. Cheery bright sunlight streamed in through the windows. The men's cots were neatly made up out of the way of the breakfasters.

The gentlemen were discussing whether or not Jackson would be elected this time to the presidency and what a shame it was that John Quincy Adams had stolen the last election from their fellow Westerner. A traveling judge with grease spots on his vest argued with particular vehemence in favor of Jackson's claims to the highest office in the land.

At any other time Margaret would have taken considerable interest in this conversation, but that morning she had no heart for it. Her eyes felt red and puffy, though she had cried for only a brief period of the night. The din of the men's booming voices and the shrill chatter of the ladies grated on her ears. Though the men represented the upper levels of frontier society, their table manners were crude. The favored utensil for conveying food to the mouth seemed to be the knife.

Chewing and spitting tobacco was a universal habit. Margaret pushed her plate aside. All the same, she berated herself for being so delicate and such a snob.

At that moment Edmund Blair eased his bulk through the door. He nodded to her tersely, then sat and began to help himself vigorously to the food.

"Isn't that Edmund Blair?" Margaret's neighbor Alice Simpson whispered, her eyes wide.

"I believe so," Margaret answered.

"My husband says he's a thief and a blackguard," Mrs. Simpson said.

"He's going to conduct me to my sister's house from Memphis," Margaret told her.

"Well, my husband wouldn't let me walk down the same side of the street as him in New Orleans." Mrs. Simpson's eyes were bright and birdlike. Her hair was arranged in an elaborate style that overpowered her thin neck and body. "I'd be very careful if I were you—a little thing like yourself so far from home."

Margaret did not explain to her that Mr. Blair had told her she no longer had any close family in this world.

"When do you think we'll arrive in Memphis?" she asked instead, smoothing her skirts with open palms, trying to quiet her spirit as well.

"The captain expects it'll be early afternoon." Mrs. Simpson raised one finger delicately as she brought her fork to her thin lips. Her manners were in marked contast to the men's.

The steamboat slowed to take on wood, and Margaret went to the ladies' cabin for her poke bonnet. It was already too warm and bright for her shawl.

She was no sooner out on the passengers' gallery that formed a second layer over the deck below, than she caught sight of Mr. Blair coming toward her. She swallowed nervously as she made up her mind to meet him resolutely. After all, he had much to tell her. He must have been at Athena Hall at the time of Elena's death

16

since he seemed familiar with the circumstances and could describe the dagger.

Edmund Blair reached her side, swept his high hat off his perspiring forehead, and bowed. The checked pattern of his coat was particularly vexing.

"Miss Havershill. Perhaps we can talk about the will."

"I would far rather, if you don't mind, talk about Elena's death." Margaret determined to put her most depressing thoughts aside and pursue the work to be done. She forced herself to gaze at him steadily.

"I told you already," Blair said with some impatience. "She was stabbed through the throat. And with a fairly strange knife at that."

"A dagger, you said."

"Yes, a pointy thing. The handle was gold and elaborate." There was a bemused smile on Blair's round face.

"But who in Tennessee would carry such a weapon?" Margaret sighed. There seemed no logic to this whole affair.

"No one. It's nothing we would use around here. It looked quite old when I think about it."

"I don't believe I've ever seen a dagger in my life, outside the theatre."

"Folks around here don't go for the kind of bookish notions your sister had. Nor do they spoil their niggers. Nor do they own gold knives to kill people with."

He was making the very weapon that killed Elena seem a bad reflection on her character. Margaret turned to look over the rail. Some of the Kentucky men were jumping ashore to load on wood. A few vaulted over each other's heads leapfrog-style, uttering wild cries. Margaret watched a bony tanned man with flaming red hair swinging down onto the makeshift dock to attack the woodpile. He wore high moccasins, deerskin breeches and a rough woven shirt.

The woodcutter's thin and almost hag-like wife emerged from the door of their shack to smile a tooth-

17

less smile at all the excitement. It appeared that life on the river bank had done nothing for her health. Her cheekbones stood out. Her skin had a yellowish tinge. The woodcutter himself was a dark-haired, vigorous man who, since he had all his teeth, seemed younger than his wife. A swarm of large-eyed, sallow-complected children crawled over the woodpile.

"Whoo-ee!" the Kentucky men yelled as they scrambled ashore, then tossed the cut wood on the deck of the *Belvidere*. They paid for part of their passage with this work.

Margaret watched all this activity with only part of her attention.

"Who on earth in Tennessee would kill her?" She did not shift her gaze to Blair. Her lips were stiff. She concentrated her will on not breaking down into tears.

"Who? I have my own idea who." These words were spoken so venomously that Margaret turned to look at him. His face was shiny; his eyes bore a light that was knowing, hating, and sensual all at once. As he fought to recover his self-possession, he rocked once more upon the balls of his feet.

Margaret turned away from the repulsive emotions revealed so nakedly and watched the clean movements of the muscular men below as they formed a human chain to pass the wood along.

"Never mind the Kentucky men below. They're where they belong—under a lady's feet. Your sister stooped low enough."

"What do you mean?" He was always forcing her to look back at him.

"Your sister was with child when she died, my dear."

"With child?" Margaret was too startled to challenge his familiarity. Her cheeks flamed. The man had mangled the story of Elena's death, oblivious to the shock he had given Margaret. Now it seemed he was pawing over the remains.

A child! Could it be true? She studied the florid face

18

she was learning to loathe. If Elena truly had been pregnant it must have been because she had fallen in love. This man delighted in making things ugly.

Oh, if only she could talk with her sister. Elena had written nothing to her of love.

"How can you possibly know what you say?" she demanded.

"Maria, one of the black women, told me."

"Maria?" She had heard Elena speak of Maria as an admirable woman. She had been the first slave involved in the educational project and Elena counted her a friend. Surely Maria would not lie about such a thing. If Margaret discovered the truth about the child, would the story be as ugly as Elena's death? Whatever the truth, she must not avoid it.

"If it is true," Margaret said hesitantly, "then who—"

"Fathered the brat?"

Margaret winced.

"I told you she was educating her own murderer. Some of the people here in Tennessee might have been a little angry if they knew what your sister was up to."

"But you don't really know what happened, do you, Mr. Blair? You seem to be thinking very nasty thoughts, I must say. And explain why Maria would tell you something that could bring trouble to her people? I've heard enough of slavery in this country to know what kind of difficulties this would cause. No, I think you're a liar, Mr. Blair."

The logic and force of her words seemed to stop him for a moment.

"Perhaps she was jealous," he murmured unconvincingly after a while. "But Maria said it for a fact and your sister had the big-eyed, soft-faced look of a woman carrying young."

"And you, Mr. Blair, where were you when my sister was killed?" she pursued.

"Me? Why, I was downstairs."

"And did anyone see you there?"

19

"I was alone."

"And you heard or saw nothing?"

"No. I'd drunk a bit of whiskey and fallen asleep after my trip."

Margaret paused as she felt the steam engine start up. The Kentucky men jumped aboard and cast off with many a yell and a curse. The paddle wheel began its insistent rhythm and the boat headed for midstream, dodging snags in the shallow water near the shore.

"If you please, Mr. Blair. Tell me exactly what happened from the moment you arrived at Athena Hall. And how long ago was it?"

Blair sat down on a keg and stretched out his heavy trousered legs. His feet in their shiny boots looked small at the end of all his bulk. With one hand he pushed his high hat farther back on his pink forehead, uncovering more of his bald spot.

"It was a couple of months ago, I guess. I rode out from Memphis and got to Athena Hall just as Henry Stanley was leaving to go upriver. I cautioned him to hurry because the *Criterion* was docked overnight to leave at dawn. There might not be another boat for several days. So we had only time enough to exchange a couple of words before he hurried away on the livery horse I'd brought. He thought it would be well after dark when he got to Memphis and that's hard traveling hereabouts."

"So he was gone." Margaret paused to think a moment before going on. "So you were there and Maria and the other Africans. And who else?"

"Probably no one. Athena Hall is not like New Orleans. Not many people stop by in a year."

Margaret's heart sank. This nasty man's suspicions must not prove true. Perhaps it would all seem clearer in Athena Hall.

"Well, then, you were asleep. And where was my sister?"

"They found her in her room upstairs."

"Who found her?"

"Jason, Maria's man."

"Her what?"

"Her husband, if you want to call it fancy."

"And what did he say?"

"Jason is not a good talker. He's not long from Africa. Maria generally talks for him."

"And that is all you know?"

"That is all I know for certain." He eyed her with arrogance.

Margaret reflected that none of the free-thinking young people she knew at home would behave with such familiarity or nastiness.

"But you did see my sister alive before you fell asleep downstairs?"

"I did. She was full of spunk for a fact. We had a few sharp words."

"I shall have to question the others, of course."

"Question away." Blair doffed his hat and split his moon face with a smile that seemed shark-toothed rather than warm. "Now, if you don't mind, I'll tell you what it was your sister left you."

"I would far rather attend to it at Athena Hall where I can study the papers."

Blair looked astounded.

"Oh, come now. It's nothing a lady would want to read."

Margaret adjusted the ribbons on her bonnet, looking at him coldly all the while.

"Surely you must know my sister would have. And so shall I."

By now they were moving steadily away from the bank and edging out to midstream. But all conversation stopped suddenly when the steamboat shuddered and a grating sound was heard.

"Snag! Snag!" they heard the men below cry out.

"I think we're aground!" someone else yelled.

The door of the captain's cabin burst open and he ran out, hitching up his trousers.

"Fools! Didn't I tell you to look sharp!"

A couple of the Kentucky men leapt into the water, moccasins and all, to look the situation over. They stood up to their waists in the river. One man hung his moccasins about his neck before he jumped, slipping a packet of what appeared to be money or papers inside one and binding it with a lace of leather or deerskin. Strangely, he wore a shirt of good quality, though without a stock, of course. Otherwise it would have been hard to distinguish him from the other lean tan men who had been lounging on the sunny deck after their revels of the night before. His dark brown hair was roughly cut. There was stubble on his chin. He rolled up his sleeves and joined the others.

From the lower deck they were pushing poles into the mud. The men on shore were cutting branches and saplings to try to free the bottom.

"Looks pretty bad, Captain," shouted the man whose brown hair looked as though it had been hacked off with a hunting knife. Margaret could hear no answer from the captain.

Before he could shout again the man's glance fell upon Margaret. Though he stood some distance from the gallery, Margaret was sure that he turned pale. It was the likeness to her sister, she thought. From that distance she must look even more like Elena. He must somehow have known her. He remained like that, staring upwards, his blue eyes perfectly serious as though he was remembering something that saddened him. Nevertheless, Margaret felt moved by the sight of him as she had never been by Phillip's well-tailored looks. Finally, embarrassed, Margaret turned to ask Blair who he was.

"A rover with an eye for the ladies, no doubt," Blair said.

"But he looks as though he's seen a ghost. I'm sure he must have known Elena."

The man indeed seemed ready to discard his pole and had one hand reaching up to a rope to climb back up onto the deck. But he was discouraged by a sudden slap on the back from the broad hand of the red-haired man. With that he began work in earnest along with the others.

Edmund Blair drifted off to ask the captain when they might expect to reach Memphis. Some of Margaret's fellow passengers appeared at her side to watch the work and comment on it, only to disappear again and go into the cabins. But Margaret felt she could not leave the gallery in case the man who had gawked at her so might appear again. She might find some way to speak to him. She finally did spy him wading out to the bank to cut more poles, an axe held high above his head out of the water. His moccasins were still about his neck. As he came back he looked up and stared at her once more. At the same time Alice Simpson joined Margaret. She, too, looked down at the man.

"Why, that Kentucky man seems half out of his wits staring at you thataway," she said.

"Would you know who he is?" Margaret questioned.

"Him? He's just one more frontier wanderer. There's hundreds like him. A no-good bunch for sure."

"I thought Americans considered everyone to be equal," Margaret smiled. She had heard about this equality and how no man was better than any other daily since the beginning of her voyage up the river. It was the topic of much conversation. This philosophy suited her well enough, but she wondered how much real truth there was to it.

"Lots of them are Irishmen or Ulstermen at least. They do flare up if you call them Irish. Scotch-Irish is what you should say, I guess."

"And how do they differ from other men?"

"They're wilder. They never stay in one place very

23

long. They shun hard regular work, wander from place to place, squatting now and then, but never staying long enough to make a regular farm. They love to hunt, though, so Tennessee and Kentucky are a paradise to them, game is so common."

"But I thought these men were boatmen."

"Most of these here are. But they're all drifters and wanderers and movers along the river and in the backwoods."

"Movers? Don't they ever marry?"

"Some do, and they wear their women out soon enough." Alice covered her mouth and lowered her voice to a whisper. "Some of the men and women live together in the backwoods for years without ever seeing a preacher."

Margaret looked down at the man who by this time was working alongside his fellows, prodding into the mud, the muscles of his back straining under his good linen.

"Well, I would like a word with that man," Margaret said.

"Why, whatever for?" Alice asked with surprise.

"I think he may have known my sister."

Alice looked at her blankly. Just in time Margaret remembered that the good Mrs. Simpson knew nothing of Elena's death, nor the scandalously dramatic nature of it. She reflected, too, that the educational experiment at Athena Hall might confuse and upset this Western woman. The idea that had seemed simple enough in England was indeed radical here.

"The captain would never allow a rough fellow like that up here to speak to a lady," Alice said. "I really wonder at the company you choose to keep."

"Company I keep? Oh, I see, you mean Mr. Blair. Believe me, I did not choose him. Unfortunately it seems that I am stuck with him until I reach Athena Hall. But what I want from this other man is merely some information."

24

"Well, I hope you know what you're about. I could ask my husband's servant to carry a message. He sleeps down below with those men, though from what I hear no one sleeps much down there."

"Servant?" Margaret had thought that blacks were the servants for well-to-do New Orleans families.

"He does everything from acting as clerk to running errands for the family. He's on the way to learn the business."

"Well, could you have him ask that gentleman why the sight of Miss Havershill causes him to look as though he'd seen a ghost and what he knows of my sister?"

"He did look as though he'd seen a ghost, didn't he?" Alice Simpson said thoughtfully, studying the handsome man below.

"Can you do it?" Margaret insisted.

"Well, I don't see why not." Alice spoke uncertainly.

"And I would just as soon we kept this from Mr. Blair."

Alice nodded her elaborately bonneted head.

"How mysterious. But I can well understand how you must feel about Mr. Blair."

At this the ladies withdrew towards the cabin, for rain clouds had begun scudding across the sky and a few drops spattered the deck. Inside Margaret peered out the small porthole, the rain splashing the window. It was irritating not to know what was going on down at the river level. The ladies lay down on their bunks to rest during the length of this frustrating delay. Margaret dozed, her spirits beginning to mend after the strong emotions of the past day. She awoke suddenly after dreaming of Elena cuddling in her arms an infant whose face she could not see.

Margaret could hear the men outside shouting and feel the boat shudder and then break free of its restraints. A cheer went up.

"What happened?" she called out.

Alice Simpson stood in the gloomy interior near the window.

"Another steamboat's towed us off."

"It feels like we're drifting downstream."

"We probably are."

Then the boat seemed to shake itself and they heard the sound of the engine starting up. The two women smiled at each other as they felt the paddle wheel turn and the *Belvidere* head for midstream. Through the drenching rain beyond the window the two women could see the blurred white shape of another steamboat. Margaret went to the door to see if she could catch a glimpse again of the man who had roused her curiosity, but the driving rain forced her back.

Of course they had not made Memphis by that afternoon and evening found them all seated together again in the men's cabin for their meal.

"Well, we can thank our lucky stars that we haven't blown up at least," a jovial man said. "You never know when to expect the boilers to explode on these confounded steamboats."

Margaret did not find this thought cheering.

The door burst open and two drenched men entered, the rather stern looking Mr. Simpson and his meek, indeed cowering, employee, Peters. Margaret flushed. She hated to try to conduct such a sensitive conversation under such public circumstances. Mr. Simpson's employee was led over to her. He fixed frightened brown eyes upon her as she began to question him in a hushed voice. She glanced up now and then to find Blair's eyes upon her.

"I want to ask you about a man down on the deck," she began.

"Oh, it's terrible down there." The cowering man grew pale at the thought of the place he had just left. "They drink and gamble all night long and curse worse than any men I've ever seen. The steamboat clerk tried to find me a berth near him and told me never to part from my watch or my money."

Margaret persisted. "This man is a brown haired man dressed very much like the others, only with a very fine linen shirt."

"I know the one." Peters looked even more frightened. "He has a good riding coat, too, bundled up with his blanket."

"Yes?" Margaret said encouragingly.

"Someone tried to open his bundle while he was on shore for wood, and when he discovered the one who'd done it, I thought for sure blood would flow." The man hesitated, shivering. "They're a lot of brutes down there. The man yer askin' for, Jed, they call him, pulled a great long knife and held it at the other one's throat until he was down on his hands and knees begging for mercy. I thought there'd be a brawl for sure. Jed has some money and some papers he carries, but he keeps them tied in his moccasins about his neck when he has to go in the water."

Margaret nodded. It must indeed be the same man.

"Could you take a message for me to this gentleman?"

"Oh, indeed, missus, he ain't no gentleman. He might cut my throat if I went near 'um." The poor man began backing away from her in his distress.

"Ask him . . ." Conscious of the interest of her fellow passengers, Margaret lowered her voice, while keeping it as forceful as she dared. "No, tell him that Miss Havershill wants to know what he can tell her of her sister."

Peters looked at her oddly for a moment, then shook his head.

"I'd rather not talk to those men, Miss."

Margaret looked at him with irritation. What a frightened little man! She reached into her reticule for a coin to give him. As she pressed it into his hand, she bent close enough to whisper, "After we have finished supper, I shall come down."

The man looked at her with wildly frightened eyes, his mouth working convulsively as though he would say something. Then he turned and fled.

"Well," Alice Simpson remarked at her side. "Your sister does seem to be acquainted with some strange men. First Edmund Blair, and now this river man."

"My sister is dead, Mrs. Simpson. I have only just discovered the fact on this voyage. She is acquainted with no one any more." Margaret almost wished she could take back her sharp words as she saw Alice Simpson's face grow blank with shocked surprise.

"Oh, my poor dear, I didn't know," Alice said.

"Nor did I until a day ago."

"How did it happen?"

"I'd rather not talk about it until I can go to Athena Hall and discover more," Margaret said. But as they went together to the ladies' cabin she saw Alice watching her with intense curiosity and not a little disapproval.

Margaret gathered her things together, since they must surely reach Memphis soon. After a while the women began chattering about people they knew in New Orleans. Then Alice Simpson discovered that she was missing a glove. They all began a frantic search. At this point Margaret stepped out upon the gallery.

Suddenly she wondered if she was acting wisely. She knew that the captain would be furious if he discovered her below deck. There was no denying that the men down there were wild; she could hear the noise of their roistering day and night. But she had feared no man in her life—even when she worked among some of the poorer and rougher objects of her father's charity. They had respected her for who she was. When she reached the lower deck she could search out Peters to help her. He could at least find Jed.

She must have this chance, she thought, biting her

lip. After Memphis there would not be another. She must somehow learn whose hand had stabbed Elena. It was even remotely possible that Jed himself had done it. But a drifter, a frontiersman with a gold dagger? It was unlikely. He wore a shirt of fine linen, but that hardly meant he would own a weapon so valuable and so old as the dagger.

The dismal weather oppressed her spirits. Rain was still falling heavily. Only for Elena would she venture forth like this. Briefly she considered returning for her parasol, but it was designed more for sun than for rain. She wrapped her cashmere shawl more tightly over her bonnet and traveling dress.

As she passed the captain's cabin she heard his voice boom out. She shrank back for a moment. Then she perceived that all the steamboat sailors were too intent upon their work to notice her. Quickly she crept to the head of the ladder-like stairs, hoping her skirts wouldn't trip her as she descended.

The Kentucky men for the most part were supposed to sleep on the deck. They were, after all, used to an outdoor life. The steady downpour had driven them back against the cabin walls near the boilers and wood-piles. It was a bleak scene, barely lit by candles shining through the windows and a few lanterns on the deck itself.

Margaret peered carefully down through the opening to the lower deck to spy someone who could direct her to Peters. The men down below were slightly quieter than they had been when the weather was clear. She could see glimpses of the red hair of the man she had noticed when the boat was snagged. He knew Jed, she remembered. Perhaps the redhead would lead her either to Jed or to Peters.

She descended slowly on the wet ladder, framing a question in her mind. Suddenly she felt a rough hand close about her ankle. She gasped with horror. Chuckling laughter floated up to her as she tried to kick herself free. She could barely see the redhead's freckled face with its loose grin that revealed a missing tooth in front. Flushing with rage, she kicked more furiously. She felt her thin slipper skid on the wet stair, then lost her balance and started to fall backwards. In an instant the redheaded man had reached up and grabbed a handful of her well-wrapped shawl. He let her feet drop to the deck. Dizzy from the impact, she caught her breath in shock and anger.

One of the other men, laughing, ran forward with a lantern to see the fun. By its light she saw the redhaired man's yellowish eyes gleaming close to her face. Though he smiled, it was malicious. He was amused at her helplessness. She was a mere object in his arms.

A sharp wave of fear swept over her. In all her protected life she had never been in such a perilous situation. She could not comprehend that this strange man would manhandle her person and that all these others crowding the deck would merely stand and watch.

Smirking, he brought his face closer to her until it blotted out the dim light as he pressed a whiskey-soaked kiss on her lips. For all his skinny body, his lips felt full and bloated. He forced his tongue into her mouth. Margaret fought to turn her head aside. To thwart her, he placed one hand behind her head.

The men roared with laughter as Margaret struggled to free herself, but the redhead only held her closer, half supporting her. After a minute of nauseous close embrace, he threw his head back to look at her wildly confused face. The sour whiskey smell was so strong that Margaret gagged.

Catching her breath, she pleaded with the men who stared at her.

"Please, I am looking for Peters." Her eyes swept the crowded deck, looking for some aid. There seemed to be hundreds of faces staring at her, some plainly lit, some lost in the shadows. Several were flushed and red-eyed, their mouths stretched in grotesque, drunken grins. Some wore rags, some homespun, some deerskin, or a combination of all these. Many of them were handsome, standing straighter than working men in England. The entire deck reeked of liquor and sweat. One thin dark man stared with eyes that were black and fanatic. Some of the faces looked almost kindly, but hesitant and confused.

A tow-headed boy of about 16 stood behind the man who still clutched her in his arms. He was the first to relent.

"Aw, let her go, Davy. She's a nice lady. Let her go."

"Awr, a nice lady. Just what we need to pass a rainy night," her assailant said in a husky high voice. He stroked her rain dampened cheek with one hand. He was thin and wiry as the Kentucky men tended to be. His arms wound closer about her like steel.

"Do let me go!" Margaret insisted, trying to twist away from him. Instead, Davy placed one callused hand over her mouth. His body smelt of old whiskey and sweat. He chuckled again.

"Can't you boys do something besides fuss and fight and cause trouble?" someone called from the crush of bodies near the boilers.

"Next time I'm walkin' back," another said with disgust.

There was a low babble of voices and the splashing sound of the turning paddle wheel. The steady pound of the rain and of the engine muffled sounds farther away. Her heart sank. Even if she could scream, the captain would not pick out her voice from all other noises. But she could only make pitiful muffled bleats. And what would the captain do if he did find out she had broken the rules?

A grizzled man of some sixty years pushed his way into the circle, the lantern light glistening on drops of rain in his beard. She wondered if she could appeal to the older man in some way.

31

"Let's all have a turn, now, Davy. Pass 'er around, there's a friend!"

Oh my God! She could not bear it. Lifting her slippered foot she aimed a kick at Davy's shin. It affected him not at all. He merely jerked her head back in punishment.

"I ain't had all mine yet." Davy laughed gleefully and freed her mouth long enough to kiss her again. She felt as though she were choking. His thin brown hands were hard upon her shoulders and she was hampered by the long shawl. Her bonnet slipped back and hung by its ribbons.

Davy pulled her still closer and his lips blew hot. The sour taste of whiskey engulfed her. He freed one hand and plunged it down past the folds of the soft wool shawl to the neck of her traveling dress. Finding the sturdy material too resistant, he jerked at the cloth at her throat. Margaret felt two buttons give way as his rough hands groped towards the softness of her full breasts.

"Here, now, Davy. I ain't had mine yet," a voice behind them said. Davy looked up and Margaret took the chance to jerk away from him, choking for breath in fear and anger and disgust. She breathed deeply, preparing to scream.

Then over Davy's shoulder she stared into the face of the man she sought. His expression was quizzical.

The old man standing beside them snickered.

"Oh, I dunno, Jed. You always has women enough. Yer a frontier hellion."

"But I ain't had this 'un," Jed said, dashing any of her hopes that he might somehow help her.

"He's dressed like a lover—fine shirt, face washed." The old man cackled again.

"She's mine, you rascal." Davy staggered back drunkenly. "I catched her."

Half laughing, Jed pulled on her arm until she was free of Davy. She watched him, wide-eyed, as his browned face and laughing eyes drew closer and he enclosed her in his strong arms to kiss her. His sensual lips were gentle upon hers. He had been drinking some like the rest of them, and he had not spoken like an ally, yet Margaret felt strangely reassured by his caress. After a moment he released her and their eyes met.

"Atta boy, Jed," the old man called. "That's a real lover."

Davy bent to take a swig from a whiskey jug. The smell from the jar was so raw that Margaret wrinkled her nose in disgust. Trembling, she gauged the distance to the stairs. If only this Jed would help her. The rain pelted the *Belvidere* with unbelievable ferocity, much of it sweeping across the deck.

Davy set the whiskey jug down again. He reached a cold wet hand out for her arm, paining a spot already bruised.

"All right, Jed. You've had yer turn," he said. "Now she's mine."

Margaret tried to speak firmly, but was conscious that her lips were shaking. "I-I demand that you let me go," she said, backing away.

"Come on, boys," the youth said with anxiety. "Let her go now."

"I ain't through yet, either." Fixing a hard look upon the redhead, Jed reached out to grasp Margaret's arm to pull her his way. Margaret gasped in fear, wondering if they would rip her apart between them.

"Now, Jed," the redhead whined. "I ain't had a woman in a long time." His gaptoothed mouth opened in a beseeching grin.

Jed dropped her arm suddenly. His hand went to the waist of his deerskin breeches where a knife was belted. In an instant it was in his hand, point upwards, and he stood back, half crouching, facing Davy.

"All right, I'll fight you for her, Davy," he challenged. The light of the lantern gleamed on the naked hunting knife—a knife too long for ordinary purposes. The men around the two drew back, dragging Margaret with them, crushing her back towards the rail. Some of them called out bets on one or the other of the Westerners as though it was a cock fight.

"Jed'll kill 'um," one said. "The fool's dead drunk."

Margaret nervously placed a hand over her lips. The men pressed against her, unconsciously, caught up in the barbaric scene.

"Here, now, Jed." Davy's hand went unsteadily to where he wore his own knife. "Why, you know I'm half horse, half alligator. I kin whip my weight in wildcats! Can't I, boys?"

"Yeah," someone said unenthusiastically.

"I'm spilin' fer a fight, Jed. I ain't had one for more'n a week. I'm a poor man—that's a fact—and smell like a wet dog—but I can't be run over!"

Davy's defiant speech was slurred, but despite his drunkenness he had his knife drawn and lunged towards Jed in one motion. Blood dripped down the sleeve of Jed's fine linen shirt.

The two men circled warily, half crouched. There were flashes of orange hair as Davy lunged again and again. Each time Jed neatly evaded him. They used their knives like swordsmen. To Margaret it looked much more primitive. Suddenly as Davy lunged once more, Jed shot out a foot to trip him as he went past. The men watching hooted and howled. Davy skidded on the wet deck. His body went limp and sodden and collapsed.

A tremendous roar went up from the men.

Jed bent quickly to scoop up the knife, then thrust Margaret back against the wall near the stairs. Davy could no longer menace her. He lay in a heap on the deck in the rain, more a victim of whiskey than of Jed's skill. He would not rise again until he was sober.

Margaret fought to recover her self-possession. She must try to make her way through this mass of men. She looked over to see the cabin door open a crack and

Peters looking out fearfully. She could see that she could count on no help from him. Still further along, frozen against the wall, a weasle-faced man stood grasping bundle.

"Hey, Jed." The young boy had seen the same thing. "Look, 'Zekial's got your bundle again!"

Jed paused for an instant, holding a knife in each hand, then flung the one from his left, pinning the thief to the wall. With a cry, the man dropped his plunder and tore himself loose.

"Well, I'll be—you're as good with one hand as t'other," the old man chuckled.

Jed shook his head, grinning. "Doesn't usually work." He looked about for Margaret. Spotting her, he pulled her from the crowd, the men parting to make way. Jed grabbed her by the arm and pushed her before him up the ladder. Margaret shivered in her soaking shawl, weak with relief to feel the steps beneath her feet. Jed's hand was beneath her elbow, firmly aiding her to the upper deck.

At the top of the stairs he pulled her aside. It was dark, but Margaret had a sense that he was laughing at her. He bent to kiss her lightly on the forehead, then shoved her in the direction of the ladies' cabin.

"Miss Havershill, I think you'd be better off up here."

"But I must talk to you," she said in a low voice, glancing at the captain's door.

"The captain will throw me in the river if he finds me up here, and the men will think I've ravished you." Quickly Jed began his descent.

"But I risked my safety to come look for you," Margaret cried in despair.

His head was just disappearing from view, but he grasped the edge of the deck over his head and swung himself back up. From the flickering light of the lantern below, she could see his grin.

"We'll meet again, Miss Havershill," he said. "Don't

be surprised if we do." He was gone before she could say more.

Rain blown onto the gallery plastered stray curls onto her forehead. Dripping wet she made her way past the captain's door praying she wouldn't catch a fever. Now she knew why the captain kept the sexes separate on his Mississippi steamboat.

She never wanted such an experience again. She had always been protected. Phillip had kissed her with respect and friendship—a lukewarm kiss at best. The crude, insistent, whiskey-soaked kiss of Davy was worlds away from that.

Jed's kiss was something else again. Her face grew hot. She told herself not to go mooning after a stranger. Yet she could not banish the memory of the hard muscled body beneath the rain-soaked shirt. But he had laughed at her—grinned continually through the whole agonizing scene. His eyes twinkled and his teeth gleamed in the lantern light. And then he had bent towards her and—well, she would think of Jed's kiss later. To be sure he had rescued her—but he seemed to have enjoyed some aspects of the work all too well and taken his time about it. He had no right to unsettle her so. And she—well, her cheeks burned at the memory, for it was a sweet kiss that moved her deeply despite the onlookers. She knew she would like to be held by those arms again.

If only she had Elena to talk to about these new and confused feelings. She bit her lip to keep from weeping at the thought.

It was not until midnight and in a pouring rain that they reached Memphis and disembarked.

Chapter Three

Memphis in the dead of night, deluged with rain, was a disappointment, to say the least. They were greeted by a man from the hotel with a lantern that threatened to blow out at any moment. The riverbank smelled of wet weeds and mud. So few lights broke the darkness that it was difficult to determine the size of the town.

As they disembarked Peters had fixed a frightened glance at her, then looked away. She was sure he disapproved of her heartily and wanted no contact with anyone so liable to bring trouble.

Margaret was disappointed that there was no further sight or word of Jed. She had no knowledge of his destination. For all she knew he might have left the boat downriver. Though he'd said they'd meet again, he did not join the party headed towards the inn. Overwhelmed as she was with curiosity, she wanted to speak to the man under more ordinary circumstances the next time. The scene on the lower deck of the *Belvidere* had shaken and unnerved her, yet she could not get his face with its quizzical smile, his body pressed against hers, out of her mind.

The town stood on top of a bluff and the road was new and seemingly bottomless when one set foot on its muddy surface. Margaret slipped twice, muddying her skirts and mantua and losing one shoe entirely. She was a sorry sight, she knew.

The black man carrying her trunk bound upon his back also fell several times until Margaret despaired of the condition of all her belongings, not to mention the poor man himself. Mr. Simpson and Peters were aiding Alice as best they could, she shrieking several times with dismay as she sank into the quagmire. Then that party broke away toward Alice's brother's house in town, Simpson cursing that he had no horse.

Margaret, by nature a tidy, modest person, hesitated to present herself to the innkeeper, especially in the company of Edmund Blair, with two buttons ripped from her dress and her hem muddied. The proprietress stood in the open door of the plank building, one hand shielding a candle which was flickering wildly. She was a tall woman of ample dimensions and looked down sternly at the travelers climbing towards her.

"Halloo, Mrs. Johnson," Blair called to her. "We need hot water and good dry beds."

"Mr. Blair, is it?" Mrs. Johnson questioned sourly.

"And Miss Havershill."

"Miss Havershill?" Mrs. Johnson was obviously startled. "Oh? The sister, I suppose."

Margaret said nothing at all, only followed them all inside, thankful to be sheltered.

The house was new, smelling of fresh mortar, and rather bare. Mrs. Johnson surveyed her with disapproval. Margaret was not sure whether it was because she was covered with mud or because of her relationship to her sister and Edmund Blair. And she felt ridiculous traipsing in with one slipper.

She was lucky enough to obtain a small chamber to herself. Mrs. Johnson brought hot water and towels. Nothing in her life had seemed so glorious, she thought as she bent over the plain wood washstand. She would hang her dress on a peg, hoping it would dry enough so that she could brush the mud from it, if indeed it was not beyond repair. The buttons would be easy enough to replace. Her shawl she could drape over the end of the bed.

Margaret opened her trunk for her wrapper. She blessed the trunk maker who had made it so sturdy that although the outside was mudsplashed, the things inside were dry. She brought the candle nearer to make no mistake, then caught a glimpse of a small packet of letters from Elena half buried among her clothing. She set the candle on a small shelf built into the wall over her bed and dug down for the letters.

She found Elena's last letter on top with a description of the route all the way from Manchester, England, to Athena Hall. Elena had been very thorough, though impetuous. Margaret read once again that horses and a wagon of sorts could be hired in town for the fifteen-mile drive to Athena Hall. But though it reassured her to refresh her memory about these facts, what she looked for was some hint of Elena's state of mind.

Elena wrote that they had begun to think of a Christmas celebration. Henry Stanley had become gloomy about the outcome of the educational experiment and Elena wanted to cheer him up. She had thought of giving a party on Christmas, but Henry was dubious since it might slow down the farm and educational work. One of the teachers left after only two weeks, saying the diet and climate did not suit him, nor his wife who had planned to teach drawing. They found they had no time for drawing anyway because of the press of day-to-day work essential for survival.

"Henry at last admitted that a party might do everyone good, since in the chill December weather everyone's spirits have sunk very low.

"I have got the most elegant dress on the entire frontier, ready to be produced as a surprise on Christmas—a garment so gorgeous it is not to be believed. But this is fitting enough since I have not been to a party since I left Manchester. We plan to ask the Africans to teach us their dances!

"It is true, as Henry says, that the project is going poorly—but I have special hopes and desires as you shall soon see that the world twenty years hence will be a better one than ours as we have known it . . ."

That was all Elena had said. What, indeed, would Margaret have seen had Elena lived? The hint was so slight as to prove nothing at all. Perhaps the country ball had never been held.

Sighing, Margaret lay herself down under a quilt that though damp felt heavenly all the same.

The next morning it was still raining hard and Blair thought it too difficult to proceed to Athena Hall under these conditions. He did go out, however, to see what horses would be available should the weather improve.

Clad in calico, Margaret went down to see if she might hang her traveling dress by the fire so she could brush it and later sponge it clean. Then she was hoping to take a quiet meal in her room free of any of the society that had been forced upon her since she had set sail for America.

The hostess nodded to her when she came into the kitchen.

"Do you think I might have breakfast in my room?" she asked.

"No, Miss. We don't do that here, whatever you're used to in England. Here we're all the same and no one gets special attention."

40

"I'm sorry. I'll do whatever you wish." Margaret's tone was docile, but she was in fact annoyed. She was not sure that privacy was undemocratic. "But are the river men the equal of all the rest?" Margaret asked, remembering Alice Simpson's comments on the boat.

"They're wild," Mrs. Johnson said. "If they weren't they'd be as good as anybody."

"And the blacks?" Margaret asked.

"Here, now. That kind of talk can get you in trouble. Over in Carolina or Georgia you wouldn't dare say such a thing. We take life a little easier out here in Tennessee . . . or your sister would have run into trouble before she did." Mrs. Johnson's hard, instructive words halted as she actually fell into confusion, a state Margaret judged was rare with her.

"Mr. Blair says they don't know who killed her."

"It could have been anyone. One of those strange blacks from Athena Hall. Somebody from town or drifting through. There were a lot of questions around here about your sister and the odd things she did."

"Elena was a good woman with a strong sense of duty," Margaret replied sharply.

To emphasize her sour words, Mrs. Johnson patted a turkey she was trussing for the oven. "Her intentions might have seemed good in England, but this isn't England, now, is it?" The landlady slid the bird into a tin pan, then opened the door to the oven built to one side of the fireplace. She picked up the heavy turkey and hung it on a hook in the oven. The pan went underneath to catch the drippings.

"You look like a nice enough young woman, but you must know folks around here didn't like your sister. People didn't like what they heard about the things going on at Athena Hall."

"Elena Havershill carried the taint of the devil and the smell of hell," a voice said behind them. The two women turned quickly to regard a long thin man dressed in dingy black who had entered the kitchen

41

without their noticing. The grim-faced man seated himself at the long plank table without ceremony. He picked up a knife in one hand and a spoon in the other and rested his fists on the table with the utensils raised as if ready for attack.

"Why, sir, how dare you!" Margaret's face grew hot.

But the man said nothing more, evidently regarding his first statement as definitive. Disheartened, Margaret forbore any effort to make him change his mind. She studied him. His face was sallow, his shoulders hunched. His hair was cropped short so that he looked like a fanatic of Cromwell's day. Red tinged his nose and cheeks, from constant exposure to the elements as much as drink, she judged.

Margaret turned to Mrs. Johnson for an explanation.

"This is Reverend Brad," that lady said tersely.

Brad nodded and spat a long stream of tobacco juice into the fireplace.

Surely no one could take such a disgusting man seriously as a preacher, Margaret thought.

Mrs. Johnson stirred a pot of mush hanging over the fire and ladled some of it out into a wooden bowl. She jerked a thumb towards a milk jug. Margaret sat down at the long plank table and thought that the mush actually tasted better than the porridge she ate at home.

Mrs. Johnson set another bowl before Reverend Brad, who propelled all of the remaining tobacco and juice from his mouth into the spluttering fire. Then he began to gobble his mush.

Watching, Margaret suddenly found that she could not eat at all.

After the instant that Brad took to dispatch his food, he set down his knife and spoon and regarded Mrs. Johnson.

"Will you pray with me, Sister Johnson?" he boomed suddenly.

Mrs. Johnson looked down at the spotless floor.

"I have my cooking," she said tonelessly.

Margaret sensed that Mrs. Johnson did not like Brad.

Brad fixed a sharp dark eye upon Margaret.

"I judge you to be a stranger to prayer." His voice was as sonorous as a funeral bell.

"Whether I am or am not, I believe it is my privilege to choose not to speak of religion in public," Margaret said tartly.

Brad rose and placed his hands upon the table, leaning forward as though from a pulpit.

"She went against the will of heaven!"

Margaret saw clearly enough that he meant Elena.

"She would go against God's holy plan for the world. God created black slavery. The Bible says it plain enough. It was a wickedness from hell that made your sister teach slaves to read and write. What other filth there was at that cesspool, Athena Hall, God can see from his heaven. And he will judge."

"Oh, nonsense," Margaret said. "Slavery is the wickedness. I'm sure God wants nothing of it."

"Blasphemer! Just as your sister before you. Elena Havershill pointed her Kentucky rifle at me and ordered me off her land."

Margaret looked at this awful man.

"I am beginning to think I would have been in absolute sympathy with her."

Brad raised one hand into the air, then extended a long, bony finger pointed in her direction.

"The gates of hell yawn wide before you, Miss. Beware. Learn from you sister's end. The knife that pierced her throat was never of a kind seen here."

Margaret stared at him as she would a treacherous snake just revealed in the undergrowth.

"How do you know of the knife?" she said breathlessly.

"I know what I know," he intoned.

"Did you see the dagger when my sister was killed?"

"I know what I know," Brad repeated, then clamped his thin lips shut.

43

"I have never seen Elena touch a weapon, much less point one at someone. What did you do to my sister, Reverend Brad?" But he had for a wonder fallen silent. After a few darting glances here and there about the room he drew a long breath and again began preaching of the gates of hell.

The room was becoming steamy as the day warmed and rain evaporated from the ground. Margaret was looking for escape when she heard footsteps behind her and turned to see Edmund Blair, his reddish face almost jovial.

"Brad," Blair said. "I was hoping to find you."

Brad immediately lowered his hand and terminated his sermon. He hastened over to Blair, and the two bent their heads together, lowering their voices as they left the room.

"Who on earth was that?" Margaret demanded.

"He's a preacher fellow who travels up and down the river holding prayer meetings and revivals. Sometimes he half drives people out of their wits," Mrs. Johnson grumbled. Wiping her hands on her apron, she shook her head. "Why, they're practically frothing at the mouth with madness, so afraid are they of the fire of hell. Women love to hear him, I hear tell. They give him goodly sums of money, too, when their husbands' backs are turned. I've heard he has a good pile of gold dollars, and he and Blair work together to make it bigger."

Margaret sat again on the bench near the table.

"So he and Blair know each other well. Was he ever at Athena Hall?"

"Oh, yes. Several times. But I understand that your sister would have none of his praying on the place and threatened to expose him as a fraud."

"What kind of a fraud?"

Mrs. Johnson shook her head to show ignorance. She was a woman of few words.

Margaret arose and went near the fire to see how her

44

dress was drying and to brush the dried mud from it. She could think of nothing else to ask the landlady, but Brad made her uneasy. She would be glad to be gone from this place.

Just before dawn the next day Margaret's spirits were restored. Blair had determined that since the rain had slackened off they could now proceed to travel. The trip itself would be a difficult one and a challenge. The water was still too high, Blair explained, to take a wagon. They would take a horse—or horses if Margaret would attempt to ride herself. She must bundle up some of her things and her trunk and hat boxes would be brought up later when the water level in the streams had dropped.

Margaret nodded, worrying about how she would acquit herself on horseback. She had ridden only a few times in her life since the Havershills were never interested in the sporting life. They traveled sedately by carriage. But the thought of riding so many wild miles seated behind Edmund Blair's saddle, clutching his portly waist, was so repugnant to her that she determined to brave out horseback riding.

Her traveling dress was becoming too wretched, she thought as she resolutely tied her bonnet over her curls. At least she had clean underclothes in her bundle. The sun was just rising as she and Blair set out. She avoided muddy patches in the road and walked through the wet grass, raising her skirts slightly with one hand. Despite her efforts her hem was quite damp.

A black man at the livery stable mounted them on their horses as they set out from the rambling little town. How strange to give this place the grand name of an ancient Egyptian city! Napoleon's conquest had popularized and romanticized Egypt. She had heard that there was another village upriver called Cairo.

Blair took her to the edge of the high cliff they called a bluff to look down upon the river. The glowing rosy

45

dawn was reflected into the water below, which at that point looked more like a lake than a river. They saw many small green parrots as they rode into the forest rimming Memphis. Although they passed occasional settlers' houses, the trees soon grew so dense that no undergrowth flourished in the dim light. Stumps here and there were all that marked the road. They crossed the first of many small streams on a rude bridge formed by logs.

Margaret was even more frightened than the horse by the crossing. She clutched nervously at the dark mane and envied Blair's ability to ride astride with no hampering skirts. He looked less clumsy and fat in the saddle and rode as one accustomed to it.

It was a long ride and her body began to ache with the strain, but she clamped her lips together firmly, determined not to complain. The day grew warmer.

However had Elena planned to farm among all these dark trees? she wondered.

Blair glanced back at her.

"Getting warm, are you? You're lucky there's no mosquitos to speak of yet."

Indeed, Margaret thought. She was quite uncomfortable enough.

At last they reached a small clearing with a few tree stumps. Blair slowed and dismounted. He helped Margaret down. She gratefully lowered herself to the ground, shaking with relief to be supported by the earth instead of the unsteady beast. Her horse bent down to nuzzle her shoulder and she felt ashamed that she disliked him so when he bore her. Both horses sauntered off to drink at the stream, though they had sampled the water at each of the many they had passed.

Blair produced a packet of corn bread and slices of turkey their landlady had cooked the day before. He passed it to Margaret. She found that she was ravenous and gulped the dry food eagerly. The sun was growing steadily higher, but only a little light reached them, even though the trees were just beginning to leaf out.

Suddenly they heard sounds among the trees and three deer, two does and a fawn, walked into the clearing. They proceeded haughtily past them to drink. Margaret held her breath. She had never been so near such wild creatures.

Blair rose to his feet cautiously and reached into his saddlebag to draw out a pistol. He raised it toward the does.

"Oh, don't!" Margaret said breathlessly.

He shoved the pistol back so suddenly that the horse reared slightly and the deer fled.

"Too much trouble to carry it," he said agreeably. "Though it's a shame to miss the chance."

She wiped her fingers carefully on her linen handkerchief, conscious of a terrible thirst. Blair apparently felt the same. He rose and walked toward the nearby stream, then got down on his hands and large round knees and bent to drink with none of the grace of the deer.

Margaret hesitated for a moment, then made her way to another part of the stream to do the same.

"Look out for water moccasins," Blair called to her.

"Water moccasins?"

"Poisonous snakes."

Margaret drew back with a start. Blair laughed at her fear. Flushed, she studied the water carefully. There seemed to be no dangerous creatures in sight. Carefully she drank from her hand. She took her handkerchief and moistened it, wiping her face. The cool water refreshed her and she sighed with relief.

Then she heard a twig snap behind her and turned to see Blair's bulk looming above her. A rush of fear and mistrust of him overwhelmed her. She tried to rise. Instantly he dropped his heavy body down on his knees and reached out a pudgy hand to pin her back down upon the ground.

47

Horrified at his unexpected strength, Margaret looked up at his flushed face as he bent heavily to kiss her. His lips were moist and insistent. She felt his thick tongue press into her mouth. Margaret pushed at him with all her might, but he only paused to look into her face and leer. One hand held her shoulder, the other groped her breast, his knee planted on her skirt.

"You brainy Havershill women are better on your backs, I think," he said, pressing down upon her.

"With a knife in our throats, perhaps," she said quickly. Hampered as she was, she reached to slap him with all her might across his broad face.

He seemed momentarily confused. This moment was enough for Margaret to roll to one side, yanking her skirts free with the force of her movement. He groped after her, but she continued to roll over the pebbles and weeds of the ground well out of his reach.

She sprang to her feet, dropping her fine linen handkerchief behind her. Breathing in gasps, she stumbled towards her horse, with Blair snickering behind her. He rose in pursuit.

As she scrambled onto her horse, he grabbed at her clothing, Had she been wearing a flimsy muslin, he would have ripped it from her back. Furious, she grabbed the horse's reins and lashed at his perspiring face, gaining enough time to mount properly. He stood there a moment, wiping his eyes with the back of his hand, as she headed into the forest.

Now she loved her horse as her savior and vowed to ride him like a hunter to put as much space as possible between herself and Edmund Blair. She was bitterly angry. In all her life in England she had never been assaulted and insulted as she had been on this frontier.

She heard Blair riding after her. They rode on in this manner for a while until he called after her, "Miss Havershill, you are headed in the wrong direction."

Vexed, she halted. Whatever could she do if she got lost in the forest? She had sworn to find her sister's killer and instead she was headed into trackless wilderness.

Blair veered off in another direction and she had no choice but to follow him. She would not let him get the best of her again. She would watch him like a water moccasin.

After a time they passed a little fenced clearing with a log house. Margaret was relieved that Athena Hall wasn't the only dwelling in the whole of the forest. The door of the house stood open, but there was no one in sight. She would like to have stopped to rest there and assured herself that someone would protect her from Blair, but he pushed on past and she thought it best to reach Athena Hall as soon as possible.

They rode in silence in this manner for a few miles. It was well into afternoon. The forest seemed to grow even denser as they progressed. She could hear the flowing of a stream off to her left.

Suddenly Blair stopped and held up his hand.

"Athena Hall," he announced as she rode closer.

Margaret urged her horse forward, her spirits rising with anticipation and relief. She looked where he pointed across the rushing stream.

"This?" she said in amazement. "This is Athena Hall?"

It was not what she had expected.

Chapter Four

Athena Hall's name was grander than the building. She had pictured a gracious classic house similar to those she had seen around Natchez or New Orleans. For in this new country builders along the Mississippi thought that nothing less than Greek temples could serve as houses—no matter how rustic the setting.

Margaret sighed, studying the unkempt and impoverished scene before her. Elena had written with such love of her Greek house—"one more temple of democracy in America." Margaret must not disparage it when it meant so much to her sister. But there was no denying that Athena Hall looked very backwoods and rather raw.

It must have been hastily whitened when the house was newly built three or so years ago. Most of this was already worn away. The original builders had made their effort, then abandoned the place within a year. Fever, Elena had written, discouraged them from finishing the work of plantation building.

As was the fashion, the front of the house was completely symmetrical. The stairs centered the veranda, the door the house front. The pillars were not the elaborate Greek or Roman columns of more substantial houses downriver, but left square and rough-cut. Athena Hall rose a meager story and a half, which left space for only two small rooms at the top.

Margaret looked with dismay at the crude log outbuildings and rickety rail fence. Beyond were a few ragged fields under tillage. All of it was surrounded and hemmed in by dense forest. Surely no one but wild Indians could live there.

It was childish, Margaret supposed, to feel depressed because this frontier house was not more substantial. Elena had been made of sterner stuff than she. Elena could drink nothing but water and gnaw on coarse corn bread and deny herself all the pleasures of a young woman as long as she had her work. Margaret wondered if she would be able to do as well, since as the youngest of the family she had been much spoilt.

But no matter, this was the end of Margaret's journey. She had left all her past life behind her. Whatever Athena Hall was in reality, she must become a part of it. Bracing herself, she rode forward, anxious to cross to the other side.

"The creek's up and has washed the bridge away," Blair called to her.

"What will we do?" Margaret asked.

"Swim the horses." Edmund Blair plunged ahead, looking unconcerned over the fate of his checkered suit. Really, he was such a strange man there was no understanding him. One minute he was happy and serene, the next vicious and mad.

Margaret urged her horse towards the water. She would not think of her fear of drowning or of the unreliability of horses. Her mount waded cautiously into the stream, then seemed to sense the habitation ahead and struck out boldly. This swim might be the fatal blow to her blue traveling dress. She was soaked almost to her waist.

But she would not be stopped. To have some companions beside Edmund Blair and to rest at her sister's house she would have been willing to swim the Mississippi itself.

As they reached the shallows on the other side, a Negro came running from beside the house. He looked at Blair with a startled, almost fearful expression, then ran rapidly uphill into the house.

As her horse surged out of the water and up the bank, she was overjoyed to see the familiar angular form of Henry Stanley in the doorway alongside the black man. It had been several years since she had last seen Henry. He came running down the grassy, weed-covered hill as she dismounted.

"Margaret, my dear." He bent to kiss her cheek in a gesture warm for him. He possessed a dedicated and scholarly nature, narrow and pinched when it came to the emotions. Still, he was as a brother to her, and indeed all she had left.

She stepped back a pace so that she could examine him. Henry looked every bit of his thirty-five years and more. His hair had grown thin on top. As his eyes met hers, his lean and somewhat yellowish face contorted with grief.

"Henry," she said. "Mr. Blair has told me about Elena."

"Oh, my dear Margaret." Sadly he took her arm to lead her to the house. "I did write you a letter, but it is so difficult to get word to England."

Margaret bit her lip to control herself. She feared his sympathy combined with the fatigue of her long journey would cause her to break down altogether.

Henry checked himself and wheeled to survey Blair, who trudged uphill cheerfully in his soaked clothes. Behind him the black man was leading the horses away.

53

"Why are you here, Blair?" Henry demanded.

"Business, of course. Business. And to take orders for anything you might want shipped from New Orleans." Then Blair seemed to reconsider, changed direction, and followed after the horses.

"How did you team up with this scoundrel, Margaret?" Henry's features looked pinched with anger. "For all I know it may be his fault that my letter missed you. I entrusted it to him."

"He introduced himself on the steamboat."

They were walking onto the veranda and into the house by then. They stood on a handwoven rug in the entry hall. Margaret lifted her skirts with one hand, worried that their dripping would ruin the floor. To the right she could see a dining room with a simple table, to the left a sitting room with some shelves of books. Directly ahead of her were the stairs.

She was anxious to change into dry clothes, but there was so much she must know. She took a deep breath, thankful to be inside and safe, yet not at ease.

"I do want to ask you about the killing, Henry. Why was the responsible person never found? How could it happen?"

"I don't know, Margaret. I go over it again and again in my mind—but—you see, I was not here at the time." Henry spoke almost with a sob. "If only it could have been—prevented . . ."

"I know it must be terrible for you, Henry." Margaret felt that she must comfort him some way. He was not yet recovered from the death of his old teacher, Mr. Havershill, and now there was this added tragedy. At least Henry and she could understand one another's losses in this strange land.

"But my dear," Henry said. "I am forgetting. You are wringing wet."

"My trunk is still in Memphis. I brought only a few things with me." Margaret took another look at him.

"You are not wearing the clothes you wore at home, Henry."

He smiled at that. He was in fact wearing a coarsely woven smock over deerskin breeches.

"These are more suited to my life here than my clergyman's clothes. Elena sewed two of these coarse garments for me with her very own hands." He halted suddenly, turning very pale as though grown suddenly faint. These constant reminders of Elena must be bad for him.

"But we must make you comfortable else you will be ill. I, myself, am troubled with fever here."

That would explain his yellowish color, Margaret thought as he stepped past the stairs and called out for Maria who appeared in a few moments.

She was a tall woman with her head wrapped in a turban. Her dark skin had a bronze cast. Her classic straight nose and strong profile seemed meant for the face on an African coin. There was nothing servile about Maria; she seemed born to command. Incredible that this woman was considered a chattel to be bought and sold like a farm animal.

Maria wiped her hands on an apron tied over her dark brown homespun dress. It was high-waisted as was the style of the day, though fashion would be little thought of in this setting.

"Maria, this is Margaret Havershill," Henry said.

Maria extended a firm, callused hand to grasp Margaret's.

"You are very wet. I will take you to your sister's room." Maria's voice was melodious and she spoke slowly as though she chose her words with some care.

She led Margaret upstairs to one of the two bedrooms with their sloping ceilings. It was clean and bare. A single dormer window with small panes of glass looked out upon the clearing and the ever-present forest.

"It is quite a grand house for this part of Tennessee," Maria said, smiling. "But not so grand as the house of my master when I was a child. They taught me to read and write there, which is quite against the custom in most places."

"Oh, I am so glad you are here, Maria. My sister wrote about you in every letter. I cannot believe yet that she is gone." Elena had indeed written often of the genius of this woman she had rescued from slavery, of her kindliness and the grasp of her mind.

"My dear . . ." Maria began, and then hesitated, wrinkling her forehead. "What shall I call you?"

"What did you call my sister?"

"Elena."

"Then you shall call me Margaret." Impetuously she reached out both hands to clasp Maria's. "Whatever was customary for her shall be customary for me, for our ideas were the same."

"I am glad to see that Elena is not completely lost." Maria gave a slight grimace, as though to fight against her sorrow. "You are so much like her. You will bring back memories of her."

Margaret felt tears fill her eyes. She blinked to keep them from spilling over.

"I am only a pale shadow of Elena," she protested. "She was always so full of energy and ideas. I am much lazier and more pleasure loving. You will have to teach me to be like her."

At that the two women embraced each other, since each had lost a cherished companion and had found a friend.

"But I must bring you some warm water and towels. You are quite soaked." Maria straightened and started towards the door. "All your sister's things are still folded in her chest. I could not bear to touch them except to put away whatever was about the room." Maria hastened out to the stairs, closing the door behind her.

Margaret was overjoyed to strip off the heavy, sod-

56

den traveling dress. She laid it over the end of the wooden bedstead. The bed was neatly made up with a quilt.

Elena's leather-bound chest was standing below the window. Margaret opened it and found a dry petticoat on top, which she exchanged for her own. Under that was a dress of the same homespun cloth and cut that Maria had been wearing, only in Elena's size. Elena was only slightly taller than Margaret.

As Margaret reached down for the dress, she felt several articles of clothing underneath. As she groped, the mass of cloth slid aside and she felt something strange at the bottom, silky to the touch. Before she looked further, she hastily put on the brown dress, buttoning the buttons on the bodice, grateful to be warm and dry once more. Then she bent to examine the contents of the trunk more closely. She held her breath for a moment as she glimpsed a dress that lay underneath a pile of petticoats. She had never seen anything like it in her entire life. It was a beautiful Grecian-style dress of white silk, embroidered here and there with tiny seed pearls. Margaret sat back on her heels with amazement. Here, in this plain room in the middle of the wilderness, to find a dress like this!

Spreading it out on the bed, she looked at it more closely. The silk seemed to be slightly yellowed and the skirt cut less generously than more recent fashion allowed. The work was very fine and undoubtedly done by the best of dressmakers. No countrywoman could sew so cleverly and with such sophistication, even if such fine silk should fall into her hands.

"I have got the most elegant dress on the entire frontier, ready to be produced as a surprise at Christmas—a thing so gorgeous it is not to be believed. But this is fitting enough, since I have not been to a party since I left Manchester."

Margaret could almost hear Elena's voice as she recalled word for word the passage from her letter. This, indeed, must be the most elegant dress on the entire frontier. But how had it come here to lie in Elena's chest?

Margaret folded the dress and slammed the lid down as she heard Maria's step on the stairs. This find so mystified her that she did not know what she could say to Maria about it.

Maria had a pot of warmed water, and Margaret rolled up her sleeves to wash.

"Jason has shot us some ducks for supper," Maria said. "They let the black men shoot here."

"Oh." Margaret thought that in most places blacks must be thought too ready to revolt to allow them to be armed. Perhaps this was the kind of thing Mrs. Johnson had meant.

"Ducks sound wonderful," she said, preparing to go downstairs.

In the evening, by the light of the tallow lamp and candles, some instruction was to take place. Henry Stanley, with a slate, was teaching simple words to a young woman who had joined them recently. She was very shy with long angular arms and legs. Margaret could only see the back of the young woman's head, since she kept glancing down at her hands, clasped tightly in her lap. She and her husband lived in one of the log houses in the back. He was supposed to be tracing letters on a slab of wood, but was nodding off after a hard day's work in the fields. The farm work must be done first at Athena Hall if they were going to be able to continue.

A little farther away Maria and Jason bent their heads over a flickering candle. Jason was even taller than Maria and very black with broad features. He spoke English haltingly; Africa was not all that far behind him. Maria had told Margaret that he spoke a dialect no one else could understand. In general he seemed inarticulate, though Maria understood him, somehow.

Jason looked up to find Margaret watching him. He obviously did not like to do this unfamiliar work under her eyes. He said something in a low voice to Maria and the two got up quietly and left for their room at the back of the house opposite the kitchen.

A girl of about twelve was lying in front of the fire. She began to snore audibly.

With a sigh Henry set down the slate he had been using to instruct.

"It is too hard to learn when you have worked all day in the sun," Henry said. "And the farming is going badly enough. Go to sleep, now, all of you." He rose and opened the door for the drowsy scholars, who filed out one by one. Then he came back, thriftily extinguished the extra candles, and sat in a wood chair by the fire.

On the wall over his head hung a portrait of Margaret's father, painted in oils. Teacher and pupil, there were many similar characteristics about the two, Margaret reflected. Both were thin and scholarly. It was Henry's love of the poor of humanity that had led him to take Mr. Havershill as his model.

But Father had had his flashes of humor, moods of playfulness and great warmth. He well knew the limits of human existence and that he alone could not wipe out poverty. For Henry there was no relaxing. He would surely work himself to death unless she could persuade him to spare himself.

"You must rest more, Henry."

"There is not time enough for everything." He leaned his head in his hands wearily.

"I shall help now that I'm here," Margaret promised. "Where is the fine Mr. Blair gone?"

"I sent him upstairs to sleep on my bed. There is no other place for him, though I despise the man. I lock my trunk while he's here."

While she watched him, Henry began to shiver and shake. He took up a shawl from the arm of his chair and wrapped it about his shoulder, moving closer to the fire.

"Henry, what is it?" she asked with something close to fear.

"It's the fever. It comes and goes like this. Drat that Blair, occupying my bed."

"But what can you do about the fever?"

"It will go away in time. It always does, but it leaves me weak and less able to do my work."

"My poor friend," Margaret said. "You must often regret that you have left England."

Henry said nothing, only looked into the fire, the light and shadows playing on his gaunt, yellowish face. Margaret guessed that he was thinking of Elena.

"Perhaps you should lie down, Henry," Margaret said.

"No, no, it will go away."

"Well, then, would you mind if I ask you about Elena? Do you feel able to discuss it?"

"If you wish." Henry stared into the flames, his hands trembling.

"You were gone?"

"Yes." Henry's voice was low. "Blair had told me the *Criterion* would leave shortly. I was to deliver a lecture in Cincinnati. There were people there interested in our work. I hurried away, leaving him behind here, so that I would not have to wait several more days for another steamboat."

"Blair thinks one of the Negroes might have killed her."

"That dreadful man. He has no sensitivity. Those raised in slavery are frightened enough of being sent back to cruel masters and of what might happen if we fail here. We are but an island in a sea of slavery. No, they would not touch her. Besides," and here Henry's voice almost failed him, "they loved her."

"Then who could have killed her?"

Henry sighed, but said nothing.

"What about Blair?"

"I do not want to malign Blair unjustly," Henry said after a moment's reflection, "but he is a violent man. Elena particularly told me she did not want to be left alone with him. He had forced his attentions on her several times. I asked Jason to make sure she was safe from him while I was gone."

"Then it might well be Blair who killed her."

"There is no way we can tell." Henry sighed. His shivering seemed to be abating somewhat.

"Well, I must say he tried to force his attentions on me on the way here," Margaret said indignantly.

Henry looked at her, a deep frown between his sharp brown eyes.

"I do not understand the fellow. He upset Elena several times. We were trying to think how our business in New Orleans could be done without him. We had no trust in him by this time. Yet he has made a friend of the strange, half-mad preacher who travels up and down the river."

"There is very little logic to him, I'll agree." Margaret could see that Henry no longer had the stamina and energy she had known him to have in England. He seemed to be defeated in some way. Why had he not made more of an effort to find the killer? She felt almost reluctant to push him on these matters, yet it must be done.

"I should very much like, if you don't mind, Henry, to speak to everyone here to see if I can discover anything. And I should like to see the curious dagger that was the weapon."

"Yes, of course," Henry said. "Only I'm not sure anyone knows where it is. There was no trace of the crime by the time I returned from Cincinnati. It did not occur to me to ask about the weapon."

He rose and lit his candle from the fire. His thin, knobby fingers were steady now.

"I shall be off to join our friend, Blair." Then he turned back to add, "At any rate, we will have to consult with Blair, much as we both dislike him. The way it was arranged, Athena Hall belonged to Elena and to you, since it was purchased with your inheritance. We pay small wages to the Africans, who are buying their own freedom. The money for the educational work and the Africans' money is in trust in New Orleans in a branch of the Bank of the United States. Blair is in charge of the trust. We can't rely on these local banks. They print useless money."

"Good heavens, Henry! That man has no sympathy for our plans. He may well be spending the money on the pleasures of New Orleans."

Henry frowned, seeming to consider the matter, then he shook his head.

"We must soon consult with the trustees. You're right, there's no relying on Blair, it seems. And if the plan is to go well, we must hire teachers soon. Ah, there is so much more to think of all the time." He sighed. "Sometimes I feel it is all quite beyond me."

Margaret picked up her candle and they walked up the stairs together. Their shadows loomed large on the wall as they climbed. His words and the general atmosphere darkened her mood.

She had not asked if Elena was expecting a child. She could not bring up the subject to such a bachelor as Henry. Elena's supposed pregnancy might yet be some strange fancy of Blair's.

She smiled fondly at Henry as he turned to go into his own room. Shutting the door of Elena's room behind her, she set her candle down on a wash table. Beyond her window in the darkness lay the small clearing of Athena Hall; beyond that the endless, oppressive forest.

She reflected with a shiver that here in this room her sister had died—and that the crime was as yet unsolved.

No one could tell her what Elena's last thoughts had been as she lay here in a pool of blood. The room seemed bleak and dismal at night. Margaret felt chilled and homesick.

How lonely it was! It had seemed to satisfy Elena. Margaret was not at all sure she would be equally satisfied to spend the rest of her life here. Yet where else could she go? Many of her friends already had husbands to cherish them and babies to care for. She might well become an old maid.

Somewhere in Manchester, Phillip was probably seated in a warmly lamplit room—perhaps thinking of her. Or maybe that far around the globe it was daylight. She had had her chance with Phillip, but nothing had happened between them. What on earth is it you want, Margaret? she asked herself. But she had no response to give.

She glanced about the small room. There, near the window, were there not dark stains on the floor? She had not noticed them earlier in the day. Was that the very spot where Elena had breathed her last? Margaret pressed her fingers to her lips to suppress a wave of nausea, wishing that she could reach back through time to comfort her sweet sister at that moment of suffering and pain.

She undressed and put on the nightgown she had brought with her. As she bent preparing to blow out her candle, she saw it flicker to one side suddenly. She straightened and saw to her horror that her door was opening slowly. She stared at it, transfixed. It opened a crack, and then halted.

Shaken, she called, "Is someone there?" The door opened farther and Maria's turbaned head appeared.

"I thought perhaps you had gone to sleep with your candle lit," Maria said apologetically.

Margaret sat down suddenly on the bed, her hand nervously at her throat. She breathed a long sigh of relief.

"Oh, you frightened me! I have never in my life before slept so far from the rest of the world. I feel as though beyond those trees I could travel to the ends of the world and never see another human."

"This is the room where your sister died," Maria said softly.

Margaret nodded.

Maria came to stand in the middle of the room. The candle she was carrying lit her face from below, giving her an awesome appearance. Though Maria's words were warm, Margaret felt chilled by her presence. But perhaps it was only the fatigue of the long journey added to the depression of being at last in her sister's house with her sister so finally gone.

Maria walked to the window and bent down so that her light shone on the stains on the floor. Then she straightened and set her candle next to Margaret's. From her apron band she drew an object that made Margaret draw in a long breath with surprise. The light of the two candles fell upon the gold handle of a small, antique, theatrical-looking dagger.

"Where did you get this?"

"I myself drew it from your sister's throat. I saved it for you."

Margaret shrank back. The calm voice Maria used to describe her act seemed frightful. Leaning over the two small flames, wearing her exotic turban, and extending the dagger towards Margaret, the black woman seemed some savage spirit from a primitive age.

"You hid the dagger?" Margaret's voice shook.

"Yes. I told them all that the sister of Elena was coming and that she would see to it that we were free, even though Elena was dead. That's why I hid the dagger for you. May it protect you as it failed your sister."

Seeing that Maria meant no menace, Margaret reached her hand for the intricately wrought weapon. It was clean and shining—free of all traces of blood—and obviously an old weapon. No one in England any longer

64

carried a dagger, much less anyone in Tennessee. She would have thought it something made for actors, but the quality and workmanship were too fine.

"It is very strange." She quickly set it on the table. It was loathsome to her touch. "Whose could it have been?"

"Why, it was hers—your sister's."

"Elena's?" Margaret looked at the black woman to read her expression, but Maria was serene and serious. "But it was not like Elena to have a weapon. She believed in moral persuasion." She remembered Brad and the rifle. What had Elena turned into here in Tennessee?

"It was hers, though. She kept it on the table, I think because she was afraid."

"Where did it come from?"

Maria picked up the dagger again.

"It seems very old. I thought she had always had it."

Margaret shook her head. Then she sat on the bed and looked at the dagger once more.

"But why was Elena afraid?"

"She was afraid of Mr. Blair. She feared the preacher, but not enough to carry a knife, I think. And then like you she was afraid of the wilderness at times."

Maria smiled slightly as though the wilderness held no fear for her. It must to many blacks seem a refuge from slavery, Margaret thought.

"You're speaking of Preacher Brad?"

Maria nodded.

"In Memphis he told me that Elena had actually pointed a rifle at him," Margaret said.

"That half-mad hellfire shouter. There was very bad feeling between him and your sister. He's come here two or three times damning your sister for her sinful ideas. I don't know what made her turn him off, though. I'm not sure it was just the preaching, but some other business he's about. Mostly he just travels up and down the river, but they say he has plenty of money, though he doesn't look it."

"I hope I never see him again. I wish I could say the same of Blair."

"They are troublemakers, I agree." Maria fell silent, then walked to the window and looked out at the vast darkness. After a moment she spoke without looking at Margaret.

"You will keep on with Athena Hall? You won't sell it and send us back into slavery?"

"Oh, of course not. I could not destroy Elena's work. I intend to continue with Henry."

Maria turned to face her, the expression on her austerely beautiful features becoming as light as a girl's.

"Oh, Margaret!" Just as suddenly her expression changed again and her eyes brimmed with tears. "We have, many of us, been growing quite afraid. I am to have Jason's child, you see."

Margaret looked at her with sympathy. More than all the stories in England of brutal beatings and killings of Negro slaves and the degradation of women, this wish of Maria's to have her child in freedom brought the reality of slavery to Margaret.

"It was Jason, was it not, who discovered my sister's body?"

Maria nodded.

Margaret pondered this fact. Why had Jason come up to Elena's room? What had brought him here? There was something puzzling about it.

But Maria was mulling over another problem. She spoke with a shyness unusual for her. "Do you think, Margaret . . . do you think that you could continue to teach me French?"

"French?" Margaret was surprised. The request seemed strangely out of place in Tennessee. "I can teach you as much as I know. I am not the best of scholars myself."

"I have been reading Rousseau and would like to read him in his native language."

Margaret leaned back on her pillow, her eyes growing heavy. It astounded her that Margaret was so anxious to learn. She herself had often shirked her French lessons in favor of livelier pursuits. And reading philosophy in any language put her to sleep.

"You are an unusual person, Maria, far more serious minded than I am. How were you able to learn so much in slavery?"

Standing as she was near the dormer, Maria's turban almost grazed the sloping ceiling. She stood very straight as one used to long hours on her feet. Her smile was a wry one.

"I am a freak, if you would speak the truth."

"Oh, no, Maria!"

Maria looked away and out into the star-studded darkness again. She spoke lowly, almost as though she were speaking to herself.

"What good is a slave versed in European philosophy?"

Margaret was struck by her literary way of speaking.

"What happened?"

Maria sat down at the foot of the bed and began the story of her life. Exhausted as Margaret was, she had no trouble keeping awake as she listened. Though Maria spoke in an even voice, the scenes she described were as vivid to Margaret as though they were being staged before her.

Maria's first mistress had noticed how bright and quick the child was, Maria began. Maria's mother, it seemed, had known some reading and writing.

"I do not know how she learned. A law was passed to make sure none of us would ever read the papers by which we were bought and sold. My mother never told me about her early life. She worked at the next plantation, and walked over now and then all the way to visit me. It was a long walk and she worked hard, so she seldom came.

"To amuse herself my mistress did the forbidden and taught me to write. When her husband discovered it, he forbade her to teach me any more. But she did in secret. It was too late, anyway, for I had developed a passion for books.

"It was also her pleasure to dress me for playacting when I was a little thing and to teach me to recite poetry. She devised turbans for me. I was an African princess or the Queen of Morocco. She also taught me some songs, but I never sing her songs now.

"As I grew older I interested her less, especially as I developed a mind of my own. I would sneak into the library and read when I had time. But I had no one to speak to of books.

"When hard times came to the plantation, my master sold me and my mistress lost her toy. She scarcely noticed by then, for she had taken a lover." Maria sighed and looked off as though her eyes could pierce the night all the way to her old home. "I cannot forgive my mistress for letting me be sold despite her early fondness for me. Yet it was she who educated me—whatever good that might bring me."

"And then how did you come to Athena Hall?" Margaret asked.

Maria's narrative continued.

"I had always been a house servant, you see. But for some reason my new master put me to work in the fields. Perhaps it was because he sensed something odd about me. My speech, for one thing, was more refined than the other slaves'. Indeed, it was more refined than my new master's. It was hard work, men's work. All my learning only made my life the more bitter.

"Then I heard through the grapevine that someone was to establish a plantation where slaves might be taught. I stole away and walked many miles to speak with your sister. When I returned, my master had me

68

beaten. But in a few days Elena came to the plantation and I became her property. I promised her I would help teach, and she in turn taught me."

"She was overjoyed to find you. She wrote me an entire letter about it," Margaret said softly.

Maria smiled a sad smile. "But though I loved being here, there were other considerations. After a while I told Elena about Jason, whom I had married. Africa, his homeland, was still a very important influence on him and it would be hard to teach him the things that Europeans value for a fine education. Even I am but a shadow to him. His mind often dwells upon his home and I cannot usually follow his thoughts there. Elena bought him also, and eventually we all came here. Though he is not a scholar, he is a good worker, and Henry Stanley has come to treasure him."

Maria picked up her candle and came over to stand near Margaret, looking down with a half smile. "So, you see, the two of us are freaks. He has never learned to bow and beg. His thoughts still return to Africa and mine to the great scholars of Europe. Neither is of much value to a slave."

"But you will be free in time, Maria."

"A freed slave has very few rights and less money," Maria said. "So you can see how important Athena Hall is to us."

Margaret nodded sleepily. The seriousness of the work at Athena Hall struck her with more force than it ever had in England. She hoped she would be equal to it.

Maria helped tuck her in, almost motherly in her solicitude. Then the black woman picked up her candle.

But—there was something undone, Margaret thought drowsily. Something she forgot to ask. Oh, yes . . .

"Maria, is it true that you told Blair my sister was to have a child?"

"Yes. It was foolish of me to tell him."

"But how did you know?"

"Three times I found her spewing her breakfast near the woodpile. Then she admitted it quite warmly to me."

"Who did she say was the father?"

"She would not. It was some game of her own." Maria smiled her strange smile—as though she was enjoying a secret joke. "And you, Margaret, have you no lovers?"

Margaret shook her head. "Not even half a one, it seems." She gloomily wondered if she might end her life here, alone, doing good works. But she could think nothing more that night for her eyes were so heavy she was almost asleep.

Maria blew out Margaret's candle and scooped up her wet traveling dress. Then she carried her own light towards the door.

"If you are ready to ride out tomorrow, perhaps you can find out more about Elena's child," she said, turning back for a moment. "I think, my dear Margaret, that your journey will prove interesting."

As she drifted into sleep, Margaret reflected that Maria's presence made her no longer afraid of the dark at Athena Hall.

Chapter Five

Maria walked down the slope wearing her blue-striped red turban regally. Her back was strong and straight, her long neck graceful and muscular. She moved beautifully in the warm spring morning. The landscape was a mass of budding green.

Margaret followed her to where her horse, fitted with a man's saddle, grazed out on the open space in front of Athena Hall. Margaret stopped dead and looked at Maria in amazement.

"Maria! What have you done with the sidesaddle?"

"That foolish thing? You could break your neck riding that way." Maria folded her arms with a look of disgust.

"But how can I ride astride in skirts?" Timidly Margaret advanced to pat the horse's nose. He snorted and laid back his ears.

"By pulling them up, of course. We slaves believe that even the daintiest ladies have legs to walk upon."

"But what if someone sees me?"

"There are no people between here and where you

are going. Henry is away working with the men, and Blair is asleep in his room. I made sure that you could depart unnoticed." Maria had a strange smile on her face.

There seemed nothing else to do. Flushing and hiking up her borrowed homespun skirts, Margaret placed a slippered foot in the stirrup and settled herself uncertainly. Her bonnet slipped to one side and she straightened it. She tried to pull her skirts down as far as she was able, but Maria was no help to her in this.

"I shall become as abandoned as one of the ladies at the court—and besides I shall get saddle sores," Margaret grumbled.

"Perhaps you should learn to ride bareback, then." Maria smiled, but as always Margaret could sense a fixed purpose behind her actions. "Go along quickly, now." Maria's voice grew crisp with authority, but then she laughed. "I am the slave giving orders. In some places I could be whipped for it."

"But not here," Margaret said with horror. "Never here."

Maria laughed again, then struck the horse's flank with the flat of her hand and Margaret was off at a jostling trot. As she looked back, she saw Maria raise one hand in farewell, then bend to remove her shoes before she walked towards the fields.

Margaret wished Maria hadn't bullied her into riding bareback. Margaret was an uncertain rider as it was. She thought she saw someone look out an upstiars window. Maria was wrong! Someone had seen her bare legs! If it were Edmund Blair, there was no telling how the sight of them might enflame him, since a soiled traveling dress had set him so afire. She shrugged with irritation, hoping the deadful man would leave Athena Hall soon.

The horse's hooves clattered over the newly replaced log bridge. Margaret restrained herself from looking down into the rushing river.

Maria had told her where to go—back along the crudely cut trail to the log house Blair and Margaret had passed on their way. "Someone there would tell her about her sister," Maria had said mysteriously. She only smiled when Margaret pressed her to tell more.

Margaret rode at a slow trot for about an hour, she judged. She had to admit that it was easier to control the horse riding astride, but the flesh of her legs rubbed uncomfortably against the saddle. The sun became quite warm to a person used to a gentler climate. Though her bonnet shielded her creamy English complexion from the rays, she felt flushed and knew her hair was curling wildly with moisture.

After a time of riding in isolation through dense forest she heard the blows of an axe at some distance. Then the pleasant domestic sound ceased and she heard nothing more. The trees thinned and the little log house came into view. She urged her horse toward it off the track, wondering if anyone was within.

"Miss Havershill!" she heard a strong voice say suddenly quite close beside her. "Why, I do believe Miss Havershill has come to discover what I know of her sister."

Stunned, Margaret turned her head to see Jed with his rough-cut hair standing by the rail fence. The broad brim of her bonnet had screened him from her view. For a moment she had a sense of shocked dislocation. She must have jerked her reins, for her horse reared slightly.

"Well, sir!" Blood rushed to her face as she realized that her legs were bare to the thigh and there was nothing much she could do about it until she dismounted. But it seemed hardly to matter since Jed stood below her, naked to the waist, having no doubt discarded his shirt to work. He looked up at her with a wild smile.

"If you don't mind, I think it would be easier for me to talk to you standing on the ground," she said.

Raising his arms to brace her, he helped her down.

73

She dismounted shakily, half wishing to flee. Shrinking a little under the touch of his sun-warmed hands, she thanked God that her skirts and petticoat were settling about her ankles and her slippered feet securely resting on the earth. She withdrew her hands from his bare arms primly. She must be careful with this man.

"Now, Miss Havershill, don't worry. I rescue more ladies than I attack." He laughed with amusement.

For the first time in her entire life Margaret found that she was unable to open her mouth to speak.

"You're lucky at that." He took her hand and led her past a rail fence. "If you go deep enough into the woods along the frontier and come unexpected on a cabin without warning, you just might find the husband and wife out cavorting around without a stitch on, and the baby as well. Of course we're getting almost civilized now and have to be more careful. We're a state in the Union, after all. But still, clothes are hard to come by in the wilds."

She flushed as all the things the man was or might be rushed through her mind: He was the daredevil knife fighter of the *Belvidere* who had kissed her—then carefully led her to safety; he was a man who carried some papers or property that he fought to protect; and he was the homesteader and farmer of this little corner of Tennessee.

But what was he to Elena?

The question was disturbing. Margaret's steps were so uncertain that she tripped over the uneven weedy ground. He tightened his grasp to support her. She looked down at the lean brown hand covering hers and wished she had forced Maria to tell her more. At any rate, he seemed not to have been drinking this morning.

As he led her towards the cabin, it occurred to her that there was something strange about him. Then she realized that though he spoke with the Westerner's nasal twang, he had dropped the coarsely spoken language he used on the *Belvidere* with the other men. It was almost as though he spoke two distinct languages.

She crossed the threshold into his cabin and looked about, wondering if Elena had been there before her, surprising herself by feeling a pang of jealousy.

Oh, if only Elena had written something of the child she was to have!

He led her to a split log bench. Rough as it was, she was glad to sit on anything besides the back of a horse. He filled a round iron kettle with water from a wood bucket, then placed two split logs and some kindling on the dying fire, watching it flare up. She removed her bonnet and dabbed at her damp brow with a handkerchief.

Jed suddenly dodged out the door without explanation and she sat there alone, looking around the small log house. She had passed many on her journey to Athena Hall. There was little to distinguish one from another. Jed's house contained a single room with a loft. Split logs, flat side up, formed the floor. Jed was no great housekeeper, she noticed. The hearth was unswept—in fact looked as though it never had been swept, nor the rest of the place.

Although the cabin was crude, there were some surprisingly civilized touches. A long Kentucky rifle lay across pegs near the door. Above it on rough shelves were several pewter and silver tankards and cups and two books. One was plainly a Bible and the other, she saw, a copy of Shakespeare. They looked to be well worn.

"Well!" she said half aloud. But the next thing that caught her eye was a small painted chest in a corner. Dancing, white-wigged figures covered the side, framed by gentle curves topped by a carved sea shell. Surely it had been made in France before the Revolution! The elaborate style made her wonder if there was not some relationship between the chest and the gold-handled dagger that had ended Elena's life. But the dagger looked older still.

She wondered that her host should leave her with so little ceremony. She could not see out the single window, which was covered with oiled paper. She leaned forward until she could look out the door. Jed strode across the newly cleared field from the trees where he'd retrieved his shirt, not the quality linen shirt worn on the *Belvidere*, but a rough woven linsey-woolsey one. So even he was conscious of appearances!

She stood back as he came in. He barely looked at her, but strode purposefully to the fire.

"My mother used to drink tea when she could get it, but mostly she picked whatever she could find and brewed it up in boiling water. I only know some of her secrets—most of them she gave to my sister at an early age. But then it's not every day I have English ladies by for tea."

He dropped some leaves into the kettle, then turned to look at her directly.

"These are blackberry leaves. Unless you'd like a sip of whiskey?" The corners of his mouth turned up.

She shook her head, flushing as she remembered the whiskey on his breath on the *Belvidere*. The whole situation was not one for which her upbringing had prepared her.

"Ladies don't seem to appreciate our western whiskey. It is a little on the raw side." Jed leaned against the rough chimney piece.

What ladies? she wondered. She remembered that Davy had called him a frontier hellion, but surely he couldn't have entertained many out here in the forest. Except Elena . . .

She cleared her throat. She couldn't let this moccasin-shod man reduce her to imbecilic silence. She remembered many afternoons spent in Phillip's company with conversation flowing freely between them. She, in fact, had done most of the talking.

"You live here alone?" Then she wished she had bitten her tongue.

He looked at her again, almost laughing.

"Most times—"

Blushing, Margaret folded her hands in her lap.

"I suppose it's not mannerly on the frontier to ask people about themselves." Her voice was wavering and uncertain.

He dipped the boiling tea into two silver cups standing on the rough table. Seeming to concentrate, he said nothing.

"These are lovely old cups." Margaret reached for one, but the handle was burning hot. She must wait for the tea to cool and settle.

He seemed still to be thinking of her words. "No, it's not bad manners to ask people about themselves in the wilderness," he said finally. "But you may not get an answer. You see, you may be surprised that a rascal like myself sets part of his table in handmade wood, and part in silver. But I feel free to tell you that the cups come from my mother's home in Virginia—a place more refined than any I've lived in. My father, though, was a mover like his rascal son. He never stayed in one place long, and never stored up much worldly goods, but he could lick his weight in wildcats just like me."

"Is she still alive? Your mother, I mean," Margaret asked tentatively. Standing there, one hand draped on the crude chimney piece holding his cup, and the other relaxed at his side, he looked stronger and more vital than any of the well-bred men she had known at home.

"No. The wilderness can be hard on a woman from Virginia. The Bible and the works of Shakespeare went from place to place along with the rest of us. My sister died at sixteen in childbirth, my mother about three years ago, and my father dropped in his tracks last year when he was moving on again." He paused and smiled his mocking smile. "That's why the Bible and the works of Shakespeare and the silver cups and spoons and pew-

ter tankards are here. I sold my daddy's rifle—mine
was better. I've been a drifter most of my life, but I've
had this place about a year now."

"And the little French chest?"

Startled, he glanced towards it, then looked back at
her warily.

"That comes from someplace else."

"Mr.—"

"Jed. Sawyer, if you have to."

"Jed. Do you know where my sister got a gold-
handled dagger?"

He looked at her steadily, his blue eyes unwavering.

"The one that killed her?"

Margaret nodded.

"I gave it to her."

His answer gave her a kind of shock.

"Where did you get it?" she said hoarsely, looking
again at the French chest.

He shrugged, but would not answer.

"But you know it killed her." Her words came indistinctly.

"Maria rode over to tell me about it."

"Why did she do that?" Margaret studied his
browned, expressionless face—a face that for years
must have hidden his feelings from the other men along
the river.

"I don't ask Maria why she does things. She's a good
woman, though."

Margaret sat silent for a moment while he took a
small piece of sugar in its purple wrappings from the
shelf along with a silver spoon. Looking very serious, he
broke the sugar into the spoon and added some to both
their cups.

Cautiously, Margaret took a sip. It was surprisingly
good.

"Well, then, perhaps you can tell me why you gave
Elena the dagger."

The muscles of his jaw tightened slightly.

"Because she was afraid of Blair."

Margaret frowned, puzzled, thinking back to what Blair had told her on the *Belvidere*. "Blair told me he didn't know you."

"I know he sent your sister flying over here in fear and anger. He'd begin to maul her every time Henry Stanley turned that skinny back of his. I know Blair by sight, but he doesn't know me."

"Why did they let him on the place, then?"

"He was the only one willing to travel this far upriver to do their banking business. But then, I've heard a lot of Blair here and there. He has plenty of business up and down the river. The worst seems to have to do with that hellfire preacher." Jed set down his cup of tea and reached for the whiskey jug on the floor. He seemed to find it more to his taste.

"But couldn't Henry do anything necessary in New Orleans himself?"

"It looks like your English Henry hasn't got the constitution for much, and he travels too much as it is. Your sister was always afraid of worrying him into an early grave."

"Have you been to Athena Hall often?"

"Only once or twice. I didn't think much of it."

Margaret looked at him sharply. "We mean to get rid of slavery, you know. Would you stand for that?" she said.

"It isn't anything to me one way or the other. Slaves are nothing to me. This is the first land I've ever owned. I work it myself—that is, when I'm in the mood."

"Then what didn't you like about Athena Hall?"

"It means trouble. They—your sister and Stanley— didn't know what they were dealing with. People around here can go crazy if they think you're for Abolition."

Margaret sighed. She felt his words made a frightening kind of sense.

"You mean that things are different here than in England."

"I don't know how they are in England. I only know what they're like here."

Margaret drank her tea for several moments without speaking. Then she steeled herself to ask the question she had to ask. His head was bent over his cup, presenting more of his roughly cut, sun lightened brown hair to her than his face. A flush warmed her cheeks as she spoke.

"Mr. Sawyer—Jed—what was my sister to you?"

He raised his eyes to look at her. His expression grew stubborn and once more the muscles of his jaw tightened.

"I can't tell you that, Miss Havershill." He rose to his feet and was looking down at her.

"My name is Margaret." Tears of frustration filled her eyes. Then she grew angry at his unresponsiveness. "I must find out who stabbed Elena with the knife you gave her. You must understand that. I'm not here just for idle conversation. I have traveled all the way from England only to find my sister dead. Whatever I do with the rest of my life, I must take care of this part first."

He looked down at her gravely, his eyes piercingly blue. "I understand that you have to find out who killed her, Miss Havershill, but I have nothing to tell you."

She still regarded him with suspicion, despite what he said. There were too many unanswered questions here.

"Then please don't be angry with me for asking questions."

"I'll try, but it don't come easy to an old ringtailed roarer like me, Miz Margaret." He adopted the rivermen's form of speech, smiling broadly at her and looking very handsome in a way that undoubtedly attracted many women.

She found that she was not charmed. She needed help and was not getting it.

"If you have nothing more to say, perhaps I should go," she said stiffly.

He stared at her thoughtfully, then spoke slowly. "I don't know what good poking up the ashes about Elena's death will do." Then he paused. "Maybe I can help you—maybe I can't."

"Perhaps you would like me to go, then?" She was not a little irritated; he was so much the master of his thoughts and so sure of himself.

"I can't control your comings and goings, Missus."

Margaret bit her lip, then stood, awkwardly tying her bonnet. Perhaps she was running away too soon, but he seemed to be daring her to leave. The two of them walked out the door together in silence to her horse that sought forage near the rail fence.

Margaret saw the fields that Jed was clearing. The one nearest the house was as clean as any European farmer's would have been. The next one over was ploughed around the still standing stumps. Still farther along some of the trees were girdled and left to die; some were partially burned.

"You've done a lot of work here," she said.

"Not that much. The place was first settled by somebody else. I bought it from him. Any other time in my life I've just squatted for a year or so and poked some corn into the ground with a stick. This place needs a woman on it to make it really work."

"Oh." Perhaps he was trying to embarrass her again. Then she saw that he was merely stating a fact of frontier life. She extended her hand to him.

"Well, goodbye, Mr. Sawyer." She hoped that he would leave her so she could scramble up onto the horse unobserved.

"I'll help you up," he said.

"That's not necessary." She blushed wildly.

"If you're worried about your legs, I've already seen them." He was looking at her sideways out of the corner of his eye, trying not to laugh.

81

Wildly confused, she allowed him to help her into the saddle, then she arranged her skirts as best she could.

"Wait here," he said with perfect seriousness. "I'll ride with you a ways."

"It's really not necessary." Margaret was still conscious of her nakedness. But, she reflected irritably, he had no doubt seen many women's legs. What would the bookish Phillip think of this behavior? At that moment England seemed very far away to her.

Jed had walked off to the other side of his cabin, but soon returned astride a brown mare. It was no beauty, but looked sound enough. No doubt it was the same horse he hitched to his plow.

They set off together, Margaret with her bonneted head held high, a flush staining her bosom and cheeks. For that matter, what would her friends at home think of her? Elena, of course, would be fully equal to the situation. Her ideas had been very advanced. She would consider superficial modesty a hindrance to her work.

Perhaps Jed, riding so silently a little behind her, was contrasting the two of them in his mind. She looked back at him uncertainly.

"Don't worry," he said, chuckling. "I won't look at them."

She snapped her head around to look at her horse's ears. Then it occurred to her that he had after all gone out of his way for her and it would be well to be civil. She glanced back.

He reined in his horse suddenly. She, too, halted.

"It's only a mile or so now. You should be safe." He had stopped laughing at her as he looked about with narrowed eyes that assessed the forest with a frontiersman's understanding. "No one usually rides out this far."

"Well, Mr. Sawyer," Margaret said crisply. "I did not expect to see you again so soon."

"Didn't Maria tell you that I asked about you?"

She shook her head, feeling her eyes widen in surprise. What on earth was Maria about?

"At any rate, I see that Peters did give you my message."

"I asked him a few questions. He didn't seem ready to talk to me until I encouraged him a little." He smiled at the memory, his teeth showing very white in his deeply browned face.

"You could have answered my questions on the *Belvidere*." Margaret heard petulance creeping into her voice.

"I had a feeling I'd see you again."

"But I had no way of knowing that." It seemed he could only be serious when looking at the trees. Every time he looked at Margaret he was convulsed with laughter.

"You did want to see me again, then?" he teased.

She blushed furiously, remembering his kiss on the *Belvidere*.

"Of course. I wanted to ask you some questions. It was certainly not because of your behavior on the *Belvidere*." Was it not? she asked herself to be sure. She remembered the feel of his arms about her.

"Yes, Miss Havershill, we river rascals are a bad-mannered lot. It's up to you ladies to teach us better ways." Laughing, he rode his horse close to hers, seized the reins with one hand, dropping his own. He circled her waist with his other arm and bent to kiss her. Her bonnet slid towards the back of her head.

Margaret felt his lips meet hers with a shock. Her knees grew weak. For a moment she met his kiss without resistance. Then she dug her heels into her horse, which reared. She clutched her saddle, almost losing her seat.

"Really, Mr. Sawyer," she said. "Can I trust no man in this country to keep his hands to himself? You are as bad as your friend Davy, or Blair."

He gave her a startled, angry look, then thrust his

moccasined foot against the flank of her horse, pushing the two of them farther apart. Wheeling, he rode off.

Margaret remained where she was for a moment. In fact, his kiss had not been like Blair's or Davy's, but much pleasanter. Still, she had been mauled enough. She would not have it. Nor would she let Jed Sawyer think he could kiss her without a by-your-leave.

Straightening her bonnet, she waited there, feeling a pang of regret. It might be difficult to see him again. He did not like Athena Hall and she had no excuse to desert work she might be doing to ride out to see him. Indeed, the horse on which she sat would be taken back to Memphis soon.

She raised her head suddenly. Was he coming back? She thought she heard slow, cautious sounds as though a horseman was riding through the forest. Then the sounds stopped. She waited a moment to see if they would begin again, but heard no more. She picked up her reins, chuckling to the horse, and rode on.

After she had gone but a few yards, she stopped to listen again. Was someone following her, hidden in the trees? But she heard nothing. Again she started off, again she heard indistinct sounds, again she stopped to hear nothing.

She began to feel a little lightheaded with fear. She did not yet know who Elena's killer was. If it was Jed following her, why was he behaving in such a peculiar manner?

She urged her horse to go faster and he broke into a canter. So unused was she to riding, much less astride in skirts, she could only pray that she would not fall off. After a while she began to adjust to the horse's rhythm and felt more confident as a rider.

She stopped suddenly.

Behind her somewhere another horse stopped.

Panicked, she urged her horse into a gallop. The wind dislodged her poke bonnet from her head so that it hung down her back by its ribbons. She felt the warm

84

afternoon air blowing through her curls and her skirts climbing higher. At last the log bridge to Athena Hall came into view.

She slowed, crossed, then stopped to turn back once more. No one was following. But it could not have been her imagination, she was sure.

Tiredly, she urged her horse up the hill.

Maria came out of the front door to meet her. After studying Margaret's face, her own took on a look of concern.

"What has happened?" she said.

"Someone was following me, hidden in the trees."

"Are you sure?"

Margaret nodded.

"Jed?"

"I don't think so. I don't know why he would."

"Help me up behind you. We must have a look."

Margaret reached down a hand. Maria hiked up her skirts and nimbly sprang to a seat behind the saddle. Margaret rode back the way she had come, over the little bridge to the spot she thought she had last heard the mysterious rider. Then the two of them dismounted and searched through the trees.

Margaret's bonnet snagged on a branch and she untied the ribbons to free it. As she did so, she looked down into the rich forest soil and clearly saw the fresh track of a horse's hoof.

"Maria," she called. "Here it is."

Maria hastily came to her side and the two women followed the tracks back to the road where they had veered off. Then they slowly made their way again in the direction that the rider had taken. The prints were fairly shallow since the mysterious person had evidently ridden slowly. They followed them to the river bank.

"It's the deep ford to Athena Hall," Maria said thoughtfully.

"Then whoever followed me must be there," Margaret said.

Chapter Six

A building as slipshod as the stable barely deserved the name. Spaces between the bark-covered logs allowed not only insects, but bats and small birds to fly through. Still, it protected the horses from marauding animals. Margaret looked about cautiously to make sure no strange rider hid there, yet whoever followed her had had plenty of chance to attack her in the woods if that were his object.

One horse alone occupied the stable——the one Blair had ridden to Athena Hall. The two horses belonging to the place were in the fields.

Blair's livery mare wore a bridle, but no saddle. The unused sidesaddle lay near the wall. Margaret walked up to Blair's horse and saw that the mare's sides were warm and sweaty—too sweaty for her to have been standing here so idly.

She heard a step behind her and turned swiftly to see Mose, a Negro she had seen about the place. Moving slowly, glancing sideways at her now and then, he took her horse from her.

"Has Mr. Blair's horse been here all day, Mose?" she asked.

"I dunno, missus." He waved his hands helplessly. His whining voice protesting ignorance irritated her. But Maria explained that that was what slavery had done to him—so robbed him of responsibility and power that he feigned a child-like ignorance.

As Margaret emerged out into the warmth of the afternoon she heard him call to her.

"Missus."

She turned. His head was bent, but he looked up at her out of the corner of his eye as though he were embarrassed.

"Miss Margaret—you keepin' on with Athena Hall like yo' sister?"

"Of course," Margaret reassured him.

He nodded, satisfied.

Mose could have been the one who followed her—he had access to the horse. But why on earth would he?

As she approached the house she stopped and glanced up at her bedroom window, remembering the bloodstains. Surely anyone standing here could have seen the murder! She stood there a moment, staring, the hairs on the back of her head prickling. She felt as though a cold wind had blown across the clearing. Nervously she looked about, but no one was in sight to view her agitation.

Hastily she began to consider. Why had Jason gone to Elena's room that day? He had been told by Stanley to guard her, it was true, yet Jason might really either have seen the murder from here or actually done it himself. The thought filled her with a peculiar kind of grief.

She was silent as she walked into the kitchen which was filled with blackish smoke. Maria was scraping out an iron baking kettle that was filling the room with stench. Margaret looked at her sadly, unable to voice her suspicions of Jason. Why, after all, would Jason kill Elena?

But the black woman's thoughts were on the kettle.

"I swear to you, I have never before in my life burned the johnny cake. I don't know what has got into me!"

"Perhaps it's the baby." Margaret had a sudden thought. "Oh, you shouldn't have ridden with me! It might be bad for you."

Maria laughed. "To a slave such concern is amusing. Slave women must not miscarry valuable slaves. Yet they must work. I would have been beaten for burning the food. Still, our corn here is very valuable to us and I hate to see it wasted." Maria shook her head with disgust at the burned pot.

"You must teach me to help you, especially now that you are becoming a mother."

"Very well." Maria handed her the smoking pot which was still hot to Margaret's soft hands. "Scrape this pot."

Margaret worked slowly with the dull edge of a knife. Her thoughts were busy. She must ask Maria more about Jason and if possible talk to him herself. She dipped a little water from the wood bucket that sat near the kitchen hearth and rinsed her pot. She stepped out the kitchen door past the woodpile to empty the water. In the distance she could barely see the men and women working in the fields along with Henry. A little smoke was curling from the chimneys of the rough slave houses as some of the women prepared food. Someone there may have watched for her return from Jed's house, possibly the same person who killed Elena.

Despite the warmth of the spring afternoon, she felt chilled as she returned to Maria's side.

Maria stirred some mush in a pot, having revised the supper because of the johnny cake disaster.

"We have no game because the men are too busy."

This would be the worst supper Margaret had ever had. America might be a place where the poor could get ahead, but the diet had little to recommend it to one used to better fare.

"We don't seem to eat much but corn here."

"Henry has bought a few pigs, but they are too valuable as breeders yet. It would be nice to have a few laying hens."

"Indeed. We must have some, I think."

"Henry seems to begrudge the money."

"He never was one to notice what he was eating. But game and corn make a poor diet." Margaret wrinkled her nose with distaste. Then she felt guilty. Elena had thrived on the diet.

"You know," Maria moved the stew pot away from the fire, "I have an idea." She handed Margaret the water bucket. "This needs to be filled. And while we are at it, we will hunt for greens."

"Greens?"

"They grow wild. In the springtime slaves try to find time to seek them out. They thin the blood. And with this baby coming, I have a craving."

Maria picked up an extra bucket, slipping her hand into the handhold cut in the side. She still looked slim, and the high waist of her dress would hide her condition for a while yet.

"We cleared this meadow last year." Maria gestured to indicate the area surrounding the springhouse. There were a few stumps remaining. "We pasture the two horses here and some day we hope to have cows."

Maria dipped her bucket at a place where the water sprang from behind a rock.

"At my old master's we had a beautiful stone springhouse. There were always butter and cream set to cool. But they were not set there for us. My mistress used to give me special tidbits sometimes when I was little, but when I went out to the slave quarters and saw the hunger in the other children's eyes, the tidbits didn't sit well on my stomach." Maria frowned at the memory of her childhood.

"So this life is better for you, even though you eat mostly corn and game."

Maria looked at her with surprise.

"Of course. Have I not told you?" Leaning to one side because of the heavy bucket she held, Maria set off towards the river edge of the meadow. Margaret followed after with her own wooden bucket.

"I think I shall miss good food," Margaret said.

Maria showed Margaret where the greens had leafed out freshly from the spring soil. She could not tell Margaret their names, but she knew which ones were good to eat. The sun was pleasantly warm on their backs as they picked. Then the two women sat on the weed-grown ground to wash each leaf carefully. To Margaret it felt like a picnic.

Margaret was only beginning to realize how hard life was so far from civilization, even though they had begun Athena Hall with money and the house already built. Still, however little she knew about farming, instinct told her the place was poorly managed.

She began to realize how hard Jed's life must have been. And that of his mother who died. She had a sudden thought.

"How did Jed get the money to buy his farm?"

Maria looked surprised.

"I don't know. The other family tired of being so close to people and moved on towards Texas. There are a lot like that. Jed had been squatting further upriver, above Athena Hall. We used to see him now and then in the woods. He only had a poor shack and his fields were barely cleared before he planted his corn. A bachelor like that has nothing to hold him to the land."

"Now he seems quite settled."

"Jed is too easygoing. He needs a woman to cure him of his wandering habits. He stopped work when your sister died and went downriver for a while."

"Yes." Margaret brushed back a curl that had fallen

91

over her forehead. Her brow was damp in the drowsy warmth. She felt her fingers tremble slightly. Then she asked the question that had been nagging at her all day.

"What was he to Elena, Maria?"

"I don't know. I know she wanted to invite him to our Christmas party, but then Henry went into a temper and said we could not afford a party, that it would take all our doing to keep Athena Hall going another year."

"And so you had no Christmas celebration?"

"We did. At the last moment one of the men shot a deer and we roasted it. We had nothing but water to drink, but we danced and sang. Even slaves celebrate Christmas." Maria expertly doused a leaf in the water, checking it for grit.

"But Elena was not able to dance with Jed, if that's what she had in her mind." Margaret glanced up at the square, plain house, wondering what it had been like that wintry day.

"She enjoyed herself. I do not know what she felt for Jed, but I know she loved Athena Hall."

"Yes. I believe Elena loved her ideas more than she could any man."

"But her ideas could not get her with child." Maria looked amused.

They finished washing the greens and emptied the buckets, then returned to the springhouse for water for the house.

"I have met Jed before." Margaret studied Maria's face. "On the steamboat coming here."

Maria gave her such an assessing look that Margaret felt herself flush.

"So he told me when he came to ask about you last night. He wanted to know if you had arrived safely."

"You might have called me—or told me."

"I thought it best that he tell you himself." Once more the light in Maria's eyes was amused. "For if it is true that Jed needs a woman, it is also true that you need a man. I suspect that without physical love you

92

will never be able to concentrate on what must be done for Athena Hall. You are right when you say that Elena was more disciplined."

"Maria!" Margaret said with shock and shame. "I know almost nothing of this man except that he can prove to be quite odious."

A cry from the river interrupted them. The two women went down the long dark central hall of the house and out onto the veranda. A black man with horse and wagon labored across the crude bridge, the wagon swaying so on the rough logs that Margaret was afraid to look. Margaret's trunk and hat boxes were piled perilously on the jolting wagon.

"My boxes have come!" Margaret said with satisfaction, happy that the embarrassingly intimate conversation had been interrupted.

The driver went around to the stable to get Margaret's livery horse while she went up to her room for money to pay him. When she came down, she looked at her horse sadly. Though she was so sore in some places that she limped, she had come to rely on him. And it would be difficult for her to ride out again as she had that morning.

"Miz Johnson got a letter for you at the inn," the black man said, handing it to her.

"Why, thank you." Margaret pressed some coins into his hand.

Though it was a several hour ride back to Memphis, the driver was determined to try it. It would be very dark by the time he got there. He waved to Margaret as he drove away.

Margaret examined her letter eagerly. It was from Phillip, all the way from England. She marveled that a letter was able to find its way to the interior of America. She sat down on the veranda steps to read.

Phillip had written the letter the day after she had left. It had followed her closely all the way here.

Margaret,

When I said goodbye to you yesterday morning at the docks, I was already conscious of having made the greatest error of my life. I know not to what danger you may be traveling so many miles from home.

I should have made my feelings towards you clearer, my dear. Who but we two can know the many thoughts and ideas we have shared since childhood? Though we are not rich, we do possess between us enough to live comfortably. We share a concern for the poor and for music and friends and books. It seems to me that we could live well together as husband and wife.

I shall wait however long it may take you to consider this matter and answer me. I regret that I delayed so long in addressing you.

I am your loving friend,

Phillip

Margaret sighed, and for a moment allowed herself to picture Phillip comfortably seated before a dining table in Manchester enjoying the substantial cuisine of his housekeeper. It seemed so safe and comforting.

Yet she could not think of answering Phillp when Athena Hall was so new to her. She had promised everyone she would continue as Elena planned. But still—Phillip was there if she needed him. And the way things were going, she might. She pushed Maria's embarrassing words to the back of her mind. Maria was a fine woman, but she would not have her dictating to her about her personal life.

Margaret put Phillip's letter in the bodice of her dress and went into the kitchen.

Those in the fields had worked late to finish, so the candles were lit when Henry, Blair, Jason, Maria and Margaret all sat down to supper together. Obviously

Blair felt the whole situation—the meal's delay, the poor fare, and the blacks at table—as a great offense. He addressed himself to his food, half turning away from the rest of them, glancing up now and again at Jason with an expression of burning hostility.

Margaret, too, felt the situation to be novel. For all her advanced ideas in England, she had never sat down with the servants. She would have been hard put to accept the brilliant Maria as anything but an equal, but Jason made her uneasy. His face was dark and brooding and he spoke hardly at all.

Both Jason and Henry ate tensely, avoiding each other's eyes.

"Is anything the matter?" Margaret hated to sit at table with so much friction in the air.

"You may as well join the conflict," Henry said. "Jason thinks we need more help for clearing and planting, and I think it is time we had more teachers here."

"But Henry, they are all so busy working now they don't have time to learn."

"The work should slacken when summer comes after everything is planted."

Margaret had no answer to this. She knew nothing of farming, yet it did seem to her that even if the seed was in the ground there was much clearing to do. Jason stared down at his plate, a look of anger on his face.

"What do you think, Maria?" Margaret asked.

"I think we need more field workers," she answered.

Henry sprang to his feet, his yellowish face turning white.

"None of you understand. What we do at Athena Hall is not just for our immediate survival: It goes beyond that. I know I could not do without Jason and that he understands farming a good deal better than I. Yet you must all remember that it was Elena's plan to strike a blow at slavery, and it is a good plan, even though she is dead." He stamped out, no doubt to tramp about the place until he cooled off.

Jason's dark face looked blacker still in the deep shadows of the room. His glowing eyes fixed on the spot where Henry had disappeared.

Nervously Margaret put down her fork. She looked up to see Jason watching her with a stern expression. He breathed deeply, expanding his muscular chest.

"No corn . . ." He struggled to get the words out, then to bring forth the next ones. "We all gone bad . . ."

Margaret nodded encouragement. She wondered at him. She knew that Maria communicated with him and even said he told stories of his life in Africa. She felt he was a thoughtful and reasonable man who understood very well the workings of the farm. Yet it was so difficult for him to talk, even with Maria to teach him English. It was as though he had some impediment. Maria said his suffering on the slave ship and with a cruel master had marked him so that English speech was a terrible trial to him—that he had been whipped for speaking his own language.

It was illegal now to import new slaves, yet the trade continued. Jason was one of those who had been spirited in against the law from his native village. He had been still very young at the time.

Margaret could not judge between Jason's view and Henry's where Athena Hall was concerned. Still, Henry must modify his ideas in the face of necessity. The four of them sat there in silence in the little circle of light cast by the candle.

"Well, Miss," Blair said finally, leaning back in his chair and stretching. "I'm about to take leave of the table. Neither the fare nor the talk is much to my liking. I have a bottle of sherry in my room, if you care to join me. Henry may even come if his mood improves." So saying Blair reached across the table to place a finger under her chin, bringing her face up to look at him.

"No thank you," Margaret said coldly. She shook her head to relieve herself of his touch.

He shrugged.

"In time maybe you'll stop looking at us with English eyes and realize that we have our own ways. We don't like others to mock them." He left the room and they could hear his heavy footsteps creaking up the stairs overhead.

"That man makes my blood run cold," Maria said. "When he is most friendly you must be the most afraid."

Now, Margaret thought, was the time to question Jason while Maria was able to help. She pushed her plate across the plain table, then sat quietly, her hands clasped in her lap.

"Jason," she began. "Why did you go to my sister's room the day she was killed?"

He looked at her warily.

"Henry tell me—watch." Each word was painfully uttered.

"But tell me, did you not see her attacked through the window? Did you see anything?"

Jason stared at her. His face grew stiff and impassive. His strong hands, ebony black in the dim light, clenched once, then rested on the edge of the table.

"No—no—" He brought out the words with such a hoarse hollow sound that Margaret looked at him with amazement. He lied, she was sure. But why? Her stomach knotted as she realized that she had ventured closer to the barriers that blocked knowledge of Elena's murder from her.

Maria looked at Jason with fear and apprehension. Her coppery brown skin turned dull and opaque. Her eyes looked darker and more liquid as though she beseeched Margaret not to go on. It pained Margaret to probe so deeply and to upset people she admired. Yet her duty to Elena demanded that she continue.

"Is that all you can tell me?" She spoke as gently as she could.

"Henry say—watch Elena," Jason repeated doggedly. His hands clenched once more.

97

"Yes." If only she could speak to him with greater ease. Margaret bit her lip.

He rose slowly to his feet, his brooding dark eyes piercing her.

"You say—Henry—corn first. Not book first. Tell—we not go back—whip." Again the slave gave orders.

"Yes, yes," Margaret whispered. "I do not want you to go back to slavery to be whipped."

He stood there looking down at her. Neither his poor speech nor his condition of slavery detracted from his native African dignity.

Maria's and Margaret's eyes engaged, full of unspoken thoughts.

Brooding, Jason took out pipe and tobacco from a pouch at his waist. He could not wait to arrive at the kitchen fireside before preparing his smoke. He fixed his eyes on Margaret as he filled his pipe. No further words passed his lips.

As he left the room, Margaret thought of Phillip's letter. Whatever she must do eventually, whatever her life might prove to be with or without Phillip, for now she must attend to the problems of Athena Hall.

Maria smiled and spoke with fond sadness.

"Jason says that in Africa his people are buried with their pipes and tobacco—they are so valuable to them."

Margaret hesitated, then forced herself to speak.

"I know you love him, Maria, but if he knows anything of Elena's death, I must find out."

Maria did not answer, but bowed her turbaned head over her clasped hands.

Again she settled herself in the little room. Margaret was beginning to feel at home in it, yet when she glanced at the window and the dark stains nearby she could not suppress a shiver.

She closed her eyes briefly without extinguishing her candle, then peered sleepily through them to see her door begin to open once more.

"Maria?" she called hesitantly.

But the figure who stepped through the door was not Maria, but Edmund Blair.

Margaret drew her quilt up over her bosom with one hand and reached for the dagger still lying on the table with the other.

"Mr. Blair!" she said indignantly. She was clad only in a light bed gown.

"Picked up the little dagger, have you?" he chuckled from the shadows. "You may recall it didn't help your sister much."

"Really?" Margaret spoke rapidly, breathlessly. "What do you know about Elena's murder, Mr. Blair? Were you there?"

He made no answer.

"I advise you to get out of my room before Henry comes." If only he would, she prayed.

"Stanley is out tramping about the place somewhere, brooding about the future of Athena Hall and avoiding my company. No, my dear, there are only the two of us." His voice was oily, his smile cheerful. His eyes fixed upon the spot where the quilt was drawn to her bare throat.

Was this the way her sister had died? Margaret wondered with a rush of panic. She still held the dagger pointed in his direction. Never having used such a weapon she feared it was more a danger to her than to this powerful fat man. But he was still smiling. Perhaps she could talk to him.

"Whatever possesses you, Mr. Blair, so that you cannot see a woman without having to put your hands upon her?" she said faintly, her lips trembling. "This is certainly strange behavior in a man who is such good friends with Preacher Brad."

Blair moved slowly towards her, unchecked by her words.

"Brad and I know what weakness you women hide under your skirts," he said insinuatingly. "I know your sister could not brag of her chastity. She went off into the woods after a few sharp words with me. Twice, she did it, and who knows how many other times when I was not here. And then she vomited up her sins because she'd got a brat. And now I see you've taken to riding in the woods as well." Blair's face was flushed. Wisps of thin hair floated about his bald spot.

Margaret tried hard to reason with him: "Your hatred of women must be deep indeed, Mr. Blair. Think, though, your mother was a woman. You must not be so hard on the rest of us."

"Her?" Blair spat. "You speak of her? Many a time in our cabin along the river I heard her screaming, screaming as my father beat her. Then she ran all the way to New Orleans, dragging me along, a mere boy. When we got there I found why he beat her and called her whore—I discovered what a whore was!"

"Perhaps she had no other way to live," Margaret said sadly. "Perhaps your father was only jealous."

"He knew! I tell you, he knew!" Blair thundered. "Just as I know about you, Missus. Where do you lie in the woods and who do you lie with?"

"So it was you who followed me today." It all seemed plain enough. He was obsessed. Margaret felt a chill of fear creep over her.

"Followed you?" For a moment he seemed genuinely confused. Then his obsession returned. "I had no need to follow you. I saw you through the window when you left and when you returned. I know the look of a woman whoring about the countryside." Blair looked at her intently, his eyes wild.

"But whoever followed me used your horse—the livery horse."

"One of the niggers, mayhap. Was it he you lay with out in the forest?" Blair's hand stole forward to lie upon the quilt.

Margaret drew a deep breath, trying to summon all her sanity in the face of his madness.

100

"I didn't—as you say—lie with anyone, Mr. Blair. And if I had it would be no concern of yours. Your behavior is disgusting for a man who is supposed to confine himself to the business affairs of Athena Hall." Oh, why had Henry chosen this time to go walking through the night in anger?

She did not lower her knife.

"Yes." Blair stood for a moment, stroking his round chin. Then his voice sank to a kind of growl. "Brad and me see things alike. We don't like trollopy, book-reading women, nor nigger slaves who get beyond themselves."

"Then I think the affairs of Athena Hall are better off in other hands. And now I pray you, Mr. Blair, to leave my room. You will have to account to Henry when he returns."

Blair's eyes glittered with rage.

"Threaten me, will you? A little bit of fluff lying on your back on your bed?"

At that he grabbed the quilt and jerked it out of her grasp. The candle flickered wildly and blew out. Holding the bed cover in his hands, he came over to the side of the bed, then threw it over her head and arms, locking her tight with his massive arms. Half smothered and panicked, she twisted and fought like a fish in a net. Her dagger was nothing but a danger to her now. With all her might she lunged over the side of the bed away from him and slid free onto the floor, striking one knee a sharp blow as she landed. Breathing raggedly she felt for her dagger. It had disappeared. She rose shakily to her feet, her eyes fixed on Blair. He lunged to her side. Her back was against the corner of the room; there was no retreat. Seizing her by the flimsy stuff of her bed gown, he threw her down upon the bed, ripping the cloth from one shoulder, knocking the breath from her lungs.

Kicking, she fought for air, then screamed, "Maria! Maria!" Would no one hear?

Heavy footsteps were heard on the stairs and Jason's

dark form burst through the door. One strong blow from his fist landed with a sickening dull impact, knocking Blair aside and onto the floor. Blair's skull hit last with a crack that would have shattered a head less thick. Margaret stood for a moment in shock, then Maria came up beside Jason, carrying a candle. Her dark eyes showed a concern that was almost pain.

Blair lay on the floor, disheveled, his face an alarming red. He breathed heavily, shaking his head in a daze. Slowly he rose to his feet, his eyes finding first one, then another of them. Finally they rested on Maria.

"If you want to keep this nigger in your bed, you'd better tell him to keep his hands off white men, or to save this bitch's honor he may get killed. It would give me pleasure to haul him to the law."

Maria stood frozen with fear, all her usual courage and strength drained away. Her eyes never left Blair's.

But Jason, still, upright, and menacing, held his ground.

"That's enough, Blair," a voice said from the doorway. Henry stood there, looking pale, yellowish, and haggard.

Thank God, Margaret thought. It would take a white man to deal with Blair, since the law went ever against the blacks.

Blair's rage knew no bounds.

"You'd better keep this nigger on your place, Stanley! If he sets foot off of it, you're liable never to see him again!" Margaret thought Blair would burst in a fit of apoplexy.

"You must be mad, Blair." Henry strode towards him as though to threaten the much larger man. "Perhaps whiskey is weakening your brain. It is obvious that you were harassing Margaret just as you harassed Elena. I thought you were capable of conducting our legal and business affairs. I think so no longer. I shall inform the trustees that we cannot rely on you. Now, if

102

you don't mind, you can sleep downstairs on the sitting room floor. I want no more of you."

Blair looked at all of them with hatred in his eyes, then wheeled and made his way heavily down the stairs.

Margaret went to Henry's side and kissed him on the cheek.

"You were wonderful, Henry. And I don't know what I would have done without Jason."

"Yes," Maria said, "but I fear we have not heard the last of this. Blair grows worse by the day. If drink doesn't destroy him first, hatred will. He despises Athena Hall."

Margaret sat herself down on the bed, covering herself with the quilt for modesty's sake.

"We must take our affairs out of his hands as soon as possible. Someone should go to New Orleans when we can arrange it to see the trustees. There's no knowing what he may have stolen from us."

"I cannot be spared from the farm," Henry said. His features looked even more drawn, if that were humanly possible.

"Then I shall go," Margaret said.

"Good." Maria spoke from her place near the door. "I am sure you will be more valuable there than in the kitchen."

"I fear I am poorly trained for that work." Margaret laughed, but felt the sting of Maria's words.

"How can you deal with such a man?" Henry wearily mopped his brow with a handkerchief. "He is a complete degenerate and I don't like to see you travel so far without a companion."

"I shall try never to see him alone," Margaret said.

Henry considered the problem for some time. The frown on his narrow forehead deepened.

"It makes me very uneasy to agree, but I have no choice," he said at last. "Promise me that you will not see him alone and that if you need help you will contact the authorities."

103

Margaret nodded.

"Don't worry. I am determined never to give him an advantage again."

Jason stirred, as though from a dream. His eyes met Margaret's with a self-assurance that few men raised in slavery could muster. But then Jason was an African still struggling with American ways.

"Fix Blair," he said slowly. "No whip Jason, no more, nobody."

"Yes, Jason, no more," Margaret said. "Nevermore."

Chapter Seven

By morning Blair had taken his horse and departed even before the early hour when the rest of them arose.

"I must surely go to the trustees at New Orleans before he makes any more mischief," Margaret said. She was wearing one of the simplest of her own calico gowns and hoped it would do good service at Athena Hall.

"I must insist that you rest a week or two before beginning to travel again," Henry said. In truth it was he who looked drawn and exhausted.

"You must spare yourself, Henry."

They stood together on the veranda, looking towards the stream and the roughly cleared road over which Blair must have traveled. Henry gnawed on a piece of corn pone that would serve as breakfast for him.

"I will give you detailed instructions about what to say to the trustees and how to find teachers," he told her. Margaret saw him tremble as he spoke.

"Perhaps I can do some things that will help the

farm, also." Margaret was mindful of the discussion of the night before.

"Perhaps. I do not want to slight the farm work, yet I urge you, Margaret, to do everything in your power to speed our work so that we can continue as we planned with your sister in Manchester. As for me—I am most anxious since I am not sure how long I can continue."

"Henry," Margaret gasped. He had whitened under the stress of his emotions as he uttered these last words. "Oh, Henry, please spare yourself. We can do little without you. And you have lost the health you had in England."

"I shall rest once I know Athena Hall is a success." He walked down the stairs, then turned towards the fields at the back of the house.

Why, he looks almost old, Margaret thought. She vowed she would help him as much as she could. She would recuperate from her long journey and prepare herself for her return downriver. And she would also help Maria and Henry in any way possible.

She went into the kitchen to ask Maria what she might do to be useful. Maria was sweeping the floor with a crude splint broom. She seemed lost in thought and without her usual self-possession.

"Yes, indeed. What might you do? Tomorrow I thought to wash clothes and you can surely help there. Today I will lend a hand in the fields and then spin some linen when I begin to tire."

Margaret had once spent some hours with a nurse who had shown her the workings of the linen wheel. Her yarn had been lumpy and uneven, though of course she had been but a child then. She despaired of having any skills but French to offer the competent Maria.

"Well, then, perhaps I can work in the fields, too."

Maria stopped working to look at her thoughtfully. She said nothing for several moments, wiping one hand on her apron. She was surely not herself today, Margaret thought, but vague and preoccupied. Perhaps it was the baby. Finally Maria spoke with the air of one who knows some words are expected.

"Field work will ruin your hands and your complexion, my lady."

"I can't let that stop me, Maria," Margaret protested. Suddenly Maria dropped all pretense and spoke directly.

"Have you seen Jason, Margaret?"

"Why, no. Why do you ask?"

"I have not seen him since last night."

"Really? Perhaps he is out working on the place."

"Perhaps." Maria looked doubtful, but her expression brightened as masculine footsteps were heard outside.

But it was not the barefoot Jason who stood in the doorway, but the moccasin-shod Jed. Margaret flushed as she realized how good it was to see him. She hoped Maria did not notice her reaction.

Maria stared for a moment, then began to sweep again.

"Mr. Sawyer," Margaret stammered.

"I've come to get you for some sweetnin'," he said. Margaret gawked at him in confusion. He wore a roughly woven red shirt and his eyes looked very blue like those of his Scotch-Irish ancestors.

"I think I have found a bee tree. You might like to share it."

Maria stopped her sweeping and looked at him as though he were dimwitted. He nodded to her, looking a trifle embarrassed.

"Oh dear, I really know nothing about bee trees," Margaret said. "Does that mean you're after honey?"

"Yes—with your help."

"My help? Why me?" Margaret's face grew warm.

"For the company."

Margaret glanced at Maria to see if she should go. Maria only shrugged and kept on working.

"Well, it would be nice to have honey." She could

hear her own voice ringing in her ears—high, uncertain and unconvincing. She sounded like an infant flirt.

"Bring a kettle." Jed turned his back on them and strode past the woodpile. Without going for a bonnet, Margaret hurried after him, kettle in hand. Really, Margaret tried to persuade herself, going for honey would be a useful thing to do.

"Don't get stung," Maria's wry voice came after her.

Jed tied the kettle on his saddle. There was also a jug fastened there which he untied for a moment so he could take a swig of whiskey He wiped his mouth with the back of his hand.

"What's that for?" Margaret asked.

"Pain." He might have been smiling had the corners of his mouth turned up.

Margaret looked at him with alarm. He fastened down his jug, then leapt into the saddle and pulled her up behind him. She was forced to ride with her arms around him, which she found embarrassingly pleasant. They rode out into the forest and she leaned her face against the warmth of his shirt. He seemed not to notice. She tried to tell herself she was a fool and that she should keep a greater distance from him, but the day was so beautiful that she seemed to have lost her will to do so.

They rode in this manner for some time, then Jed pulled up the reins and they halted. He looked about a sunny clearing.

"That looked to be a bee that just went by." He helped her slide off, then dismounted.

The little glade was warming under the sun and Margaret was beginning to miss the shade of her bonnet.

Jed was peering through the trees to see what had become of the lone bee. He reached into a pouch belted near the knife at his side and brought out a small piece of old cloth. As he unwrapped several layers, Margaret saw that it was sticky with honey. He put a dab of it on a rock and came over to stand next to Margaret. Placing one arm across her shoulders, the other over the horse's neck, he remained standing lazily in the sun for several minutes before they saw a bee fly unerringly to the rock. As it flew off again, Jed gauged its direction, walking through the trees after it. Then he came back and began to lead the horse further back into the forest.

Margaret followed like some primitive dumb beast. She was drugged by the sweet smells of vegetation under the sun. They might be a man and his woman from anywhere on earth since Paradise was left behind. The direction of her thoughts embarrassed her, yet he seemed to notice only the job at hand.

After a while he stopped and daubed another sun warmed rock with honey, pouring a drop of whiskey over it for good measure. He flung himself on the ground to watch. Margaret, too, sat.

When the bee came, Jed watched it carefully, then raised Margaret to her feet. Again he leaned one arm over her shoulders. Slothfully she enjoyed his warmth like the warmth of the day.

"Y'see, it's as good as surveying," he told her, gesturing with his free arm. "The first bee lighted on that rock and flew straight that way. The second landed on this one and flew that way. If you pace off two straight lines, they'll come together. That's where you'll find the bee tree."

He grabbed for the horse's reins and they walked slowly along the bee's line of flight.

"There it is!" Jed said with satisfaction.

It was a ruined tree, most of its branches gone, hollow and rotten inside. Bees were busily exiting and entering, buzzing and droning.

"What shall I do?" Margaret whispered.

"Gather tinder."

She began to search for small dried twigs and grass. He was thrashing about in the undergrowth, amassing great pieces of dead branches and other inflammable matter with the aid of his axe. In the background she could hear the rippling of the wild stream.

"Don't get too near," he warned her as she went toward the bee tree. She dropped her material in a pile and retreated.

"What shall I do now?"

"Set the kettle in that little clearing, then take the horse and get out of the way."

She went to the mare and moved her still farther into the undergrowth. Jed carefully avoided the bees as he piled the branches and tinder about the base of the tree. Then he busied himself with flint and the horseshoe-shaped steel, cursing until the fire had caught. As the fire burned upwards, he went to the stream bank for green grass and damp leaves to make it smoke.

The startled bees began an angry snarl and rose from the tip of the hollow tree in a cloud.

"Ouch!" Jed said, as one angry victim found its mark. He retreated once more to watch. Margaret cowered behind the horse. Finally Jed ran over to her and loosened the whiskey jug from its fastenings. Thirstily he drank a couple of good swallows, then re-corked it and put it back.

"More pain?" Margaret asked. He grinned at her.

"Give me your apron," he said.

Margaret had forgotten to take it off. She undid it now and handed it to him. He wrapped it about his right hand, then picked up his axe. Then he was off and running towards the smoky fire. With two sharp blows he opened up the side of the rotten tree, then flung his axe out into the clearing. Reaching inside the hole, he grasped a chunk of comb, then ran like a madman, angry bees after him, thirsting for vengence.

Leaping in great leaps and yelling like a maniac, he ran towards the open kettle, dropped in the comb, then slammed on the cover. He barely paused in his running, heading towards the stream, a plume of bees strung out behind him. Margaret could see nothing more, but heard his splashings and splutterings. Countless bees still swarmed about the little glade. The horse stamped her feet, whinnying. A stinging pain struck Margaret's hand.

"Oww!" she yelled, pulling the horse back even farther. The mare rolled her eyes wildly, but came obediently enough.

"Got you, did they!" Jed called from the stream.

Margaret studied her hand and saw the tiny black stinger still disgorging. She had not been stung since she was a child in the clover fields at home. She pulled the stinger and put her hand to her mouth to suck the pain away.

Margaret heard one more yell from Jed, then dropped the reins cautiously and made her way to the stream. He was just coming out of the water, soaking wet, his hair plastered on his head. Her apron lay a rag on the bank. The bees had returned home, so he stripped the wet shirt off his back, then lay on the bank, reaching into the gooey mud and plastering it on his arm and at the side of his face. Near his eye there seemed to be some swelling.

"Here," he said, scooping up a gob of mud. "Where are you hurt?" She held out her hand, and he dumped the mud on the spot. It was soothing, she decided.

Exhausted, he lay back on the bank, face to the skies, breathing heavily.

"Bring me my whiskey, woman," he said. Feeling slightly resentful, she did as she was told. He took a couple of swallows.

"Ah, the pain is better now." Handing the jug to her he smiled. "Have some."

"It smells awful," she said, setting it down. Then she bent to look at him more closely.

"Jed, you fool, your face is swelling. Was it worth this for that bit of honey?"

"Honey is mighty sweet," he said, then threw one arm around her neck and drew her down. His kiss was

111

gentle and warm like the day itself, and the smell of what might have been honeysuckle drifted through the air. She lost herself in these sensations, soft as the honey itself, and did not think beyond the moment. They lay there, languidly embraced, with him holding the muddy side of his face away from her. The whole day seemed turned to honey, and she as well, her brain, her breast, her very bones. It was something she had never known before. The barriers she had always felt between herself and Phillip dropped away.

Jed reached with thumb and forefinger to feel one of her dark curls. She gently rubbed at the flaking mud as it slowly dried on his face. When their lips came together again it was as though neither willed it—it just happened. But their lazy feelings warmed. She stroked the hard muscles of his browned back while he pulled aside her bodice until the milky white breast was revealed under the heavy sun. His mouth sought the nipple. Deeply stirred, she moved her hips towards his.

"Oh, lady," he murmured painfully. "There's all this cloth between you and me." Smiling gently, without a second thought, or any thought at all, she slowly stripped herself of the calico gown until the two of them were as naked as Adam and Eve.

For a moment he studied her lean curves, then he roughly pulled her to him and entered her.

She gasped at a brief pain, then at the pleasure of being filled by him.

Oh, but she could not have enough of him. He stiffened suddenly, and her untaught body rose in response as they exploded together with tender burning joy.

When she arose, she threw on her mussed dress, then hiked her skirts to wade into the stream to wash herself. It scarcely mattered now whether or not he saw her legs. Below the sun-warmed surface the water was cool. He watched her from the bank, touching his fingertips to the dried mud on his face.

112

"You look grotesque," she said, looking back at him.

"And you don't look much like a lady."

Sighing, she supposed not. The whole beautiful drunkenness of the day and his craziness with the bees had robbed her of the ability to think. For a few moments at least she had forgotten the worry of the future of Athena Hall and of her own future and whether or not she had behaved properly.

When she came back and lay down beside him on the uneven ground, he reached for her and kissed her again.

"I told you I came out today for a bit of sweetenin'," he said.

She drew away from him, not liking the tone of what he had said. Would any sweetenin' have done as well? Then all the thoughts she had put away during the day came swarming back into her mind. She hesitated, biting her lip for a moment before she spoke.

"Jed. Elena was to have a child. Was it yours?"

He sighed, and looked at her as though she were a silly woman who must intrude on a man's pleasure.

"I guess that it was," he said.

His words pierced her with a shock. She felt betrayed by and betraying of both of them. She put on her slippers, rose, and walked away from him. She went over to the horse, throwing one arm over its back and resting her head near the saddle.

Oh, what would Elena think of this day's work? And what had she thought of Jed? She could hear him stirring and walking about, the clank of the kettle as he set it near her feet. He drew her away from the horse and wrapped his arms about her.

"Now what's this?" he said. "You're biting your lip again." He touched her lip gently with a forefinger, then leaned his head against hers.

Why couldn't he understand? she wondered. Her sister who was dead had lain in his arms just as she had.

"Did you love her?"

"Love her." He set Margaret aside then, and sat on

113

the ground. "No, I don't think I did. Yes, maybe. I don't know what that means. I've known a lot of women here and there."

A lot of women. Margaret felt a great pang of jealousy and a feeling of offended pride in Elena's as well as her own name.

"Yes, Davy did call you a frontier hellion." She stiffly walked away towards where she thought Athena Hall lay. He pursued her and grabbed her by her arm.

"Hold on, there. You'll get lost, you foolish Englishwoman. Now stay here a minute while I gather up my things." He retrieved his axe and fastened the whiskey, kettle, and jug back onto the saddle. He threw his drying shirt on top of everything, then stripped the moccasins off his feet and squeezed the water out of them.

"They'll be stiff as boards tonight," he said. "It's better to put them back on to soften." And so he did, and mounted once more and pulled her up behind him.

She swayed forward and leaned her head on his bare back as they rode. Oh, why was she so weak that she could not find out the truth of how things stood before she let her emotions move her? The sting on her hand still twinged now and then like her conscience. She could see the mud flaking off Jed's face when he turned towards her.

What would Maria think of her? But then she had as much as told Margaret she wanted this to happen and was herself deeply in love with Jason.

Henry might be another matter.

"You say you've known a lot of women?" she asked, her lips close to Jed's back. She felt as though she was seeking to be tormented the way he had sought honey through the bee stings.

"I've lived on the frontier and the river all my life. There's not a lot of women, but it's not like living in town and going to church every Sunday."

"Evidently."

"Why do you ask questions if you don't like the answers?"

She was forced to admit to herself that he had a point.

"Well, I guess it's true that you don't understand me and the way I've lived. Nor did you probably understand Elena."

"All women say the same things," he grunted.

This remark particularly offended her.

"What happened between you and Elena?"

"I don't like to talk about it. I don't understand it myself."

Margaret felt as though she were riding the jolting horse with a broken rib. Each step brought more pain to her. It would be simpler if it were a physical pain. She was shocked at her feelings of jealousy, yet protective of Elena at the same time. She wanted nothing more than to get to Athena Hall and hide inside the room where her sister had died. When they could see Athena Hall in the distance, they both dismounted. He turned to face her.

"You don't really want to hear about it, but you won't rest until you do."

She nodded. All the sweetness of the morning was gone.

"Your sister ran to me twice because of Blair."

She nodded again.

"I know. He attacked me also, last night."

"She was afraid that Jason might kill him in her defense and that the law would get him—a black man killing a white. It was only her word, since Henry Stanley was gone. There are no close neighbors and she knew me a little from the years I was in the woods."

"She was upset," he continued. "I supposed that she was not a woman usually upset."

Margaret nodded in agreement.

"And so we sat together by the fireside, then went

the way of a man and a woman on the frontier. There's no preacher but one hereabouts to tell us we shouldn't."

"Did she love you, then?" Margaret whispered.

"How should I know?" he said angrily. "There wasn't time to find out. Make no mistake, it wasn't a thing coldly done, but there was not enough time."

"And me?" she said. "Me?"

He smiled very slightly.

"You? There hasn't been enough time for you, either."

"And for none of your other women, either, I suppose." She was suddenly very angry.

"For God's sake, woman, I've been a mover and a river man all my life. I've only begun to settle down—and then Elena died."

She looked at him thoughtfully.

"And then Elena died." One thing seemed plain enough. He could not have caused her death—could he? Even though the dagger was his to begin with.

"Where did you get the dagger, Jed?"

"I've already told you it's none of your business!"

Was it not? she wondered.

He untied the kettle and handed it to her.

"Here."

"But the honey. Don't you want any?"

"I can always go back," he shrugged.

It had certainly been a ruse to get her out. Maria would raise her eyebrows at the scant results of her day. She was feeling very small, indeed. Lovemaking did not seem to have a very good effect on her. Yet she always would remember the wonder of this afternoon and wish she could return to the innocent pleasure of it.

"I will take you back with me, if you like, when I go again."

"I don't know," she said slowly. "I must think." She had set such great tasks for herself, and already she had forgotten them all.

116

He shrugged again, looking down at the ground. Leading the horse, he began to walk away.

Margaret pressed her fingers to her lips. It might be difficult to see him again. Yet it was true that she must regain her wits and control of her life.

"What's this?" he said.

She turned to see what he was looking at, but he was merely studying the dirt at his feet. He swung his axe free and began prodding the soil. She could see nothing at all until she moved closer. There were some flakes of black material.

"It's nothing but burned cloth," she said.

"What's it doing here?" He continued his digging until he unloosened a great clout of homespun not destroyed by fire. He straightened it out with the blade of the axe, seeming not to want to touch it. Only the very center was free from rot. But they were able to see brownish stains soaked deeply into the lighter colored cloth.

"Maybe someone was hunting," she ventured.

"And so burned a sound shirt instead of washing it?"

Their eyes met. Margaret was sorry that she had angered him because she felt afraid.

But he mounted his horse before he looked back at her again.

"Be careful at Athena Hall. Is Blair still there?"

"No. He left this morning."

He nodded, then turned and rode away.

Margaret wanted to call him to come back, to explain herself to him. But then she remembered that he had said all women said the same things, and she turned proudly away. She picked up the kettle and her soggy apron and walked towards the house, swinging around towards the front.

Maria was standing there, her hands clasped tightly in her apron. Margaret felt her face blaze. She thought that Maria had probably half expected her to come home dragging her crushed skirts and shameless memories with her—half wanted her to tie her to Athena Hall.

Still, Margaret felt that Maria needed help with the countless tasks about the place. Margaret had let her down badly there. Tomorrow she would work hard with the washing.

There was something strange about the way Maria stood there, so still and unmoving. Margaret hoped that the baby was not coming so many months before its time. When she drew closer she saw that Maria looked grey and drawn, her eyes dull and stricken.

"Maria! What is it?"

Maria looked at her dumbly, unable to find words, though her mouth worked painfully. Margaret dropped her kettle and ran to the black woman's side.

"Maria!"

"Jason!" The word burst from Maria's lips hoarsely.

"What is it? Where is he?"

"Lying in the hall."

Margaret broke away and ran into the house. There were Henry, Mose, and some of the others bending over Jason's body on the floor. One of the men was holding the axe and wiping blood from it with an old rag. Sickened, Margaret forced her eyes downward. Jason's skull was crushed and he was covered with dirt. Margaret covered her mouth with her hands to keep from retching. There were spots of dried blood on Jason's clothing. He must have been killed some hours before. Incongruously, the man was laboring hard to free the axe from its bloody stains. Even when it came to murder the people of Athena Hall were thrifty, she thought. The axe must be saved for its more ordinary uses.

"What happened?" she said in a low voice.

Strangely enough Jason still looked strong and vital even in death.

"They found him in the woods." Henry's voice quavered like that of an old man. He seemed thinner and yellower than before.

This will kill him, she thought.

Mose and the others volunteered information. Remembering the charred cloth Jed had found, she questioned them closely. Jason had been gone all day. Finally they had stumbled upon him behind some felled trees at the edge of the cleared area. The bloodied axe that belonged to Athena Hall lay near his side.

But the charred cloth looked long buried, Margaret thought. As long as—perhaps since Elena had died. And it had been found on the other side of the clearing from Jason's body.

"Was it Blair?" she asked them.

They all looked at her blankly. No one knew.

Oh, my God! Maria! She must go to her in her suffering. Margaret went out the door and looked about. Maria was nowhere in sight. Margaret walked down to the stream and then through the clearing. Surely Jason's wife would be back soon when the first of her grief had begun to abate.

But she was not. As night fell and they laid Jason out for burial, Maria had not returned.

In the morning they buried Jason with his pipe and tobacco as befitted an African. Even as he was committed to the ground Maria had not returned.

Chapter Eight

The journey to New Orleans was a long and uninteresting one. She had so recently come upriver that the sights were familiar to her. Besides, her mind was weighed down with the tragedies at Athena Hall. Justice was haphazard in the American west. No inquest was summoned to look into Jason's murder since he was but a slave. There was no way of telling that Blair had actually killed him, otherwise he might have been made to pay for destroying one of their chattels.

They had been careful to avoid advertising Maria's disappearance. The law could fall heavily on runaways. Margaret only hoped that her friend was safe, whatever her reason for leaving.

Margaret passed Jed's cabin on her way to Memphis in the wagon. The little house was closed and deserted-looking. She told Mose to give Jed word of her departure. Jed was a matter that would require more thought upon her return. But late at night when the American moon shone brightly upon her pillow and her defenses weakened she dreamed of him.

Once more she partook of Mrs. Johnson's hospitality at the inn while Mose turned back with the horses towards Athena Hall. While she waited for the *Captain Blake*, Mrs. Johnson told her that Henry Stanley had arrived in a lather on a livery horse borrowed from Edmund Blair just in time to catch the *Criterion* for Cincinnati the month that Elena was killed.

Margaret had to admit to herself that she enjoyed New Orleans—so far from all that had troubled her and away from the discomforts of the steamboat. Not that the town was comfortable. For one thing, there were the mosquitoes. The swampy situation was hot and humid and often filled with early morning fog. But it was an exciting and foreign town, quite strange to her English eyes.

The streets were filled with delicious and exciting smells, smells of the sachet shops and of magnolia, cape jasmine and honeysuckle from lush gardens. Negro vendors wandered the streets calling "Blaack-ber-ies," "Waat-er-melons," "I got fresh corn, butterbeans, cantaloupe, oranges . . ." Margaret couldn't wait to taste all these things after the restricted diet at Athena Hall. Other vendors called in French, "Charbon! du charbon, Madame? Bon charbon?" Down near the wharves the smells were of tar and rope and products shipped in from the Caribbean.

Still, New Orleans was a dirty town. Only a few streets were paved with cobblestones. She had been told that brawling river men tied up their boats at a huge flatboat harbor at Tchoupitoulas Street. She was warned away from this underworld section of town where drunken men staggered from tavern to brothel. She thought of Jed and wondered what he might have experienced of the riverboat harbor.

As she walked through the streets from her hotel she heard church bells ringing and the pleasant sounds of French rippling past her ear like some refreshing brook. She had enjoyed a fragrant cup of coffee, French bread and strawberries in her shuttered room before setting out and was relaxed and pleased with the world.

She sighed, reflecting on her own frivolity. As long as she had a few creature comforts she could so lazily forget the missing Maria, the murdered Elena and Jason, and the problems of Athena Hall. In so relaxed a setting, pleasurable thoughts of Jed seeped past the barriers in her mind. She must arm herself against all these distractions until the work she must do was finished.

Now she walked through the streets to Mrs. Henderson's house. Mrs. Henderson was a trustee of Athena Hall. Since the sun's glare was increasing, Margaret wore an enormous straw hat, brand new, bound under her chin with a scarf. Her thin sprigged muslin dress with its puffed sleeves, high waist, and single band of ruffles just above the hem was as cool as anything could be in the climate.

It was 11 o'clock when she presented herself at the door of Mrs. Henderson's house, a small shaded dwelling with glass doors opening into a pretty garden. Margaret had sent her a note by messenger the day before.

A young slave girl ushered her into a cool parlor. Her hostess came forward to embrace her.

"My dear Miss Havershill, we are all so grieved about Elena."

"I have not got used to it yet," Margaret admitted.

Mrs. Henderson was a rounded woman of middle age. Her expression was concerned and motherly. Her two children, a son and a daughter, sat on the floor leafing through books.

"The gentlemen and some other ladies will join us for dinner at two. I have asked the few people in New Orleans who profess a belief in the abolition of slavery. But now we must discuss the problems of Athena Hall."

Margaret settled into a comfortable chair, feeling pampered indeed. She explained the situation to her pleasant listener.

"It is too bad the trustees are so far from Tennessee,"

Mrs. Henderson said. "Yet the plan of Athena Hall is a good one. We cannot let the activities of Edmund Blair interfere with it. We will investigate his activites and place our concerns in other hands."

"At one time," Mrs. Henderson continued, "I wondered why we did not place all authority over the funds in the hands of Henry Stanley and your sister—but now it seems all for the best."

Margaret nodded.

Mrs. Henderson rose and looked out into her garden.

"It seems we must see about buying more slaves—a strange thing when abolition is our aim. Whatever slaves we buy must be suited to the work of Athena Hall."

Wondering, Margaret looked at the little black girl arranging their coffee and claret.

"We ourselves are slave owners." Mrs. Henderson's face showed some embarrassment. "We found all other help unreliable. But we hope to help our slaves buy their freedom."

Margaret thought this a somewhat curious state of affairs.

Mrs. Henderson very kindly gave her the name of a French lady, Mme. Sevestre, who had fled the Revolution. Though this lady was not a strong abolitionist, she would make an excellent teacher.

The children stirred restlessly. Mrs. Henderson fixed a critical eye on them.

"We take the children out when the wind blows from the lake, otherwise we keep them home in warm weather as it only makes them more languid to go out."

"It is a very feverish climate, I believe," Margaret said.

Mrs. Henderson shrugged in an almost Gallic manner.

When the gentlemen and other ladies arrived for dinner, Margaret found the conversation interesting and the company lively. M. Charles Petit, who came originally from France, she found particularly amusing.

"The city is unhealthy for the body, and some say also for the morality," M. Petit said.

"Indeed?" Margaret replied. Fanning herself, she sighed. She did so love civilized conversation. Maria might have provided it had she not disappeared; Henry was very learned but terribly serious; Jed could hardly be called a conversationalist in the English sense. She looked about at the pleasant group. Athena Hall seemed gloomy compared to all this light talk.

Mr. Henderson, a lawyer, told Margaret that he and the three other trustees would find someone to replace Edmund Blair since they had had so much trouble with him. Margaret nodded gratefully.

The party left the dinner table early. The gentlemen trundled low stools and some light chairs into the garden so they might all enjoy the shade. There they chatted throughout the afternoon. Mr. Potter and Petit sang some amusing French songs that had come down the river from Canada with the French river men. Margaret wondered if Jed knew these songs.

The heat settled down in earnest and some of the ladies talked listlessly of the need for a siesta, but no one moved. Finally tea was brought out and then Mrs. Henderson suggested they retire around the piano inside for the mosquitoes were becoming fierce.

"Ah, no," M. Petit suggested. "The afternoon has been too wonderful! I think we should go to the opera."

Mrs. Henderson was hesitant.

"Yes," M. Petit insisted. "The Orleans Theatre can be most enjoyable. And I have my carriage here."

"It might be nice for Miss Havershill," Mrs. Henderson agreed.

Several other gentlemen and ladies wished to go.

"And Miss Havershill may get a glimpse of the quadroon beauties going into their ball," Mr. Henderson added.

"Quadroon ball?" Margaret wondered.

"Yes." Mr. Henderson puffed contentedly on a cheroot. "It is one of our more colorful, though sad, customs. The women are *gens de couleur*, or free women of color—neither white nor black, generally at least three-quarters Creole. The most beautiful of these lightskinned women become the mistresses of rich white men, though they are not allowed to marry. For many years there were more men than women in New Orleans, you see."

"It is often tragic," a lady added, fanning herself with a palmetto fan. She was rather heavy, and her doublechinned face was glistening with moisture. "I have heard touching stories about couples separated by the man's family and children brought up with much love, but no official recognition." Her sigh made Margaret suspect that the lady was a habitual reader of romances.

"The ver-ee richest men keep their mistresses in fine houses on Ramparts Street." M. Petit stood with one arm resting on the chimney piece, and the other gesturing elegantly. "They are kept very well indeed and the children are baptised at the cathedral. The women are faithful all their lives to their protectors."

"They say the quadroon balls are the grandest in town. But white ladies are not allowed there, only white men." Mrs. Henderson rocked slowly in her carved rosewood chair. "The quadroon women are often highly educated as well as beautiful. If they are able they go to France to school. It is no wonder many men lose their hearts to them in a way legitimate wives can never inspire."

Margaret had been a secret reader of romances, and these descriptions of the quadroons whetted her appetite. Elena had never approved of light novel reading, but surely she too would have been curious about these ladies. It was a great injustice, after all, that families were separated by race and by law.

"The opera will be tame by comparison, but never-

126

theless we shall enjoy ourselves," M. Petit assured them.

In no time Margaret and Mrs. Henderson set off with M. Petit in his carriage and another couple followed behind. The famous Orleans Theatre was at Bourbon and Orleans streets. As they turned to draw up before the theatre, Margaret saw some of the dandified white gentlemen and the tall, elegant, copper-complected quadroon beauties going into the ball. They were accompanied by older women wearing turbans. Margaret judged them to be the women's mamas. Margaret felt dowdy in her simple muslin and wished mightily for a glimpse of the ball.

The comic opera inside seemed bland compared to the events next door. There were some quadroon women in the audience casting languorous eyes at gentlemen who seemed anxious to retrieve a dropped handkerchief or glove. Margaret sat next to M. Petit. She turned to him.

"M. Petit, I do so wish I could have a look at the ball."

"But my dear Miss Havershill, white ladies are not allowed."

Margaret glanced at Mrs. Henderson, seated at her left. That good lady seemed absorbed with the events on the stage.

"If only I could disguise myself in some way," Margaret whispered.

He raised his eyebrows and spoke gently. "That would be an adventure, indeed, but might mean trouble and cause gossip about your reputation."

"But I am not known in New Orleans." Margaret's cheeks flushed with excitement. What a lark it would be! It was like some of the schemes she and Elena had hatched as children.

M. Petit nodded, his eyes twinkling. He brushed back a strand of his thick dark hair. He really was an awfully nice man, Margaret decided.

127

Jane Tracy, another woman of the party, leaned across M. Petit to whisper, "Oh, Margaret, I do think it would be exciting to go! Let me send my coachman for some feathers for our hair and some veils and perhaps we can at least get through the door."

"I do not want you to do this, Jane," her husband whispered loudly. "With your blond hair you will be discovered immediately."

"Oh, but it would be such an adventure!" his lady responded. "They say our masquerade balls are nothing compared with quadroon balls. But perhaps Margaret with her curly brown hair could pass, though she is fair of skin. Do let me send Ajax for some disguise!"

"I suppose I cannot control Miss Havershill," her husband grumbled.

"Good. I will speak with him during the intermission. Miss Havershill can disguise herself in our carriage and we will wait until her return for her story."

Mrs. Henderson's eyes never left the stage.

"Do not tell Mr. Henderson," she said. "But give me an account as soon as you can. My own carriage will come at the end of the performance."

Now that it was decided, Margaret felt apprehensive. She had no wish to mock or upset the quadroon beauties or their mamas. Surely their lives were filled with problems enough.

It might once again be a case of the Englishwoman stepping in where angels fear to tread. Questions of race in this country were filled with unexpected pitfalls. But her own impetuousness and the Havershill curiosity overcame her caution.

"Will you accompany me, M. Petit?"

"I would be delighted. I am very fond of little adventures myself." He patted her gloved hand.

Ajax was quickly dispatched for pieces of the costume under which Margaret must hide her muslin dress. Ladies of color wore silks and taffetas and gold embroidery to their ball. Jane helped Margaret don a white silk cloak, a veil, and some decorative feathers for a headdress. Jane Tracy also lent her a valuable diamond set in a necklace.

"The quadroon ladies have many jewels," she said, "and hopefully the doorkeeper will be so bedazzled by the diamond he will forget to look at the rest of you."

Doorkeeper? Margaret thought with some nervousness.

Jane stood back to inspect her, then nodded approval.

"It is the best we can do in this short time. What a lark it would have been had we thought of it sooner. It is too bad I cannot pass as your mama!"

The party had by this time lost all interest in the theatrical performance. M. Petit offered his arm, and he and Margaret swept off to the ball.

There was a crush of people waiting at the door, and Margaret and M. Petit entered with them while the liveried black doorman's attention was momentarily diverted. M. Petit swept her aside so that they were standing screened by a cluster of handsome men and women attentive only to each other. Margaret raised the fan that Jane had given her to screen her face.

The Bal du Cordon Bleu was a dazzling sight. The light from hundreds of candles glistened over the beautiful fabrics and jewels. Ladies in their silks, often trimmed with gold, danced with grace and decorum. Their turbaned mothers sat about the room, judiciously watching their daughters. White gentlemen bowed before the older ladies respectfully before addressing the younger ones.

"No arrangement is made without the mama's consent," M. Petit explained in a whisper.

The conductor raised his bow and the violinists raised their instruments to their chins. Partners were chosen for a quadrille.

"You see," M. Petit said, "There are no *gens de couleur* who are men attending, except in the orchestra."

Margaret nodded, spellbound by the elegant scene. She shifted slightly for a better view, then became aware that people were watching them. It must be obvious that they were strangers. She hurriedly scanned the room for whatever impressions she could take away with her, for she suspected that they were about to be thrown out.

"Monsieur, Mademoiselle," a polite voice came from a liveried black man who had made his way to their side.

"I'm terribly sorry," Margaret feigned ignorance of French. "I am an Englishwoman."

M. Petit began to speak volubly in French, concocting a story to explain their presence. Margaret glanced about the room in agitation. Directly opposite on the other side of the door, three figures stood observing them: a beautiful young woman with fragile narrow wrists and bare shoulders above her silk robe that was fastened at the bosom by a diamond; her stern-looking mama; and a gentleman—Margaret gasped. A gentleman who despite his new boots did not look quite a gentleman—who in fact was Jed Sawyer!

Margaret raised her fan again to cover the lower half of her face and stared over the top of it at him in disbelief. For a moment she thought one of her sleeping fantasies had materialized.

Equally startled, he stared back, their eyes meeting. There was no doubt that he knew very well who she was. His shocked eyes swept past her to fix upon M. Petit, who was still occupied with explanations. The delicate girl at Jed's side looked at him questioningly. Her mama took her by the arm to whisper something to her.

Margaret felt a wave of giddiness sweep over her. She had been promising herself to think rationally of Jed when the proper moment came, but her emotions would no longer wait for that proper moment.

M. Petit turned toward her.

"My dear Miss Havershill, I fear our little adventure

is over." Speechless she nodded and they moved towards the door. As Margaret pulled the silken cloak closely about her in the hot evening, she looked back over her shoulder. Jed's eyes were fixed upon her. Margaret felt her face burning.

When they arrived at the Tracys' carriage, Jane leaned out eagerly.

"Margaret, what was it like? Were you discovered so soon?"

Margaret searched her memory for impressions, but could only see Jed Sawyer, the delicate girl, and her proper mama.

"It is the strangest thing," she confided. "There was a man there I knew."

"How dreadfully unfortunate," Jane said. "He must be seeking a quadroon mistress. And for that it would be well if he has a good deal of money, for her mother is not liable to allow her daughter to make a bad bargain."

"It doesn't make any sense at all," Margaret said.

"Few things do in this life," M. Petit remarked cheerfully. "But were not the young women beautiful, and their mamas wise?"

At this Jane bombarded them with questions, which Margaret tried to answer as best she could in her shocked state.

"But I think, Margaret, that you are wondering about the gentleman you know," Jane surmised.

"Is he to be considered a gentleman?" Margaret wondered.

"An arrangement with a quadroon mistress does not take away from a gentleman's standing," Jane explained, "though it is not spoken of in public."

"But this man is from the back country. He is a Kentucky man."

"That is strange," Jane admitted. She gathered up her finery. The Tracys bade Margaret and M. Petit a

131

reluctant goodbye and M. Petit escorted Margaret to her hotel.

"If the subject of the quadroon women interests you that much, Miss Havershill, perhaps you would like to ride about the city tomorrow evening and go down to the levee to see more of them."

"Yes," Margaret said thoughtfully. "I would like that."

When she arrived at her room, she found that her head was aching from the heat and from her disturbing thoughts. A black maid filled a tub with cold water so that she might bathe before sleeping. After the first shock, Margaret found the water soothing and forgot the oppressive heat. Even her headache began to recede.

But her distressing thoughts did not. Who was this man in whose arms she had lain only a few weeks ago? Where did he get the money to buy his land and his new boots and court a quadroon maiden? He had described himself as a river rascal, but was he in fact a scoundrel?

She had felt so sure that he had known nothing more of Elena's death than the facts he had told her, but now she saw there were whole areas of his life that were as mysterious as the gold dagger and the French chest. What business had he in New Orleans for these last two trips? Why had he left his farm?

And it seemed that women meant nothing to him beyond a quick embrace—unless he would prove faithful to the quadroon.

Then her feverish thoughts began to circle again. How could he afford to buy off a quadroon mama?

She stepped from the tin bath and toweled herself dry. She almost hated to don her night dress before she crawled under the mosquito bar. She had left no candles lit, relying on the brightness of the moon and the flashes of summer lightning for illumination.

But there was no sleeping. She rose and stepped out on her balcony looking down on the wicked city in the night. Even late as it was people were still walking about.

And where, she wondered, was Jed? Ah, it was not bad enough that she could not understand him, but she found that she missed him, too.

The next morning when she arrived at the graceful wrought iron gate of Mme. Marthe Sevestre's house she felt herself to be quite haggard and hollow-eyed from lack of sleep.

She walked through a dark narrow carriageway between two buildings into a shaded courtyard brilliant with flowers. She paused a moment to savor the sight, then went to ring the bell of the house which was fronted by a double row of handsome galleries.

A slave girl answered her and she was announced to Mme. Sevestre, then led into that lady's presence. Mme. Sevestre did not, in fact, own the house, but occupied two rooms within it. The slave girl was sent to fetch coffee and some wine.

Mme. Sevestre was dressed neatly in black taffeta. She might have been a great beauty in her day, but evidently had reached the age of no longer being interested in decorating her person, because of her bereavements and her resignation, although her dress was of a good quality and finely made. She did, however, paint her cheeks with rouge as was the custom of French ladies of the town.

As they sat in the room overlooking the garden, the shuttered windows screening out the light, Margaret explained her errand. Mrs. Henderson had wondered if Mme. Sevestre would like to go to Athena Hall to teach. As she spoke, it occurred to Margaret to wonder where on earth they would put her should she come.

Ideas of the same sort must have occupied Mme. Sevestre, for she questioned Margaret in great detail about Athena Hall.

"Ah, but Mrs. Henderson concerns herself too much

about me. It is true that I was a child in much grander surroundings. Long before I married Comte Sevestre I expected a life much different from the one I have led. Poor Mama. Had she known that I would end my life in two rooms in a foreign land she would never have rested easily—but then Mama did not survive the Revolution."

Margaret nodded, wondering if Mme. Sevestre might not prove too much of a royalist for Athena Hall even if she were willing to come.

"No, my dear. I am quite content to live modestly here among many French people where I can hear my language spoken. I take an occasional pupil for music or drawing, and it is quite enough, for I am not destitute, you see."

Again Margaret nodded. Mme. Sevestre's present life was indeed more comfortable than the life at Athena Hall.

"And then Claire de Longueil, the dear friend of my youth, went to live somewhere where I gather your Athena Hall lies. Like me, she had wandered a good deal of the world since the Revolution. She had a fine husband, Césaire, a son who died in infancy, and a beautiful young daughter—about your age—who arrived unexpectedly late. They were terribly lonely there in the forest and not at all suited to farm work, though they had two or three slaves to aid them. They wrote to me a letter saying they had sold their land and were coming to New Orleans. They hoped they would have better luck here. Unfortunately they were never heard from again."

"They never arrived?" Some unpleasant thought was tugging at the back of Margaret's consciousness. There was no avoiding it. She remembered the little French chest in Jed's cabin, the lady's dagger from another era, and the beautiful pearl-trimmed silk dress.

"They have disappeared from the face of the earth."

"Your friends, Mme. Sevestre," Margaret began with hesitation.

"Yes?"

"Were they able—did they bring many of their possessions with them from France?"

"Some. I don't know how many. Why do you ask?"

"Because I have seen some things in our neighborhood that look to be French. No one can explain to me how they came to be there."

"I don't know how I could tell that they had belonged to Claire. That is what you are saying, Miss Havershill, is it not? That somehow things belonging to Claire and her family are still in Tennessee even though the family has disappeared? That is a very frightening thought. I often wondered if they were set upon by bandits. Césaire might very well have been carrying money, since he had just sold his little farm."

He had just sold his land, Jed has only recently bought his, Margaret thought reluctantly.

"Would you know if the family owned a small lady's dagger?"

"I would have no way of knowing that, though such things have come down in many families."

Margaret thought of the beautiful dress, somewhat oldfashioned and narrow of skirt, its silk yellowing. It was obviously of a style later than the Revolution itself—but perhaps of the time of Napoleon's empire.

"Did your friend attend balls—after the Revolution?"

"That is a very strange question. Yes, certainly she did as she traveled to England and through Europe. They returned to France during the Empire. Unfortunately Comte de Longueil fell out of favor with Napoleon. They were able to salvage some of their fortune—much more than my late husband—but Césaire did not handle it wisely. The little farm was his last investment. Alas, I fear my friends were not meant for the life of the frontier."

135

Margaret set down her delicate china cup and gazed seriously at the French woman.

"I question you in this way, Mme. Sevestre, because my sister at the time of her death had an extraordinary gown—could you recognize it as belonging to your friend?"

Mme. Sevestre's eyes seemed fixed on sights of long ago.

"Ah, we both were very fond of dresses when we were younger. I could recite all Claire's gowns to you. There was the Grecian robe with the gold key border, for instance, and the red woolen with silver embroidery, the grey taffeta trimmed with lace that she wore when she was older—but most expensive of all was, I think, the pearl-sewn silk in which she was presented to Napoleon."

Margaret rose from her chair in agitation, feeling herself becoming pale.

Mme. Sevestre forgot her daydream and gave Margaret a piercing glance. "So your sister had in her possession a dress belonging to Claire?"

Margaret nodded.

"But you do not know how she got it?"

Margaret shook her head. "I will try to find out for you," she promised.

Mme. Sevestre sighed and fanned herself with a lovely fan of a bygone era painted with Grecian figures.

"If it is your pleasure, Miss Havershill. But I fear that it is clear that my poor friend, her husband, and daughter are no more."

Margaret, too, could think of no other explanation.

At dusk M. Petit came for her in his carriage and they drove about the rutted streets. Petit pointed out the small cabriolets of the great quadroon beauties who drove themselves with the relaxed ease of long practice. An elegantly dressed Negro boy or girl stood behind.

M. Petit explained that quadroon women who failed

to attract men of large fortunes were often set up with cottages, or even offered regular support in their parents' homes. Of course many quadroon women married quadroon men and conducted businesses. Some owned slaves in their turn. They had thrived under the French; American black laws weighed harshly on people of color.

Margaret reflected that had she not had the questions of Jed and of Athena Hall on her mind the story of these exotic beauties would have fascinated her, but instead she found herself seated sulkily in a corner of the carriage, straining to maintain ordinary politeness.

Then she and M. Petit went to walk along the levee as the sun was sinking.

"It is the chief market for the quadroon traffic *de coeur,*" M. Petit said, taking off his high hat to bow to an acquaintance. The man did not return his bow, prefering to remain anonymous.

It was cooler on the levee. The beauties were assembled, walking up and down or seated under orange trees. A fan dropped, a gentleman picked it up.

But Margaret was looking for a particular group. She was not disappointed. As she scanned the crowd, hardly responding to M. Petit's comments, she thought she saw the smooth-skinned, rounded mama seated upon a bench. A man was bent to speak close to her ear, but he was partially blocked from view by the elegart skirts of the fragile young girl.

Margaret shifted for a better view. Yes, she thought wearily. It was he. Perhaps he was making final arrangements with the mama. But what could he offer among these aristocratic and wealthy gentlemen?

Jed straightened and met her eyes as he had the night before. He glanced at her companion, frowning.

"What is it?" M. Petit asked, noticing her preoccupation with the three. "Oh, it must be the man you described last night. It is best not to interrupt him while he is about his business of love, I think."

Margaret raised her chin proudly.

"Yes, you are right. I would not want to slow his progress." She wheeled and walked stiffly back to the carriage.

M. Petit left her at her hotel with many felicitous words.

Again the little slave brought her bath and she settled into it, wounded in spirit. Angrily she took a cloth and wiped her eyes of a few tears she was unable to suppress. Jed must be preoccupied indeed with the quadroon beauty to make so many long trips to New Orleans. But then why did he have to take her, Margaret, honeying?

"Oh, Jed," she whispered. "Who are you and what are you doing, in heaven's name!" She swore that it would be some time before she again felt warmth for any American, no matter how engaging and handsome.

Somewhere outside someone with a guitar was serenading an unknown woman—a legacy from the days when the Spanish had ruled. The passionate music only made her mood more bleak. She slipped into her bed gown and was lifting the mosquito netting, when suddenly she thought she heard a sound on her balcony. Looking around, she saw the shadow of a man upon the shutters. She sucked in her breath with shock.

"Who is it?" she demanded loudly.

There was no answer. Then the shutters opened a crack and she and Jed Sawyer were standing face to face. His eyes looked dark and angry in the moonlight.

"Jed!" she breathed with relief. She tried to caution herself to be distant with him, but words she could not suppress rushed forth.

"Jed—who on earth is that girl?"

He drew back in surprise.

"Girl? What do you mean? Who the hell is that man?"

They looked at each other with incomprehension.

138

Then Margaret could feel a giggle rising in her throat. The hot night and the whole wicked atmosphere of the city swept over her and she burst into loud and unlady-like laughter.

Chapter Nine

"I've been to three hotels telling 'em I've a message for Miss Havershill," Jed explained. "If you'd stayed at a boarding house I'd never have found you."

All her doubts of him fled with scandalous haste. Margaret could not keep a note of joy out of her voice.

"You must be mad, Jed. Did you climb the face of the hotel?"

"I did," he admitted.

"Hush," Margaret whispered suddenly. "I hear the girl coming back for the bath."

They fled to the balcony, pressed close against the wall hidden under the elaborate grillwork. Margaret was fearful that the summer lightning flashing over the city might reveal them to passers-by. She hung onto Jed's sleeve, burying her face in the shoulder of his coat, trying not to laugh.

"Mademoiselle?" the girl called. "Where are you?"

"Here," Margaret answered.

"Are you through with the bath?"

"Yes, quite through." Margaret barely suppressed a giggle.

He tightened his arms about her. As the girl dipped her buckets to empty the tin bath, they stood quietly in each other's arms.

This is ridiculous, Margaret told herself. You have determined since coming to New Orleans that Jed is the worst of rogues—and now you are nestling quietly in his arms. But those arms comforted her as they had on the day of the honey tree, and she could not recapture her anger at him while he held her.

The moon was enormous over the river and there were still more flashes of lightning in the distance. The guitarist still played. Finally she heard the little maid dragging the bath out of the room, banging the door behind.

They stepped inside and Jed bent to kiss her, his hands pressed against the flimsy stuff of her bed gown. He paused to take her chin in his hands.

"I'm glad you're too much of a woman for vaporings about how little you're dressed."

"I didn't even think of it," she said with surprise. "I am debauched, indeed. I never would have behaved this way in England, even though we were an unconventional family." She sighed. "Maybe it's the huge moon you have here. But you surprised me so that I did not think. You seem to have that effect on me."

"I'm just as happy you did not think." He smiled, with a little too much self-satisfaction, she thought, and kissed her again.

Reluctantly she pulled away as she felt her knees and her resolve weakening.

"Jed," she whispered with what force she could muster. "I think you owe me some explanations. Why are you in New Orleans? What on earth are you up to?"

He looked at her with irritation that was plain to her even before she struck a flint and lit the candle. He was wearing a gentleman's riding coat and his good linen

142

shirt without a neckcloth. His linen had been washed. She could not see if the nick in the sleeve from Davy's knife was mended.

"Are you trying to get me to spend a night like this in talk?" he said in a low voice.

"Yes, I think you'd better." She tried to remember Elena and Mme. Sevestre and the quadroon beauty so that she wouldn't melt into his arms before he'd given her some answers. She breathed deeply. He leaned towards her with that familiar maddening glint in his eye. Despite herself she swayed towards him as though her body had a will of its own.

"Come here, honey-sweet," he said, grasping her wrist to draw her to him.

But unbidden, the elegant figure of the quadroon floated into Margaret's imagination like a cold dash of water. Her fingers dug into him and she pushed him away.

"No, Jed, I will not have this before you tell me what is happening here. I am not so soft as that."

She went to a little table and shakily poured a glass of wine for them to share. He sighed heavily, and sat himself down in a chair. It was the first time she had ever seen him sit in a proper chair, and she was not quite sure he looked natural that way. He stretched his legs to look at his shining boots.

"I was hoping even an Englishwoman would appreciate my boots," he said.

"And a quadroon?"

"Her, too."

Margaret drew back angrily, but he took her by the wrist and pulled her towards the other chair. Grudgingly she sat. He handed her the glass for a sip of wine.

"Just what is it, my sweet, you want to know?"

"Everything—back to the French chest and dagger and ballgown and how you got your money."

"I can see," he sighed, "that I am bound to tell you

more of my story than I've ever told anyone else, except Michaela Beaulieu and her mother."

Margaret felt a pang at the familiarity with which he spoke of them.

"I knew you had come to New Orleans, sweet, but never suspected you would appear at a quadroon ball to give me so much trouble. It was a silly thing to do, by the way. But New Orleans is a small town at that in many ways and I suppose our paths were bound to cross sooner or later." He smiled. "Not that I'm complaining." He took a long drink of wine, then threw back his head and began at last with his story.

"You've guessed right if you've supposed I could not have bought my land with money I made squatting or working on the river—even with more industry than I've ever shown. It all happened long before I ever set eyes on you, sweet. I was squatting down in the back country and drifting up and down the river like I'd always done. Finally I built a shack not far from Athena Hall.

"But it was lonely and I didn't see much sense in just sitting and watching the corn grow. I didn't mind if the deer or the bears had a little, just as long as they left me some.

"So I thought I'd go down river and see if I could pick up some cash one way or another. I'd see if I could get some keelboat men to pick me up and I'd lend a hand.

"Well, I was walking along the river bank and I saw a flatboat tied up and heard a kind of wailing coming from inside. I stepped aboard and found a woman some sixty years old, rocking back and forth and crying to herself over the body of a dead man. Nearby a young woman lay burning up with fever.

"I thought I'd set about to help them as much as I could—and at the same time be carried downriver later on for my Christian act."

Jed paused at this point to refill the glass and take

another drink of wine. She placed a cautionary finger over her lips, then opened the door a crack. There was no one in sight, fortunately, for his voice had been growing louder. But in wicked New Orleans the natives turned their backs on much inpropriety—as long as it did not involve their own wives. She sat down to hear the rest.

"I buried the old man with his wife standing at my side, but her grief was too much for her and she collapsed. While the young girl rallied, the mother died."

"Was it cholera?" Margaret asked.

"It was a bad fever, that's all I know. I never got it, thank God. And so I buried the mother, too, and the daughter, whose name was Adèle, said some words in French over her mother's grave."

"And did the daughter, then, become one of the loves of your life?" Margaret asked, raising an eyebrow.

"I kissed her as she lay dying and held her hand as she breathed her last. I could not speak French over her grave." His eyes, fixed on Margaret, held an expression of reproof.

"She had told me that the boat and everything in it were mine, so I took it and hid it in the swamp, covering it with boughs. The small chest, the dagger, and the money I took away with my own things. I took the dress, too, figuring the pearls might be worth some money. The man's clothes were so small and worn that I couldn't wear them. The family was down on its luck even before they caught fever. They had a few slaves that they sold long before. But the place they sold was big enough so that I could take the money and buy my own and still have some left." He lay his head against the wall for a moment, thinking back. She sat quietly watching him. Then he took another long drink of wine.

"I meant to go back to the boat, but a couple of months passed, and there was Elena. And then she died, too."

Jed paused for a moment, then took a deep breath, looking out across the balcony into the night.

"Finally I figured it was time to go downriver. The boat was still well hidden and afloat, so I untied it and drifted away with the current. It wasn't an easy job, but I made it to New Orleans after a time. I sold everything off and set out to see the town with more money than I had ever had."

"Was that when you met the young quadroon?"

He shook his head and filled the glass again and frowned at her.

"I told you before, Margaret, all women ask the same kinds of questions. They want to know they're the only woman you've ever known. But if you tell them that, they'll despise you for a weakling. It's my story and I'll do the telling of it."

Rebuffed, she reached for her fan on the table and began to use it furiously. Then she thought she must look a little foolish sitting there in her nightgown expressing her rage.

"Then, sweet, my conscience grabbed me in a terrible grip. Did the money really belong to me? I wondered. On the frontier a man usually takes what falls across his path, but what if there were orphans or other kin of the French family?"

"So you do have a conscience after all," Margaret murmured.

"I do. Since there were so many French people in New Orleans, I asked around a bit with only a little luck. Most people seemed to have forgotten the name. I thought I'd better go back to my farm if I ever was going to settle down there. So I hopped the *Belvidere*, and—"

"And that is when you met me."

"Yes."

"But you haven't told me yet about the quadroon."

"That," he said, "is another story. And while we're telling them, where'd you get that Frenchman?"

146

"Oh, Jed," she laughed. "He's just a very nice man."

"He damn well better be."

She turned away from him thoughtfully, biting the nail of her thumb.

"Jed, was the name of the dying family de Longueil?"

"Yes." He was obviously startled. "How did you know?"

"That, too, is another story. Tomorrow I can show you someone who knew them."

By now the guitarist had finished playing. Margaret hoped he had won his lady love. Then Jed set down his glass and began a suit of his own.

"Well, little Englishwoman, have you had talk enough for tonight?"

"Oh, indeed," Margaret yawned. "It's past my bedtime."

"Past your bedtime? Past your bedtime!" With a roar of rage he leapt from his chair and grasped her about her waist as she rose to her feet, then dodged to evade him.

"Hush, Jed," Margaret cautioned, bursting into giggles.

"I'll bed you, you teasing woman," he said, lifting her light form for a moment right off the ground. "Ah, how do you manage to wrap me around your finger when you're no bigger than this."

Margaret looked up and smiled into his eyes. She loved these light moods of his, though she sensed he had a melancholy side. He set her down. His eyes were unmasked and tender.

"Well, Margaret, do we have to stand here all night when we might lie down behind mosquito netting?"

"Oh, Jed, you fool," she said, parting the gauzy drapes.

He lay down beside her and she held him fast and unashamedly.

147

"Ah, a good woman in a good bed in New Orleans—what more could a man want?"

Margaret rose on an elbow, laughing.

"I will not stay in the same bed with a man who goes on with such foolishness."

He pushed her back.

"Oh, honey sweet, you are about to find out how serious I can be," he said, kissing her nose.

"Oh, Jed, I have wanted you so," she admitted with a sigh.

"Have you? Have you? I—" But he could not quite tell her what his feelings were.

"Never mind," she said, and pressed her lips to his. They said nothing more, but he held her as though he could not get enough of her. Her body stirred in response to his until, shaken to the core, she knew that all her dreams of him were but shadows of the reality. This is dangerous, she told herself. You will never want to let him go. But then all thought left her as their bodies moved together, each touch more magical in the moonlight that swept across the balcony.

She knew she could not put off seeing Blair any longer and was relieved that Jed offered to go with her. He waited for her on the ornate gallery of the hotel. Jed looked out of place——no mustachioed Frenchman, he! Though he had shaved, his hair had probably never felt the scissors of a genuine barber, but was roughly cut. His riding coat showed signs of travel and his linen shirt was quite limp. But he had obviously just shined his new boots.

Margaret had donned another light muslin newly made for her, with cool puffed sleeves. Waists, she had noted in passing in New Orleans, were growing longer. She wore her large straw hat and carried a parasol. From the glances they received on the streets she judged they made an odd couple. The thought might have occurred to Jed, too, for he walked silently. By then the heat was so intense they kept to the shady side. The street was one of many shops, with the owners' rooms above.

Blair conducted his business from a very small room opening directly onto the narrow walkway. Margaret looked in through a small window. There were a few ledgers here and there and a single silent clerk. In the corner some stores were stacked, ready to be brought upriver.

She lifted the latch and walked in boldly. Jed stood just inside the door. The room was cooler and far darker than the street outside.

Blair looked up with some surprise. His eyes narrowed as they fixed on Margaret. He turned a dangerous-looking color of red. Leaning towards her, he prepared to spit out angry words, when his glance shifted to Jed. He visibly tried to restrain himself, but the hissing words slipped out.

"S-s-so, an English lady who lies with the scum of the river. You found him, I think, on the *Belvidere* . . ." Again he began that curious rocking back and forth on the balls of his feet that was the outward sign of some emotion in him.

Margaret glanced at Jed, fearful that Blair would goad him to some attack. But Jed stood quietly, looking thoughtful and deceptively relaxed. He had a good two inches on Blair and was many times stronger.

Good for him! He's no fool, she thought, and remembered his coolness with Davy on the boat. She wondered if he carried his knife belted under his coat. He must have left his long rifle down at the flatboat harbor with his friends.

"I've come to examine the records for Athena Hall," Margaret said.

"And to ask you what you know about the death of the slave, Jason," Jed added quietly.

Margaret looked at him with surprise. She had told

him nothing of the recent events at Athena Hall. But his face was guarded and closed as he watched Blair.

"No need to tell me why you've come." Blair's voice buzzed ominously. "Henderson's been here already. You've done your work well, Missus, but I'll not forget it."

Margaret ignored him and stepped to the cowering clerk.

"Get me the records of Athena Hall, please."

Trembling, the little man obeyed.

"Stop, you wretch." The man froze as Blair, beside himself with rage, walked a few steps closer to Margaret.

"Pry into my ledgers, will you! Tell the trustees you don't trust me! They are even accusing me of the death of the nigger Jason. Very well, the business I do for Athena Hall is paltry. Paltry, my dear Miss Havershill. There are planters with great fortunes and greater needs up and down the river. Save me the trouble of journeying to that bedlam in the wilds. Do you think I could get money to suit me from such places as Athena Hall?"

"No, I suppose not," Margaret said briskly. "It seems this is an excellent time to find someone less grand for our needs. Now, if you please, the ledger."

The bubble of his anger pricked, Blair nodded shortly, and the clerk produced it for her. Blair sat in a wooden chair regarding her through narrowed eyes.

A little surprised that he had capitulated so easily, Margaret set aside her hat and went to work. Jed did not move from his place by the door. Margaret went over the figures closely. Some seemed dubious to her, but not outrageously so. There was something strange about this. She rubbed her fingers over the page. There were rough spots and an unusual amount of erasures and places scraped clean. The ink of some of these did not match the ink on other entries. Some of the totals had been changed in this way. Blair had said Mr. Henderson had been there. Working hard, Blair and his

150

clerk might have changed the records so that nothing seemed amiss by the time she arrived.

Margaret glanced up to see Blair smiling. He was not by nature a truly happy man, so his smile gave her misgivings.

"You see, my dear, you were wrong to worry so. Everything's in order."

He well knew she understood the deception. Now all his anger was gone. He almost purred. Truly the man was demented and they would be well off without him.

"You can tell Mr. Henderson that he may collect everything in my possession pertaining to Athena Hall. I've done with it! Except," and here Blair seemed to be enjoying some huge joke, "for one last errand with which he entrusted me."

Margaret felt apprehensive. Mr. Henderson did not seem to realize the extend of Blair's derangement.

"It is the matter of the purchase of two slaves for Athena Hall. Mr. Henderson charged me that they be especially suited to the life there." Blair's eyes glittered.

Margaret shifted uneasily.

"We know you are a cheat and a liar and an attacker of women, Mr. Blair. We don't know whether you killed Jason or not, nor Elena, but we do not intend to let these matters stand if we can help it. I should be very careful if I were you not to cross the path of anyone connected with Athena Hall."

Again red stained his face and the loose skin that covered his bald spot.

"No! You accuse me! Have you ever seen that pretty lot of money that Henry Stanley keeps in his chest? If you think my account's a little short, maybe you should ask him about that!"

Margaret's eyes met Jed's. There was no telling whether there was anything to the accusation or not.

"And as for the nigger Jason—I would have killed him if I had the chance. Only a bad nigger strikes a white man."

Margaret bit back angry words that would have proved useless. Jason, she thought with sorrow, had been defending her.

At this moment the shop door opened and the skinny, greenish-black figure of Reverend Brad stepped through, his eyes fixed on Blair.

"Captain Fredericks has arrived," he said, rubbing his hands together like Pilate washing away the guilt.

"Indeed," Blair said with satisfaction.

Brad blinked as he looked about the shadowy room and spotted Margaret.

"The image of her sister," he muttered under his breath, then spat on the floor. Margaret moved her skirts aside in a gesture of obvious disdain.

"Well, my dear," Blair smirked. "It seems that shortly we will have one more trip to Athena Hall. Reverend Brad will accompany me on the river. He has much business of his own. But he will also help me with some of mine. Yes," Blair seemed at the point of laughter. "Now, if you will excuse me, we have to prepare."

Margaret tied on her hat and picked up her parasol, feeling that she had lost her grasp on the slippery Blair. She glanced at Jed for support. He was looking thoughtful. As he opened the door for her he turned back to Blair.

"Be sure you choose the slaves carefully," he told Blair.

"Oh, I most certainly will." Blair was smiling cheerily.

Jed maintained a judicious silence until they were out of earshot.

"Nothing but a good hiding or a bullet will ever change Blair. If I ever catch him on the river it's liable to happen."

"You may be right, but I implore you not to do it."

"Your Mr.—Henderson, is it? He seems to have walked into a rattlesnake's nest and then asked to get bit."

152

"They are all so innocent compared to Blair. I'm not sure the trustees know what we face."

"I don't think you know what you face, Margaret. Even if Athena Hall wasn't a mad idea to begin with, the way you've gone about it, it's bound to fail."

She stopped then in the dusty street and turned to look at him.

"Oh, do you really think so? I admit we're on shaky ground with Jason and Maria gone."

"I'm not sure you should go back there," he said, looking at her seriously.

"Where else can I go?"

They walked on in silence, well-dressed ladies and gentlemen brushing past them, along with black servants, sailors from every port in the world, and the general polyglot citizens of New Orleans. They stopped before the gate of a walled garden restaurant. Inside a dusky-skinned girl was laying cloths on four tables ready for dinner.

Still pondering the future of Athena Hall, Margaret turned to Jed.

"So far we've educated nobody and two people are dead." Looked at squarely, Athena Hall was depressing. Sighing, Margaret walked before Jed into the little garden to dine.

They visited only briefly with Mme. Sevestre. That good lady seemed to mistrust Jed at first when he told her of his last days with her friends.

"So. They are all gone. Even the so very young Adèle." She sat quite stiffly in her black dress holding a starched linen handkerchief between hands clasped in her lap. Her English was gracefully accented.

"I have heard so much of pirates on the river—I thought perhaps my friends became victims of these bad men."

"No, ma'am, they did not." Jed's words seemed too

defensive to Margaret. "I've been looking around New Orleans to see if they have any family left."

Mme. Sevestre cut in quickly.

"Césaire and—and Claire—Mme. de Longueil—acknowledge no other family. Their son died very young. The rest of the de Longueil family died during the Terror."

Jed nodded, then reached into a pocket and pulled out a small round object which he handed to her.

"I think this is your friend, Madame."

Mme. Sevestre stared down at the miniature she held in a plump hand.

"My poor Claire. It is she." Two large round tears sprang from her eyes and made their way sedately down her rouged cheeks. After a moment of silence she spoke.

"Thank you, Mr. Sawyer. These little pictures, the miniature and my oldfashioned dreams, are all my life now. When I am gone, who else will remember Claire? And who will remember me?" Sighing once more, she picked up her classic fan and waved it languidly.

Margaret found this encounter saddening and she and Jed left in a heavy mood.

The sun was already sinking, lighting the wide winding river with fiery touches. But it would be many hours before the city was cool. Jed led Margaret over the dusty streets in the direction of the levee. Even from a distance Margaret could recognize the quadroon mama she had seen before. To walk on the levee must be a nightly habit with them. The woman was looking about watchfully. When her eyes fell upon Jed, she placed a finger over her lips and shook her head.

"What does she want?" Margaret asked.

"Only that I don't spoil her daughter's chances."

Michaela Beaulieu was standing beneath a Pride of India tree, gazing shyly into the face of a very young man. He was obviously as shy as she, and quite overwhelmed. As though spellbound, he lifted her fragile

154

hand to his lips, then whispered some ardent words. Then he led her to her mama, who nodded her approval of him. The young couple walked off slowly for another tête-à-tête.

Jed touched Margaret's shoulder and she followed him to the older woman. Margaret found that she was very handsome.

"Madame, I've brought a lady to meet you," Jed said with more gentleness than she was used to hearing from him.

The eyes beneath the turban looked at her shrewdly. Mme. Beaulieu spoke English well enough, but it was heavily accented.

"You are a very elegant lady to accompan-ee a man who is so wild," she observed.

"They told me in England that everyone was very democratic here," Margaret responded forthrightly.

"New Orleans has its own ways. People from France, like people from England, do not quite understand them. Nor do Americans. For us quality is very clear, though." She turned to Jed and almost smiled. "Some of the richest men started out wild men like you, but now they try for quality."

"Quality comes hard to me," Jed said. "All I have is my new boots."

"If you would listen to me, you could learn some quite fine ways." Mme. Beaulieu spoke with utter seriousness. "But why have you brought this lady to me?"

"For the end of the story."

Mme. Beaulieu frowned.

"I heard today that Césaire de Longueil had no living family left—that he acknowledged," Jed said.

Mme. Beaulieu stiffened.

"That is correct," she answered.

"But that's not to say he had no other children."

Mme. Beaulieu spoke slowly, as though the words were painful to her.

"Césaire de Longueil was too recent to this country

155

to understand our ways. He did not see any difference between me and a slave woman. I did not have my mama to protect me. I was very naive. My good protector—more an angel than a man—later knew my sad story but loved me despite it. He is Michaela's father, no matter what you may have learned from old friends of the de Longueils."

"Maybe, since Michaela's future seems settled, she'd like a present from an old family friend—though I'll have to give it for him, since he's dead."

"No, no," Mme. de Longueil said sharply. "Her young gentleman will care for her well enough."

"Well, would you allow a gift from a new friend?"

"Per-haps," the woman said with dignity. "Oh, Mr. Sawyer, you are a kind man, but you do not understand our ways."

Since Mme. Beaulieu's gaze had returned to her daughter like a cat watching a venturesome kitten Jed offered his arm to Margaret and they prepared to leave. Mme. Beaulieu turned for a moment to look into Margaret's eyes.

"You are quite a lady, Mistress. This man will be very difficult for you. But I can see by the way you carry yourself that you care very little what the world thinks. If you have your own fortune, that is all very well, but if not, you will have much trouble. I hope you will find your later years as peaceful as I find mine. But this man will prove very hard to tame."

"Thank you, Mme. Beaulieu." Margaret felt her face flame. She wondered why she was thanking Mme. Beaulieu. It was surely a strange benediction. But Madame was giving her the best of her wisdom.

As they left the Beaulieu mother and daughter Jed walked very tensely beside Margaret. When they were well out of earshot, he burst out, "She's selling her own daughter."

"But Jed, as she says, it's their way. And you yourself have told me that your own sister died in the wilderness

156

at sixteen. Was that any better? And the boy loves her."

"After a while I can't stomach this town," he said moodily. "It's more your kind of place than mine."

"I have enjoyed it here," Margaret admitted. "But now I'm ready to go back to Athena Hall."

"I don't believe you."

Margaret sighed.

"No, you are right. I dread it. Athena Hall terrifies me in some way. But I have to begin living my life somewhere, somehow." Her mood was sinking as rapidly as his.

They walked in silence to the hotel. When they came to the gallery, she swung around to face him.

"And so you did not bid for the little quadroon beauty yourself?"

"No." He looked startled at the thought. "Our ways are so different I wouldn't have thought of it."

"And ours?" Margaret whispered, wanting to pierce this mood of dissatisfaction that seemed to have turned him from her.

"They are different, too. That's what they are all telling you, isn't it? That I am wrong for you?"

"And what do you think?"

"That they are right."

Margaret bit her lip to keep back tears. She felt as though a cold breeze had engulfed her as he bade her goodnight and walked away towards the flatboat harbor. But why was he such a fool that he failed to understand that it didn't matter what all those others thought? Why could he not simply tell her he loved her and let the rest of the world take care of itself?

Chapter Ten

Jed insisted that he would travel as he always had, down on the lower deck with the rest of the Western men.

Boarding and loading the steamboat was exciting. Margaret had spent a good deal of her own money in New Orleans. To fatten the larder at Athena Hall she had bought bottles of wine; packets of tea and cocoa; cases of French preserved meat; crackers, which had been called biscuits at home; gingerbread; and wheat flour for a better kind of bread. She also had two cones of white sugar, though she had sentimentally developed a fondness for honey. She only wished that Maria might share all these luxuries with her. To Henry they would mean nothing, but the rest of the people at Athena Hall would surely enjoy the change.

As a present for all of Athena Hall Margaret had purchased a brown rooster and two hens in a wooden crate. She loved to watch the pretty fowls.

Last of all, with Jed's aid, she had selected a chestnut mare for her own use. This last made her feel a little guilty, so she swore to herself that she would work extra hard for Henry to make up for the indulgence. She would provide much instruction, for she had failed to bring any teachers back with her. Henry would be displeased about that.

Jed had spent much of his remaining cash on a gold locket for Michaela Beaulieu. Once that business was transacted, he seemed anxious to leave New Orleans behind.

Margaret was to share the ladies' cabin with two other ladies and three very small children. Margaret was fond enough of children, but the beet-red faces, constant tears, and loud bellows of these frayed her nerves. She was glad for any escape outside.

Not that the gallery was restful. The captain had taken on so many deck passengers that some of them occupied the upper gallery. The whole steamboat was swarming with men. Despite the lack of privacy, Margaret was glad, because this way it would be easier for Jed to come up and stand with her. It would be a way to avoid her experiences on the *Belvidere*.

From the gallery, Margaret was disgusted to see Blair, Brad, and the captain of a sailing ship standing on the docks near four manacled and half-naked slaves. Two of these wretched slaves were no doubt destined for Athena Hall.

"I thought as much," Jed muttered. "Fresh from Africa. It seems the preacher and Blair are up to a little smuggling. And slaves fresh from Africa won't do you much good at Athena Hall—which Blair knows for sure."

"We must stop them. It's against the law!" Margaret cried. She in no way wanted to contribute to this awful traffic.

"It's done all the time." Jed shrugged. "The laws won't stop it." Then he went down to see how Margaret's chickens and mare were bearing up.

As the pilots and captains conferred and the lines

160

were cast off, Margaret spied Blair and the four slaves coming aboard. Brad trailed behind, religious tracts clutched in one hand. He spit a long brown stream into the river.

The slaves were all men, obviously sunk into deep depression at their condition, and looking slowly about themselves without comprehension. Margaret remembered Jason's trouble with English speech. He had had several years to acquire some language. These men obviously knew nothing at all. How would they ever teach them to read and write at Athena Hall? For these slaves it would prove but one more onerous task.

Jason, while she knew him, had never been crushed. These poor wretches looked demolished already.

Margaret sighed. She seriously doubted that Henry had been able to conduct much of a school in her absence. The farm must have been too much to manage, while she had been dallying.

With the overcrowding on the steamboat there was little attempt on the captain's part to keep the three women separated from the men cabin passengers except in their own room or at night. She only prayed that Blair and the preacher would keep their distance during the long upriver trip. She hoped to see none of them.

In this she was disappointed. The men and women cabin passengers ate together as on the *Belvidere*. The captain, it seemed, was a good friend of both Blair and Brad. Captain Smedly had seemed competent enough when loading the steamboat, but it soon became evident that he was overfond of the bottle.

Brad, who scrupled not to admonish the ladies at table concerning their morals, enjoyed the bottle equally with Blair and Smedly.

A gentleman seated next to Margaret bent to whisper his fears concerning the safety of the steamboat.

"You may not know how dangerous steamboat travel is," he said, "but with the captain nothing but a common drunk, heaven knows how we will fare."

161

Margaret looked across the table where the captain was having a drink with Blair and Brad. Brad looked up and his wildly glittering, fanatic eyes fixed upon her. Margaret could not suppress a shudder. But Brad had seen her revulsion.

"Miz Havershill tempts the devil," he said in a low, but carrying whisper.

Their fellow passengers looked up from their dishes and followed the preacher's pointing finger with their eyes. Margaret shrank, wishing she were invisible.

"Here, now," the captain said jovially. "Save that kind of talk for your camp meeting, Mr. Brad." He took another swig from the whiskey jug he held in his hand.

Margaret felt herself pale as many of the passengers continued to watch her. She kept her eyes lowered for several minutes, then raised them again. Brad's eyes were still fixed upon her. His sunburnt nose had reddened still more.

"The Bible warns us not to lie down with infidels. Elena Havershill went against the Word." He spoke in a high whining monotone, waiting for no response from his listeners. Margaret had heard the inmates from madhouses speaking so when she had done charitable work among them.

"Mr. Brad, I'd like you to mind your tongue," Margaret said, dangerously close to losing her temper. "As much as I can understand your gibberings you are accusing my sister of things that are not true."

"Then why'd she point her rifle at me?" Brad demanded in his high hysterical voice.

"I would like to know that myself."

"She called me a soul-destroying body seller, that's what she did." Brad's narrow beaked face was awash with indignation.

"Pay no attention to him," Margaret's neighbor, a civilized, neat man from Boston, whispered in her ear. "He has a strange delirium. I myself am a clergyman

162

and abhor these unlearned excesses in the name of religion."

The man's wife reached a friendly hand across the table to clasp Margaret's. Margaret felt some of the color return to her face with their support. Oh, if only Jed were near her! Still, it might be best that he was not. To Brad's and Blair's eyes any sign of affection between the two of them would be proof of ugly sin.

"Slavery is ordained by God," Brad continued.

"So they say. So they say," the captain chortled.

"Not according to my reading," the clergyman from Boston said stiffly. His fine fair skin was tinged with red from the emotion he was trying to control.

Margaret didn't know how she would bear it if this type of talk was to keep on throughout the journey. The preacher's twisted thinking must greatly aid those involved in the slave trade.

Margaret could not wait to get out on the gallery for some air. The Boston couple joined her there for a time.

"We are abolitionists," the lady said quietly. "But we dare not mention it here. Anti-abolition feeling seems to be growing of late."

Delighted by their sympathy, Margaret told them about Athena Hall.

"It is certainly a grand plan," Rev. Mathews said. "But you are liable to meet great—and dangerous—resistance."

"So far we have been able to do very little educating."

"Your plan may be too advanced for these times. I feel, though, that in my own lifetime I may see the end of slavery, but the cost in human lives will be great, I fear."

Margaret nodded. Her spirits were oppressed. Two had already died at Athena Hall and their plan was little, if at all, promoted.

Mrs. Mathews, with a friendly smile, withdrew to the ladies' cabin, and Rev. Mathews joined some other gentlemen. Brad and Blair were nowhere in sight, thank heavens. Margaret was alone. She missed Jed. If only he would come!

But she sat several hours without a sight of him. The air that evening was amazingly cool after New Orleans and the mosquitoes had fled. In the twilight she could see many large and prosperous plantations. Half-naked slaves chopped wood, then straightened to view the passing steamboat.

Margaret saw strange sparkles on the shore and wondered what they might be. She heard a step behind her and turned to see Jed. Her heart lightened.

"Jed," she said, laying a hand on his arm, "look at all the little lights! What are they?"

"You have one right here." He pointed to a spot on her short sleeve where a strange insect lay. It spread its gleam over half her arm.

"Why, they're fireflies, aren't they? They're beautiful!"

He took her hand silently, but said nothing. His touch was cool. He had been in a strange mood for the last few days. She now knew that it was not because of parting with the young quadroon. He had presented her with the locket to ornament her future life as a kept woman. The girl was charmed, and Jed seemed to consider that episode over.

She asked finally, "Is anything wrong?"

"I was just wondering what I'm going to do with you."

Margaret laughed nervously.

"If you have any plans for me, I think you might tell me."

He shook his head.

"I have no plans."

It was too dark for her to see his face, but she heard his words with a pang of loss. He brought their joined hands to his lips, then parted from hers.

"I keep thinking of what Mme. Beaulieu said. I think

of the way my mother and sister died. I can't see any kind of life for you that way."

"I hadn't thought that far," Margaret admitted. She loved the feel of this man's arms about her, but how on earth could they live together?

"As Mme. Beaulieu suspects, I do have a little money of my own. And, of course, I do own Athena Hall, whatever that may mean."

"I'm used to making my own way." Jed's voice was low and gruff.

"But you felt free enough to spend the de Longueil money on your land," Margaret protested.

"I haven't even begun to farm it right. I've never stayed in one place so long before since I've been on my own." He was looking past her towards the shore that glistened with fireflies.

"Can you—stay in one place—or with one woman?"

"I don't know."

Their words spread a feeling of bleak despair over Margaret. How would either of them live? She had a duty to Athena Hall—but she was unschooled in most ordinary household work. Since they were alone, she leaned her head towards his shoulder. His clothes smelled as though they had been slept in, as they had. He eased his chin atop her curly head and loosely enclosed her in his arms once more. But there was a sadness in this closeness.

Jed had said his farm needed a woman to make it work, but did that mean he needed a woman like her? She knew nothing of the frontier arts, had never made soap or candles, nor hackled flax, nor wove, nor spun, nor gutted a wild turkey.

What would Elena have done in her place? What would she have done had she lived? This thought Margaret found particularly depressing.

"Jed, tell me, did you love Elena?"

"I don't know." He just stood there, staring into the night.

She bit her lip, hating to ask the next question, thinking she was a fool to ask it.

"And me?"

She could feel the muscles of his arm tighten. For a long time he was silent.

"Yes," he said finally. "I think I do."

So he had said it. He did love her. She should have been filled with joy. Yet he had not spoken with joy, but rather as one speaks in the autumn when one remembers the spring.

"And do you love me—a river rat?"

"Yes, Jed, I do."

He was silent for a long time until they heard voices approaching. He shook himself free, although her arms wanted to cling to him. He went to pick up his blanket off the deck. She felt a pang of loss as though he might be leaving for a long time.

"Jed," she called after him, but stopped, not knowing how to continue, until finally she blurted, "How are my chickens?"

By the light from the cabin window she could see him smile at the absurdity of this.

"I'll look after them," he promised.

She did not see him again for several days. They seemed dismal days indeed. Margaret remembered the restful serenity of her voyage on the *Belvidere*—restful, that is, until Blair had introduced himself. On Captain Smedly's steamboat she could not sleep at night. If thoughts about Jed did not keep her tossing on her cot, one or another of the three children would awake. Then she would brood about Elena and Jason and Maria. If she walked on the gallery she disturbed the men on the lower deck. Bitterly she wondered if Jed was part of the noise they made.

They had picked up more passengers at Baton Rouge and Sarah Bayou. The ship was dangerously and un-

166

comfortably overcrowded. So far there seemed to be no fever aboard.

Margaret could not eat. If her fatigue did not dim her appetite, the sight of Blair and Brad seated across the table from her did. Some of the passengers invited her to join in their card games, but she could not concentrate.

"The pilots are afraid for the safety of the ship," Rev. Mathews confided to her. "They say the captain has always been a drunkard, but nothing can match this voyage."

"Do they lose many of these vessels?"

"Yes, they run into snags or sawyers, or the boiler blows up, I'm told. It is wonderful to travel at so great a speed, but it has its dangers."

At Vicksburg the three squawling children and their mama departed with many demands from the children for toys to be bought in town. Margaret and Mrs. Mathews were now the only women left on a vessel crowded with men and livestock. They did enjoy quietly conversing together, but had almost a sense of being under siege because of all the rough noises of the men.

When she could snatch a moment of sleep, Margaret often dreamed of Jed's arms around her, and woke longing for them. Could she, in fact, spend the rest of her life with no man but Henry Stanley sharing her roof? She had not been able as yet to find an answer to Phillip's letter. The experiment at Athena Hall must succeed—yet somehow she must still have a life of her own.

Finally Memphis was only about a day's journey away. The tedium of staring at the broad river and dense forest would be ended. There was no way Jed could hide from her when they disembarked.

At dinner in the afternoon Brad pushed away the whiskey jug when it was offered to him. He was preparing for a camp meeting he was to conduct near Mem-

phis when he arrived. Indeed, he had plastered hand-
bills advertising the event all over the steamboat.
Margaret was sure that his faith must be great for him
to be so certain of arrival by the stated date just three
days away. But then another minister would aid him
with his flock.

The captain and Blair more than made up for Brad's
sobriety. The captain, oblivious to the two women at
table, was telling boasting tales of his amours in New
Orleans and St. Louis.

"I opened her door suddenly," he said, "and found
Madeline standing in her petticoat. I whispered to her
and she turned a beautiful shade of rose pink. Her little
bosom was flushed, and even her little bare toes.

"When I whispered my desires into her shell ear, she
drew back with a little shriek, crying, 'Oh, monsieur, I
do not know what that is, but I'm sure Mama would not
like it!' "

Rev. Mathews arose, his face white with anger.

"Captain Smedly, I find that kind of talk in front of
my wife and Miss Havershill offensive," he said.

Blair sat hunched in a heap.

"Miss Havershill is not so innocent as the little girl in
the story," he muttered. "Few women are."

"Mr. Blair," Margaret said angrily, "How is it you
and your friends despise what you call fallen women so
when you do your best to topple them?"

"They fall easily enough." Blair's words were low
and spoken without expression.

Margaret sprang to her feet as wrathfully as had Rev.
Mathews.

"Well, as I recall, it took all the physical force I
could muster to free me from your disgusting ad-
vances."

Blair raised half-mad, reddened eyes to her.

"But you do lie down easily with others, do you
not?"

"No, I do not," Margaret said. There was only Jed,

168

and she would not let that be beslimed by someone like Blair.

Brad soberly turned to fix his dark, beady eyes upon her.

"It is unnatural to come all the way from England to teach slaves to read despite our laws. Elena Havershill threatened me. She turned her rifle upon me. She said no man selling new Africans was welcome on her land. She said slavery was unnatural." He droned on in a high nasal whine, evidently intending to continue his bizarre sermon forever. "But Athena Hall is unnatural. They live unnatural and die unnatural. The stench of hell hangs over the place. Go back to England!"

"Stop!" Margaret insisted. "All of you have these dreadful fancies about women, I think, because none of them will have you!"

"We'll have you soon enough," Blair warned in a low voice.

Margaret felt a chill of fear. Had he spoken in his usual oily, grandiose way she would have been less frightened. She turned her back on him suddenly and sped for refuge into the ladies' cabin. Shaking, she lay down on her cot. After a while her trembling subsided and she drifted into nervous and exhausted sleep.

She was awakened by the feeling of someone stroking her hair. She started up with a gasp. Jed slipped his arms about her shoulder and held her. She realized that he was stinking drunk. His hair was more disordered than usual and he had a stubble on his chin. But his expression was concerned.

"What's wrong, sweet? You look skinny and tired."

"How on earth did you get in here?" Margaret was by now fully awake.

"Through the window with the help of the laundry." He laughed.

Margaret looked where he was pointing. The laundress had indeed hung the wash between them and the deck rail. It must have screened Jed's entry.

"Someone might come."

"The minister's lady is reading on the gallery."

Margaret reflected that even if Mrs. Mathews should come in, she certainly would bear no tales to the disgusting captain.

"Oh, Jed, Blair and Brad have been saying terrible things about me!"

"We'll be rid of them soon, sweet. At least if that fool of a captain doesn't sink us first." He bent to kiss her, engulfing her in a wave of whiskey. She clung to his lips for a moment, then broke away.

"Jed, *where* have you been? I've been up here all alone with Blair and Brad and the captain."

"And the minister and his wife." He kissed her again. But she would not relax.

"Did you have to fortify yourself with whiskey to see me?"

"Yes, sweet, and it's wonderful to see you." He swayed toward her, smiling. The corners of his eyes wrinkled. "I kept telling myself that making love to you would only cause trouble."

"Trouble? Is that why you kept away?"

"Uh huh." He swayed again. She noticed that his eyes were rather reddened.

"I can see that it's no use trying to talk sense to you in your condition."

"No, sweet, it isn't."

She tried to free herself from the heavy weight he was leaning upon her, then, feeling the warmth and magnetism of his body, relaxed and enjoyed his presence as he covered her with poorly aimed kisses. Then he crowded into the little space, half lying on top of her. Their lips touched, then parted.

"I've missed you, Jed. Your kisses drive away all the devils of the last few days." Somehow his very drunkeness made it easier for her to tell him this.

"It takes a devil to drive out a devil."

"Oh, darling, you're not the devil you pretend."

"Hmmm," he sighed. "Not when I'm so close to an angel. Would you share your heaven with me?"

"Even smelling of that awful whiskey you're hard to resist."

"Have a taste." He worried her lips with his, then touched the tip of her tongue with his.

Suddenly he tensed and inhaled sharply. He drew her to him all the closer and she had no head for further foolish banter as her body was swept up with his. He felt inside her bodice and her breast flamed. She raised her hips towards him as he impatiently pushed her skirts up and aside.

There was a sudden sound. They looked up, startled to find Blair and Brad and the captain gazing at them from the door, looking like three low comedians. Margaret thought she would die. For all their foolish expressions she knew that Blair could be deadly. Her face flamed. Now she really had given them fuel for their warped fancies.

The captain could barely stand. He was drunker than Jed.

"I told you I heard a man's voice in here." Blair's watery blue eyes were narrowed and cold in his round fat face.

"So-o you did, so you did," the captain said.

"Throw them ashore. They're an affront to decent folks!" Blair's voice rose.

"I beg your pardon," Margaret said indignantly. "I paid my passage and I demand that you gentlemen leave the ladies' cabin."

"But you've broken the rules," the captain said weakly. "That there man'll have to go, too."

Margaret thought the captain wouldn't fully realize the situation until he sobered up—if he ever would. She looked to Jed, but he was just standing there, a stunned smile on his face. Really, she thought, Blair and Brad go after me as a sinner, but the lot of them are besotted. She was no longer sure that the natural life along the

171

American frontier was as morally healthy as people in Europe imagined. It seemed none of them could get along without their corn whiskey that flowed like the waters of the Mississippi.

"You want me to carry my baggage to Memphis?" Margaret by this time had no doubt but that they were all mad. Jed was no better. She was sorely tempted to claim that he had attacked her. Let him walk home alone. Then she noticed that the steamboat seemed to have suddenly changed its course.

Jed staggered to his feet and headed below, with one of the hands following him. Jed had a funny smile on his face, as though the whole episode was somehow enjoyable.

She thought that she should appeal to the law, but had no idea where on earth to find it.

"I cannot believe that you are going to drop me and this drunken man off together in the wilderness," Margaret said.

But that was exactly what they intended to do.

The Mathews came running up as a ramp was lowered to the shore. The captain's two assistants were forcefully throwing Margaret's and Jed's belongings on the river bank.

"Miss Havershill," Rev. Mathews cried. "What on earth is this?"

Margaret flushed. How on earth could she explain it? Oh, if only her father or Henry or Phillip were here!

"Let the mosquitoes eat them while they think about their salvation." Brad spat into the river.

"But this is madness. These drunken lechers are become moralists. Miss Havershill needs protection, you fools. I'll send someone out from Memphis," Mathews called angrily.

"Don't bother." Jed walked across the deck. "The way things are going we might be in Memphis before you."

"Who is this man, Miss Havershill?" Mathews demanded, pointing in Jed's direction.

"A neighbor," Margaret said weakly. She did not know what else to say. Jed must indeed look awful to them—travel-soiled, unshaven, drunk, obviously lacking in refinement. She sighed.

Mrs. Mathews came to stand beside her husband, a handkerchief pressed to her lips.

Soon Margaret and Jed stood side by side on the heavily forested shore.

"Don't worry about the slaves, Miss Havershill. I myself will deliver them to Athena Hall," Blair called from the rapidly disappearing steamboat. His voice had recovered all its usual oiliness. He seemed quite sober. Margaret remembered his threats.

As the steamboat headed for midstream, Margaret felt abandoned and desolate. The sun was already sinking and the mosquitoes were fierce. Her horse grazed nearby unconcernedly.

"How could you just stand there and let them do this, Jed?" she asked sadly.

He seemed to be standing a little straighter, thank God.

"I'm in no shape to fight off the whole crew." His speech was less slurred. "I didn't like the company much aboard. Besides, I wouldn't put it past that captain to sink her. And then, who knows when I'll have a chance to be alone again with you, sweet? I've spent the whole time down on the deck thinking that once the trip is over we can never really be together again."

"But it will be dark soon and we're miles away from Memphis." Margaret was ready to burst into tears, not sure if it was the isolation or his feeling that they must part.

"That's the way I've spent much of my life," Jed said simply. "It's lonely sometimes, and even frightening. But it has its good side, too." He set his long Kentucky rifle upright against a tree.

173

She looked off into the dense forest that surrounded her.

"Are there Indians?"

"Somewhere. Tennessee's named after Tanasi, the old capital of the Cherokee."

Margaret shivered, remembering all the horrid stories she had heard of Indians in England. But Jed seemed unruffled and had spent many a night in the woods.

She felt quite useless. She knew nothing of making a home in the wilderness. What good could her kind of woman be to him?

The rooster was sitting in his cage glaring like an offended monarch.

"Have they got anything to eat?" She poked a finger through the slats. One of the hens nipped it.

"We'll find something." He was unrolling his blanket. A small iron pot and a basin rolled out onto the ground.

"Where did you get those?" Margaret asked.

"I stole them. While you had them all busy. I figure they owe you some money."

So he had been doing some logical thinking after all.

"We must think what we are to do, Jed."

"I thought we'd have a drink of coffee." He began to gather kindling and tinder. Margaret sat herself on the ground and watched him moodily.

It was almost dark as they drank from the basin and ate preserved meat and gingerbread. The food warmed Margaret's spirits and tasted far better than anything Captain Smedly had provided.

"How on earth will we get to Memphis, Jed?"

He shrugged. He apparently had never developed the urgent sense of passing time that people brought up in more crowded and civilized places had. Besides, he was still half drunk. It would probably do little good to urge him on.

"Blair seems up to something very nasty," she said. "It makes me uneasy that he's gone on ahead."

"We'll catch up with him soon enough."

"Are you still drunk?" she said timidly.

"Yes, thank God."

"But shouldn't we be trying to get to Memphis?"

"Not without a good night's sleep." He smiled wickedly at her.

She flushed. She had been so angry and depressed at his absence. And now he was here and they were in the middle of nowhere.

"Well, you needn't think I'll fall into your arms whenever it suits you. You're always making plans for me without letting me have my say."

He merely shrugged and walked over to shake out his blanket. Then he spread it out on a level spot of ground.

"Well, there's your bed, Missus. I don't think there's any lice because I kept to myself on board."

"Oh," she gasped. "Are you sure?" She studied the blanket, but it seemed to be free of any unwelcome colonists. Sighing, she untied her bonnet and lay down stiffly. She was immediately attacked by a swarm of mosquitoes. He sat by the fire as she slapped and scratched. He threw on more wood and the flames leapt higher until there seemed to be fewer insects.

"Sweetheart," he said, laughing and crawling over on his hands and knees. "You need something to help you forget these pests." He stretched out beside her.

"No I don't," she said huffily.

"Yes you do," he contradicted. He stroked her neck until she turned to look at him. He was smiling wolfishly at her, then bent his neck to press his lips upon hers.

With a sigh she threw her arms around his neck and gave up the struggle once more. With his arms about her he dropped the attitude of foolish drunkenness he had had all day and became serious and tender. She felt a rush of sadness as she held his hard body close and with slow movements they fused their passion together. This country was as wild and unrestrained as he and her

175

feeling for it was confused with her desire for him. And yet this wildness frightened her.

Their passion spent, they lay twined together in terrible closeness. Then they began again to touch and kiss and love. The night sky was enormous and beautiful over them. In the distance they could see some lightning. But where they lay it was warm until very late.

This night, Margaret thought, they would have if no other.

Chapter Eleven

The rising sun pierced her eyelids. Clad only in her petticoat, she was a mass of lumpy mosquito bites. Jed didn't seem to be bothered at all. No doubt his hide was too tough. She had never slept on the ground before and was finding it hard and damp.

Stiffly she rolled over and looked down at Jed. He wore nothing but his linen shirt. He was a ghastly color and still smelled of whiskey.

"Jed," she whispered into his ear.

He opened his eyes painfully. Feebly he placed one hand on her shoulder and stroked it shakily.

"Honey lady," he said. His smile was faint.

"How do you feel?"

"Like I'm dying."

"But how on earth will we get to Memphis?"

He closed his eyes again without answering.

She thought she would try to start a fire and make some coffee with river water. She searched through his things until she found his flint and steel.

An hour later, in tears, she finally managed to light the tinder. She set the iron kettle on the flames and, wonder of wonders, it did boil. She crushed the coffee beans as best she could with a rock, the way she had seen Jed do it the night before. Finally the coffee was boiled. She poured some into the small basin and carefully carried it to where Jed lay.

Smelling the coffee vapors, Jed's face contorted. Shakily he rose to his feet and was sick behind a decayed tree. His shirt barely covered his behind. Then he returned to sit on the blanket and sip the burning coffee. Some of his color had returned. He looked a little ridiculous, she thought. His legs were pale compared to the rest of him.

Having finished his coffee, he lay down again. He said nothing of her great achievement in providing him with coffee in the wilds.

"Jed," she said. "We must get to Athena Hall. Blair is up to something. I know it. He really wants revenge on all the Havershills."

"You're right." He stirred as though to rise, then lay back again. "My God, that brew the boys had was raw." He smiled feebly. "But I'm glad I drank it. I wasn't going to come up to see you until we got to Memphis. Let me sleep a little." He was unconscious almost at once.

Margaret looked down on him with irritation. His brown rough-cut hair ruffled in the breeze from the river. She sighed. She, too, was glad they had spent this night together. But as always there was Athena Hall. She felt a pang of sadness. Perhaps they could never again be the same to each other.

Margaret thought in some ways Elena had placed a terrible burden upon her with Athena Hall. It was an experiment so advanced and so perilous that the fallible human material they had to work with, white and black, seemed feeble indeed. From talking with the Hendersons she sensed that hatred of emancipationists was

178

growing. Slavers must, after all, justify their inhuman practice.

She gathered their belongings together as best she could, then paced up and down the bank nervously with no other company but a brilliant blue jay while Jed slept. Suddenly she started. What was that splashing sound? And were those men's voices?

She got down on her knees beside Jed.

"Jed!" she cried. "Indians!"

He was instantly awake and listening carefully. He reached for his breeches and sprang into them, shirt tail hanging out.

Margaret, following suit, quickly slipped her muslin over her petticoat. Then Jed waded out into the water at the river's edge.

"Halloo!" he called.

Margaret could hear the voices pick up with excitement as the splashing sounds grew closer.

"Jed! Jed, you old snappin' turtle!" someone called.

So it apparently wasn't Indians after all. Instead of a war canoe she saw a keelboat come into view riding close to shore, the men on the bank side poling upstream. And on the deck—was that the flaming red hair of Davy?

Margaret's face burned. She felt like hiding herself behind some bush.

"What are you doing on the bank with all that gear?" Davy's voice came over the short distance of water.

"I got throwed off the steamboat," Jed said.

The men on board laughed uproariously, slapping their knees.

"And the lady?" Davy said. "You old lover, you."

There was no need to answer, for the men continued to laugh knowingly. Margaret prayed that she might sink into the ground. She half made up her mind to walk to Memphis herself.

"Lost your wind, have you?" Jed said when the noise

179

had died down. "I'll give you a hand if you'll give me a lift."

"Can you push a pole?" The question from the French captain, whom the men called the p'troon, was spoken sharply.

Jed nodded.

"And the lady? What'll she give?" Davy's mouth stretched into a wide gaptoothed grin.

The keelboat boss handed the tiller to another man and came to look at the two of them speculatively, puffing his pipe. He wore a handkerchief tied over his head like a pirate. His skin, like the other men's, was so weathered he could be a member of a darker race.

"Could use an extra hand," he grunted. "But the lady must pay."

"Done," Jed said. He rolled up his boots along with the kettle in his blanket.

The keelboat moved closer to the bank and Davy jumped ashore and tied her to a tree.

"But Jed," Margaret whispered. "I don't want to travel with that man."

"Don't worry, sweetheart," he whispered back, embracing her hurriedly with one arm, "they know you're my woman."

"Do they?" she whispered indignantly. "That's more than I know. What will you tell them?"

"Folks don't worry that much about what goes on between a man and a woman on the river—or far enough back in the woods," he laughed.

Margaret glared at him.

The keelboat was small for all the men it carried, about forty feet long and eight feet wide. It was pointed at both ends. The captain's eyes lighted on Margaret's horse.

"You didn't tell me about the mare. I got no room for her."

"It's only to Memphis," Jed said, shrugging.

180

"I'll pay extra," Margaret said, looking through her reticule to see how much money she had.

Jed looked at her as though he thought she was a fool with her money. But she could not bear the thought that they might desert her beautiful mare. If Jed wanted to deal better, he should have done it.

Jed was already busy preparing logs and planks to walk the horse on board. If the captain looked at the mare with dislike, the mare felt even more strongly about the keelboat. It took a good half-hour to get her aboard and to gather something to feed her.

Margaret's chickens were set on the roof of the little house that centered the boat. The men got them a little corn and the chickens jerkily snatched it up with the rooster taking the greatest share.

"Stand to your poles and push off," the captain said.

The keelboat sail was tied up and the men, with Jed to help them, began the hard work of poling upriver.

"Be nice to get a little upstream wind," the p'troon said, looking up at the sky. But none came. The men poled steadily, muscles straining, poles bending to the breaking point.

"If it w'ant for the name of riding, I'd about soon walk," Davy said.

Margaret sat on the roof, dangling her slippered feet over the edge, watching some hawks wheel lazily overhead. Her straw hat shaded her complexion. She was sure she looked quite out of place. She bit her thumbnail, wondering how this insane journey would end. Blair's oily words and malicious eyes haunted her. At the rate they were going it would take days to catch up with him. There was so much driftwood near the banks that progress was unbelievably slow. At least Brad would be occupied with his camp meeting.

When night came the men tied up and scraped together some supper. They shared some corn pone and jerked venison. Margaret opened some of her crackers.

She wondered if her supplies would make it to Athena Hall.

Davy brought out the inevitable jug of whiskey and they passed it around. Jed drank as eagerly as though he'd never suffered that morning. Margaret stuck her nose in the air when they offered it to her.

"Reminds me of yer ma, Jed," Davy said. "She couldn't stand whiskey in the house, and yer pa couldn't stand the house without it."

Jed nodded, his eyes thoughtful, then looked towards Margaret.

"Whiskey sure helps make a journey short," Davy added.

When it grew fully dark they bestirred themselves and lit a torch, which one man held aloft as the rest of them began poling once more. The captain sat on the roof for a while and played his fiddle in accompaniment.

Margaret helped herself to Jed's blanket and went below to sleep in a corner of the house. She would leave it to Jed to decide whether or not to come too. But she lay alone far into the night as she heard them laughing and talking under the stars.

She had no idea where Jed slept that first night. They barely spoke to each other the following day, though Jed was friendly enough with the men. By late in the day they had all consumed a goodly amount of the whiskey that was a part of their wages. It was a man's world aboard the keelboat, she thought bitterly.

There was still no upstream wind. Standing with their bare feet braced against the deck cleats, muscles straining, the river men pulled or rowed against the powerful Mississippi current.

Late the second night it began to shower, and Jed came inside to lie down beside her in the tiny house.

"I've missed you," she whispered.

"You shouldn't. What can such a beautiful English

lady want with a ring-tailed roarer like me?" He breathed deeply, then his eyes closed and he was immediately asleep after the hard work of the day.

Margaret sighed. What indeed could she want with a river varmint like Jed?

They were tied up for the night. The other men moved quietly about the boat or slept. They seemed unconcerned about her presence. She found it a pleasant change after the stuffy genteel attitude of the steamboat cabin passengers. Perhaps, free thinker as she was, she had more in common with these backwoodsmen than the gentry after all.

But there were other problems. She put her head down and closed her eyes again.

"I heard you bought a place, Jed."

The words entered her consciousness before her eyes opened.

"Yes, Davy."

"Settlin' down, eh?"

"I dunno. It comes hard when you're used to wandering."

Margaret sat up hastily. Looking through the door, Davy nodded to her, respectfully acknowledging Jed's rights over her. Perhaps it was just as well Jed slept near by.

The men started drinking earlier than usual on the fourth day. They knew they were getting close to Memphis and the tedium was wearing. After Jed and Margaret disembarked, the rest of them would push along all the way to St. Louis. Margaret felt more understanding of Davy than she had on the *Belvidere*; still, she did not trust him.

Anxiously Margaret peered around each bend of the river. Blair must be far ahead of them by now. Who knew how much mischief he was making? Jed, too, seemed to be worrying.

"If I could see what they were up to, I'd feel better,"

he told her. His muscles tensed and strained as he worked. But there were countless snags and half-sunk branches.

At sunset they all relaxed and ate and drank while the p'troon played his fiddle. Only Margaret sat there tense and separate on the roof, chewing nervously on a cracker.

Davy looked at her now and again, then looked away as her glance fell on him.

"Hell, boys, we ain't gonna get to Memphis tonight," Davy said.

"I bet we could if we put our backs into it," Jed answered.

"Damnation, Jed, you know me, I'm half horse, half alligator, I can whip my weight in wildcats, but Memphis tonight?"

"What do you say, p'troon?" Jed said to the captain.

"It's all the same to me," he answered with his trace of a French accent.

"I'll lay out a dollar in gold if you make 'er before dawn, Davy."

Margaret knew Jed had very few dollars left, but she shared his feeling. This was no time to hoard.

"And I'll open two bottles of claret," Margaret said excitedly. They had thought her such a snob about the whiskey that she thought she'd be generous and show them what something decent tasted like.

Margaret couldn't read Jed's expression when he looked at her in the dimming light, but she thought he was not too pleased.

"And a dollar to you, Jed, if we don't make it," Davy said. "Whoee, boys, let's go! Let's have a little whiskey to get up our steam. Why, no boilin' wash kettle kin beat a true river man! A man's a man, not a tea kettle. Here, lend a hand, now, Jed. Give your lady the torch."

Jed handed Margaret the burning pitch pine branch. She was more and more infected with their mood. A couple other men sprang to their feet, howling boasts

184

and insults. The p'troon untied them, then took the tiller.

"Watch her there, boys," Jed called as they veered in close to a submerged log.

"Oh, it's the alligator itself, waitin' to bite off your toes," Davy called, wildly swigging at the whiskey jug.

"I be fly blowed before sundown if it don't remind me of the Salt River where the snags was so thick that a fish couldn't swim without rubbin' his scales off," was another man's colorful comment.

A young boy of about sixteen took a pull at the jug in his turn, choking as the brutal stuff went down. He turned a warm smile on Margaret, who smiled back. She realized with a start that he was the boy from the *Belvidere*. He had been concerned about her then, and she hadn't even recognized him. She had been holding herself aloof from Jed's world long enough. Tonight she had caught the excitement of the race against time.

The next man in line was thin and gaunt with black hair and eyes. He drank his whiskey eagerly, then set it down to look morosely out into the darkness, his eyes catching the light of the torch. The p'troon handed the tiller to another man, took a long guzzle of his own, then sprang to the roof beside Margaret and the chickens and picked up his violin.

> "Hard upon the beach oar!
> She moves too slow
> All the way to Shawneetown
> Long while ago."

Their laughter grew louder and their boasts broader. The captain laid his fiddle down again and picked up a pole.

Margaret's torch burnt low. Jed took it from her hand and lit another. Her arms grew tired. Finally Jed took it from her and tied it to the bow. She felt sorry that she was no longer playing a part.

She sat there and listened to the strange poetry of their speech, a frontier language of men who seldom if ever saw a book. Their speech grew wilder and more slurred, their boasts of their prowess grew more absurd.

"One squint of mine at a bull's heel would blister it. Cock-a-doodle doo!" Davy said.

"Hee, haw," another laughed. "I'm the gen-u-ine article. I can outrun, outjump, outshoot, chaw more tobacco and spit less, and drink more whiskey and keep soberer than any man in these localities."

Suddenly they all stopped and hung on their poles, breathing heavily. Jed was the last to let go.

"It must be almost midnight, boys, and we're not there yet," Davy said.

"Maybe a couple of miles yet," Jed agreed.

"I'd sure like to get me into town again," the boy said. "Maybe see some gals—beg pardon, lady. Do you suppose they'll have some dancin'? We went out and busted up a dance once in Kentucky. A couple of the boys came back with they eyes black."

"Why, I hear music," Margaret said, wondering if his words had put the idea into her head.

They all fell silent then, listening to the quiet river. Then they picked up their poles with new vigor, until rounding the bend they saw a score of blazing campfires.

"By God, it's Brad's camp meeting," Jed said.

Margaret excitedly went into the house and unpacked two bottles of claret. She had a devil of a time trying to draw the corks with an old rusty knife she found stuck in the wall. Finally she pushed in the pieces, splashing wine on her thin white dress. She dashed out to the deck to present her gift to the hardworking men. The young boy took a swallow.

"Very nice," he said insincerely, handing the bottle back.

Davy took a long pull on the green glass, then spat it into the Mississippi.

"Tastes like river water," he said, turning to his work and wiping his mouth with his arm.

By torchlight she could see Jed shaking his head at her. Margaret was crestfallen that her contribution had been rejected. She could not believe that they could prefer that awful whiskey to good wine.

"Here, Missus," the p'troon said, reaching for the bottle. "I myself like the good taste of wine even if these river brutes do not."

Relieved, she handed him one bottle and began sipping from the other. It would be terrible to waste it.

By now they were drawing close to the camp meeting, which must lie some miles south of Memphis. The men worked to bring the boat up to the bank, then fell suddenly silent as they surveyed the curious scene. Whatever hymns had been sung were ended now. From over across the river now and then flashes of lightning and cracks of thunder came. The night was stifling hot.

Several acres of the wild unbroken forest had been partially cleared, and tents pitched in a semi-circle around the countless fires. Behind, close to the dark line of trees, horses were tethered and carriages abandoned. Moonlight added to the strange light from the fires that bathed the grove.

The sight dampened the men's spirits. Margaret had never seen them so quiet.

"Shall we go have a look?" the boy whispered.

The men—there were about seven of them—all rose, except for the p'troon, who lay on the housetop drinking claret. Margaret came to Jed's side.

"Let's take a look to see if Blair is too busy for mischief at Athena Hall." Barefoot, he dropped overboard, splashing, then reached up to carry her to dry land. The others were dark shadows about them.

"Be careful," the p'troon called in a low voice. "Especially you, Missus."

As they approached they saw white tents glowing from within. Low moans and groans came from one and

187

another of them. Half shadowed, the keelboat men looked at each other in amazement.

"It sounds like the gates of hell," one of the men said in wonderment.

Margaret could distinguish a few words here and there from the racket. Some prayed, some called on God for forgiveness, some screamed that the torments of hell were upon them, some confessed their sins.

Margaret felt the dark-eyed, quiet riverman stumbling at her side as she walked between him and Jed. They grew closer to the crudely constructed platform in the center of the clearing. She could smell the piney smell of blazing fires. Other spectators walked here and there among the mysterious tents looking as apprehensive as Margaret and the rivermen. Some turbaned Negro women passed, and Margaret looked eagerly to see if Maria chanced to be among them. She sighed. Maria would have the good sense to keep away from a place like this.

Suddenly the sound of a horn pierced the clearing and the strange babbling from the tents ceased. Tent flaps raised and people of all descriptions— townspeople, country people, even some backwoods people and river men—swarmed out, leaving nothing in the tents but straw on the floor and a few chairs. It was as though they were racing to Judgement Day.

The little keelboat band, the men all barefoot, cautiously made their way to one side of the circle where the firelight was less bright. Davy passed around one jug of whiskey, another man a second. Jed drank with the rest. Even Margaret felt a little tipsy from her claret.

Two preachers strode towards the platform. Brad's angular rusty black form was easily recognizable. The other man had disordered dull red hair and a full beard. Both looked as though they were too busy cleansing the spirit to wash the body.

Margaret thought wryly that Brad must have

searched far and wide for a minister willing to preach with him.

The horn sounded again, sending a chill along Margaret's spine. It was like the call to some medieval trial out of a book by Sir Walter Scott. She reached for Jed's reassuring hand.

The redhead was to do the preaching. The wretched audience clustered about the platform. Firelight turned the minister's beard to dirty copper and revealed his rotten teeth. There seemed to be something strange about Brad until Margaret realized that he was without his habitual plug of tobacco.

The strangely lit scene would have been beautiful, Margaret thought, were it not for the peculiarity of the people. Just opposite her she saw a familiar figure—Alice Simpson, come down from her brother's house in Memphis. So she was still here! Margaret was not eager to be seen among the river men with her wine-spotted dress.

But how silly it was to care more for Alice's or Brad's opinion when these same river men had rescued her!

Suddenly the preacher raised his hands to heaven, and the crowd hushed.

"Brothers and sisters!" His voice must have made the very leaves on the trees quiver. "Let us begin with a hymn."

A group of obviously primed citizens began a particularly dreary hymn which was joined in by others. Margaret was surprised to hear the black-eyed man from the keelboat join in. The crowd seemed to take heart from the singing.

But not for long, for the preaching began.

"Brothers and sisters," he began once more. "All of you know that your mortal days are numbered."

"Yes, yes, glory!" came voices from various parts of the crowd.

189

"The body dies and decays, but what of the spirit? Will it journey down to hell?"

The preacher fixed his gaze upon a spot just in front of the platform. For a full moment he stared so hard that his eyes seemed almost to start out of his head.

"I see the fires of hell—burning! BURNING!" he boomed.

Screams of terror rippled through the crowd. Faces began to contort and hands were wrung or thrown up in defensive positions. As the minister began to describe the terrors in greater and more graphic detail, sobs and moans swept through the crowd like a storm at sea. The horizon was lit by blazes of lightning, highlighting the effect. A hot night wind began to blow.

Margaret shivered with apprehension. Jed put his arm about her. She sensed that he, too, was uneasy.

"Brad is busy enough here," he whispered. "But where is your friend Blair?"

Making trouble at Athena Hall, Margaret thought.

"Beware that ye do not fall into the pit—" the minister intoned. The groan of the crowd rose to the heavens.

"Come to the Lord!" the minister cried. "Tonight is the time for sinners—sinners not ready to sink into the pit—to wrestle with the Lord. Those of you ready for redemption come forward before us here . . ." The minister pointed to an open space before the platform where before he had seen the vision of hell.

"Preacher Brad will counsel you—wrestle with you against the devil's snares."

Brad stood complacently, his thin hands folded. But no sinners rushed forward to fill the empty space.

"Who would?" Margaret whispered to Jed.

"There's no telling what they'll do," Jed murmured. He shifted his feet uneasily.

But the preacher would not let it go at that. Once more he began a hymn with Brad joining in from below. Singing seemed to loosen the crowd. The hour was late. The preachers had been working on them throughout the day. A woman began to sob, then ran forward, howling and groaning. Some dragged others. Almost all these sinners were women, which conflicted with what Margaret had observed along the Mississippi. The preacher moved among them, whispering in their ears, clasping hands. Now and then they bent to kiss a fair young cheek.

"Look at that disgusting hypocrite," Margaret said indignantly. "I wonder where he hid his bottle tonight."

Jed said nothing, but his face by firelight was grim.

A particularly lovely young girl flushed red as Brad whispered into her exposed ear.

"Lord, Lord, Lord!" one older woman called without ceasing.

The boy at Margaret's side stirred.

"Look at that!" he whispered excitedly, pointing to a young girl with hanging, disheveled hair who was kneeling on the ground.

"Oh mother, mother, take me with you into the heavens!" she sobbed. "You are gone before me. Do not leave me here to slide into the snares of hell!"

"She oughten to go on like that!" The boy pulled at the whiskey jug, then set it aside. He ran into the group of prostrate sinners, leaping over many. At the young girl's side he knelt and threw an arm about her neck. He began whispering into her ear. She appeared to be listening until the two of them swayed off balance and lay headlong on the ground.

"That boy'll be a lover yet," Davy chuckled.

"Something'll happen to him, Jed." Margaret tugged at his sleeve.

Jed merely shrugged. The whole scene did not seem to have a good effect on him. Suddenly she noticed that the dark-eyed man had begun to quiver. His eyes began to roll up to one side.

"Glory, glory!" The words sprang from his mouth at first lowly, then with increasing volume. He threw his

191

long arms towards heaven and ran towards the writhing mass of bodies.

Davy was holding the jug to his lips.

"Now he shouldn't do that!" he said, setting the liquor aside. His wiry body sprang into action. Leaping over several prostrate sinners, landing just behind the black-eyed man, he reached out to grasp his shoulder. The man half turned and Davy hit him square in the jaw, felling him like an ox. Davy bent to pick up the dark-eyed man's bare feet and pull the limp body back to the corner where all of them stood.

The boys began to laugh uproariously, sharing the whiskey, except for Jed.

"They've spotted us," he whispered, tightening his grasp on Margaret's arm.

Brad's eyes flashed from across the clearing. Behind him stood the portly yet menacing form of Edmund Blair.

"But some are come to mock their fellow sinners!" Brad cried in a high voice so loud that it dominated the rest of the racket. "Mock not, ye sinners!" He pointed a long bony finger across the clearing to where they stood. As he spoke the crowd noises ceased. "Mock not the laws of God that decree black slavery! Let not the horrid word abolition enter these sacred groves."

At the word abolition the crowd buzzed angrily like disturbed bees. They looked about to find the offenders.

"Mock not the chaste and the pure! Elena Havershill mocked and sank into the mire. She thought she was better than others because she could speak Latin and studied mathematics. Her sister who stands there brazenly is following to the gates of hell!"

"Oh, my God," Margaret whispered.

"He's talking about Margaret here," Davy said indignantly. "Jed, you gonna let him do that?"

Jed had put his arm about her shoulders and half turned away when Davy let out an awful howl.

"Yeee-ow! Come on boys, let's get 'em."

At the same time there was an enormous clap of thunder overhead. The other river men were nothing loath and followed after Davy headlong into the crowd. Fists flew. Horrified, Margaret saw both ministers go down under the onslaught. The boy still lay on the ground clutched in the arms of the young girl.

Jed quickly pushed Margaret ahead of him away from the scene.

"You can't just leave them all there!" Margaret cried, half turning back.

"Maybe not, but you're going to—" he began when they were interrupted.

"Miss Havershill," an oily voice beside them said. "It was not nice of you to bring your friends to break up Brad's meeting."

"Well, I'm sure it was not at all good of you to have me thrown off the steamboat," Margaret retorted to Edmund Blair.

"I left them all well at Athena Hall." Blair laughed, and rubbed his hands together. "I hope they will be able to replace Jason."

This man made Margaret feel queasy. She thought of Jason lying on the floor at Athena Hall, his skull split. Had that been Blair's revenge on them? Blair must have delivered the two unseasoned Africans to Athena Hall. God knows if Henry could cope with all of this. Oh, if only they could find enough proof of Blair's misdeeds to talk to the sheriff.

While figures had been running back and forth past them, Jed had been standing silently. Now he raised a fist, not displaying any great anger, but merely looking businesslike, his head tilted to one side.

"I'm looking for an excuse to lay you flat, Blair."

"If you threaten me, river rat, I might have to use my pistol," Blair said smoothly.

Margaret gasped. Jed had left his rifle on board. But almost before she had noticed him move, his fighting knife was in his hand.

"I wouldn't go for your pistol," Jed said.

"Maybe not." Blair sadly tipped his tall hat and retreated until he was out of sight.

It would be wonderful, Margaret thought, if they had seen the last of him. Jed quickly took her arm again. There was such a melee of flying fists that Margaret was unable to distinguish the keelboat men until Jed had taken her some distance and there was a chance to look back properly. Women were screaming and she could see Davy's fists flying madly and men crashing to the ground. There was no sign of the boy.

When they reached the river bank, the p'troon stretched lazily, coming down off the house top.

"So the boys are at it again. I wondered how long it would take to break things up."

"Why on earth did you let them go?" Margaret asked.

The p'troon shrugged. "The river gets very dull."

"Go inside, Margaret," Jed ordered as the first drops of rain began to fall. As soon as she had gone through the door she heard him turn on his heel and spring over the side.

"Jed," she called after him, but he was out of sight. He still was armed with only a knife. She had a terrible vision of him and Blair killing each other tonight. She prayed that Jed would be sensible.

The captain let himself down off the roof and came inside, where he picked up his violin.

"We might just as well entertain ourselves."

Margaret failed to find the music soothing. She sat biting nervously at a thumbnail. She was tempted to go back to the men, but she might add to their peril.

It must have been about three o'clock in the pitch black of a rainy morning when the boys returned. Davy was dragging the dark-eyed man.

"Is he still unconscious?" Margaret asked with surprise.

"I had to hit him again." Davy chuckled.

"And Jed?" Margaret bit a finger distractedly.

"Did you miss me, sweet?" He appeared through the darkness. There was not enough light to see how he looked.

"All here?" the p'troon asked pleasantly. "Where's that damn boy?"

No one knew. The men stood in silence in the rain for several minutes until they heard noises in the undergrowth. The moon appeared in an opening in the clouds and they were able to see the boy and the young lank-haired orphan. They came on board without a word.

"Do you expect your papa to come after you, Missus?" the p'troon asked.

"No." She would say nothing more.

One of the men untied the line and they drifted out into the current, rain deluging the little boat.

"There's an upstream wind, by gar," the p'troon said.

Quickly they lowered the sail.

"It is very dangerous to go like this in the dark. But perhaps it is best tonight. Watch well for snags, boys." The p'troon took the tiller. A torch was lit, but sputtered out immediately in the rain. Another man bent close to the water's edge to act as watch. Still another took soundings.

Despite the rain, Margaret worked her way to Jed's side. He was soaked to the skin. She touched his back to tell herself he was solid and alive. Had he not been so busy she would have put her arms about him with relief.

"I thought Blair might have shot you," she said.

"I did what I've wanted to do for a long time—knocked him flat."

"I wonder what he will do in revenge?"

Dawn found Jed handing Davy his gold dollar as the bluffs of Memphis came into view. The men cheered, then dropped in their tracks for a sleep.

Chapter Twelve

Margaret's chestnut mare was skittish and nervous from the unpleasant keelboat trip. Balanced precariously on her sidesaddle and wearing an unfamiliar riding habit, Margaret had trouble keeping the horse under control.

Jed rode his own horse which he had collected from the house of an old friend near Memphis. They had left the chickens and the rest of the baggage there.

Jed had not spoken an unnecessary word since he awoke on the keelboat. He had shaved, revealing an ugly purple bruise on his cheekbone besides the one she could already see just under his left eye. Margaret judged that he was feeling the wear and tear of the last few days—and was thinking of her. She half wished she could stop with him to escape the trials of Athena Hall. Still, from the frown he wore she was not sure she would be welcome.

In her reticule she carried a letter that had been waiting for her in Memphis. Phillip had written that she had but to send word and he would journey to America to

197

bring her home. He seemed to be far away in another world.

The sun was slanting low when they came within view of Jed's cabin. Margaret's mouth fell half open in surprise when she saw smoke curling from the chimney. She turned to Jed with a questioning look. He avoided her eyes. With a sinking feeling Margaret wondered what he was hiding this time.

But not for long. As they drew up before the cabin, the door burst open and a young woman with wild tow hair came running out, barefoot, corncob pipe clenched in her teeth.

"Jed!" she cried, almost dropping her pipe.

"Betsy!" He dismounted to give her a hug.

A sudden flash of anger swept over Margaret. To have gone through everything she had gone through on the river trip and then to find this! No wonder the river men called him a lover! She dug her heels into her uncertain mount and broke into a furious gallop towards Athena Hall. Turning to look back over her shoulder, Margaret saw the two of them standing open-mouthed, watching her with surprise. Then Jed shrugged and began to walk towards the house.

She half expected Jed to ride after her despite her temper, but he plainly decided not to. With a sinking heart, Margaret wondered if she had been childish. She continued on at the same rate for about a mile, biting her lip with vexation. The plume on her hat bobbed wildly. Then she slowed. It was fearfully hot in the thick, humid forest. Her boots and riding habit were not meant for this season. She became slightly dizzy. The mare was steaming and snorting, poor thing.

Oh, why was Jed such a liar and a fool? The image of the frowzy blond with—of all things—a corncob pipe, appeared before her. But he had warned Margaret that they could not stay together once they were home. She urged her horse forward again, but at a more sedate pace.

Mind you, she thought, the woman was probably more suited to life on the frontier with Jed than Margaret. The blond undoubtedly knew how to make hominy and how to cook venison over a fire. She could be that female helping hand he needed so badly. Margaret felt her eyes grow damp. She missed the feel of his body. She could not stand to think of his arms around someone else. She rode on, her spirits oppressed.

Athena Hall looked hot under the sun. Before crossing the bridge, Margaret let her horse drink at the stream. Dipping her handkerchief in the water, she dampened her wrists and brow. The sun was sunk quite low by now, and there was a deep golden glow over the forest. Margaret sighed. There was nothing for it but to cross the river to the other side. Athena Hall was her fate.

No one was in sight. She tied her horse to some bushes in front, then walked quietly into the house. Henry did not look up from the letters he was writing on a slate for the instruction of a young black man. Mose sat in the corner, holding his head. No one saw her. Suddenly Margaret felt a chill as she realized how the scene would appear to those rabid abolition haters Edmund Blair counted among his friends. No English person could understand the dangerous feelings the simple act of teaching reading could arouse.

"Henry," she called softly.

"Margaret." His thin, yellowish face became warmed by one of his infrequent smiles. His hand trembled slightly as though he were bothered by one of his attacks of fever. But he arose to clasp both her hands in his.

"I'm so glad to see you. We have been quite overwhelmed. How on earth did you get here?"

"I rode over on my own horse."

The expression on Henry's face clouded.

"Really? We don't need another horse so much as we need a milk cow—"

"I wanted the horse for myself, Henry." That would be his first disappointment in her. Margaret steeled herself for the second.

"And the teachers?"

"There were none willing to come."

Downcast, he looked away from her as though trying to control his emotions.

"But I do have some chickens. They're still in Memphis."

"Well, that should be very good, indeed." He paused a moment before seating himself on a chair and rubbing his eyes with a thin finger. "But are you sure about the teachers, Margaret? Would no one come?"

"No one," Margaret said. "They all thought it too risky a venture." Out of the corner of her eye she could see Mose, seated in the shadows, look up to listen to their conversation.

Henry sighed. "Blair brought the two slaves arranged for by Henderson."

Margaret sat down facing him.

"I saw them. They are newly arrived Africans."

"The bastard." Henry cleared his throat. "I beg your pardon, Margaret. But I cannot resign myself to Blair's parting shot. He knows we would do anything rather than perpetuate the slave trade. It is one thing to better the condition of blacks already here, quite another to encourage their importation."

"He will do anything he can against us." Margaret looked down at her hands which had lost their fashionable pale softness during her recent experiences.

Henry nodded. "To top it off these men are Ibos, with not a word of English. And Ibos take poorly to slavery. They become easily depressed and are known to throw themselves overboard in mid-ocean. One of our Ibos became very wild yesterday and we've had to restrain him. Imagine an abolitionist like myself binding a man!"

"The whole situation would suit Blair's warped sense

of humor very well. Let us only hope we've seen the last of him."

"Yes. Yes. I keep thinking of that poor Ibo and his fellow. They little understand that we mean them well." Henry's dry forehead creased into sharp wrinkles.

Margaret reached over to clasp his thin, cold hand.

"I must see about stabling my horse."

Henry's gaunt face clouded over again. He picked up a candle to light from the kitchen fire. The two of them stood facing each other in the doorway.

"You'll have to stable it yourself, Margaret. We must all share in the work."

She nodded. She had done little enough thus far for Athena Hall.

"I shall get myself into something cool, then attend to it."

Henry turned back once more near the kitchen door as she placed her foot on the first stair. The irritation he had been holding in check bubbled over.

"I do hope you can help me, Margaret. We are falling behind on a number of things. I realize you are very young, but the work is more important than any of us."

"Yes, of course, Henry." Margaret picked up her heavy skirts to ascend. The house had grown dark. Perhaps she should have gone with Henry and lit herself a candle. She felt her way along the passage uncertainly.

How she wished Maria were there. She had an intuitive knowledge of what really needed to be done. And she was much more understanding of the human clay than Henry. Why did Athena Hall seem to her to have none of the charm and interest Elena described in her letters? Perhaps simply because Elena was gone.

Just opposite Henry's door Margaret halted, remembering Blair's accusations. Did Henry really keep a large sum of money hidden in his room? It was probably just more of Blair's nastiness. Yet Margaret was not as sure of Henry as she had been in England. It seemed there was no one in her world she trusted completely.

Softly she lifted the latch on his door and crept inside. The room was quite bare. Blueish evening light came through the window so she could see the large chest. Henry had told her that he sometimes locked it. Cautiously, quietly, she tried the lid. It opened. In one corner she plainly felt a packet of coins and what seemed to be banknotes. There was a step at the door behind her. Margaret drew in her breath with a gasp and turned quickly.

"Henry!"

"What on earth are you doing here?" By the light of his candle she could see red suffuse his habitually yellowish pallor. He was very angry.

"I'm sorry, Henry," she said contritely, her words tumbling out in disorder. "It was wrong of me to come in without asking. I should have—well, you see, Blair, when I accused him of questionable practices insisted that you kept large sums of money here——and so you have."

"It is not all that large a sum," Henry said righteously, his candle flickering as his hands trembled. "And it was precisely because I didn't trust Blair that I kept back much of the contributions I received from lecturing. I really thought it unnecessary for the trustees to haggle over every penny. I think I understand better what is needed here than they can from New Orleans."

"I see." Margaret did in fact see that Henry took upon himself much that should be decided in the group. But there was no denying that he meant well. "I am sorry," Margaret said once again. "I should have asked you directly. It was underhanded of me to go behind your back."

"Please don't touch my chest again! Ever!" Henry demanded coldly, his face as pale as death.

"I'm truly sorry, Henry. You are right, of course."

Henry nodded his acceptance of her apology. He locked the chest and they both left, he downstairs to his

202

scholars, she to change into a homespun in the darkness of her room. But she noticed as he turned away from her that his movements were stiff and unrelaxed.

She went out to pat her horse's nose and to lead her to the little stable. Since the mare was new to the place, she thought it best to keep her confined. Henry was right. They did need a cow. When her next money came from England she would see to it. But surely there were enough gold pieces in his chest for Henry to buy many of the things needed for the place. If only he were not so set on having more teachers.

Walking through the clearing by the light of the moon Margaret felt prickles of fear creep along her spine. When would they ever be able to relax at Athena Hall without fear of an unknown assailant? The noise of an owl in the woods made her more nervous still. The tremendous racket of chirping insects that always filled the hot American night sounded to Margaret like a bad dream.

The crude stable was darker than the night outside. Margaret felt her way carefully as she took off her horse's saddle, tugging at the fastenings, and set it on the floor. She had never done this work before. As she rose, she felt something solid strike her shoulder. She jerked her body around in sudden fear, staring into the shadows above her, half stumbling over an overturned keg.

Margaret hardly knew that the screams she heard came from her own throat. Her feet were rooted to the spot. By the time Henry and the others arrived, her throat was pained and hoarse.

"My God, Margaret, what is it?" Henry demanded.

"The Ibo," she whispered hoarsely. "He's hung himself."

"Good God!" Solicitously Henry took her by the hand and led her out of the small enclosure while Mose and the other men cut the hanged man down. Shuddering, Margaret turned away as they carried his dark form past her. Still she had a clear impression of his hard dead bare foot and the leg that had struck her.

After a while she breathed deeply and steadied herself.

"One more crime to lay at the door of Edmund Blair. Oh, Henry, we must never have anything to do with that man again."

"Indeed," Henry said grimly. Taking her arm, he led her towards the house. "I shall let the trustees know how grievous a mistake they have made. We never had a chance to help the poor man." Margaret could feel Henry tremble. He was in danger of destroying himself in his concern for this place.

Henry stood still for a moment out under the stars.

"Newly landed slaves are frequently frightened by stories that they will be eaten. There was no way we could talk to this Ibo to tell him it is not so. Had I been a crueler slave master I would have bound him more securely and he would be alive now. Go along inside, Margaret. I must speak to the men and have them try to reassure the other Ibo. Perhaps something can still be done for him." As he walked off into the night, Margaret could hear him mutter lowly, "So many deaths."

When Margaret awoke the next morning she was far from rested. The day was already unbearably hot. She had never known such heat in England. She had only managed a few hours of untroubled sleep. All of Athena Hall seemed contaminated by death. Her nerves were drawn taut to the point that she would have liked to open a bottle of claret, but all her baggage was still in Memphis. The house was bleak and lonely without Maria, without Jason—without Jed. Henry was off already at work. He'd been up late last night burying the Ibo by torchlight. Henry's frail constitution was so overtaxed she wondered if he, too, might not leave her.

She must become more a part of Athena Hall. There

204

was so many needs. Quickly she arose and dressed and went down to the kitchen. The young girl, Sukey, was at work there. The room was in great disorder.

"You doin' the kitchen work, Missus?" Sukey asked wide-eyed. "I sooner work in the fields. I think Jason or Miss Elena get me here."

"Why don't you get along to the fields, then?" Margaret didn't blame her. The house felt oppressive to her, too. Sukey ran off looking greatly relieved.

Margaret stirred up great clouds of dust with a splint broom. She had no idea what to do about cooking, so she walked out to where Henry was working. Impatiently he told her that they would finish the food cooked yesterday; indeed they must before the heat spoiled it.

Feeling useless, Margaret walked back to the house. She longed for companionship. She regretted she had run off from Jed, yet what else could she do with that tow-headed woman in his house? He could not possibly long for Margaret the way she did for him. She bit her lip to hold back tears.

Perhaps she had been too hasty. She had given him no chance to explain, though he'd shrugged her off easily enough as she galloped away. Suddenly she found herself running to the stables. She knew Henry would be furious, but she couldn't rest until she set things straight with Jed. Why did Henry always manage to make her feel like a bad child, anyway? She could always excuse herself by saying that she had to find out about the things in Memphis.

She stopped short before the log building, biting her lip. She had the awful feeling that the Ibo might still be there, swaying at the end of a rope. But she must get away from there for a while at least. She was growing quite hysterical, trembling, her fingers stiff as she unfastened the door.

Mose came to stand near her as she was saddling the mare.

"You leavin', Missus?" he asked anxiously.

"Only for a little while. Tell Henry I will be back."

He nodded, looking at her with great dark eyes. Margaret left the stable trying not to let her imagination wander back to the scenes of the night before.

Once across the bridge Margaret set off at a furious pace, slowing to a canter when she realized that her horse would never stand the pace in the heat of the day. But how she longed to get away! She was hatless. It hardly mattered if she became brown as an Indian so far away from town. The important thing seemed to be to put much space between herself and the deathly atmosphere at Athena Hall.

For her horse's sake she slowed to a trot. Then she reigned up so suddenly the horse reared.

Someone was coming behind her! With a flash of fear she remembered the last time she had been followed coming back from Jed's.

Heat or no heat, she urged her horse into a gallop. It seemed an endless ride through the forest. She could swear she heard someone following her at some distance.

At last Jed's cabin came into view and she slowed and slid off, running to beat on the door. It had been made with such solid planks that the sound hardly echoed inside. Behind her the mare stood, head down, breathing heavily. Margaret pounded until her hand was red and bruised.

Strange, she was sure she had seen a trickle of smoke coming out of the chimney. The latch string was drawn inside. But no one answered.

Damn Jed! How could he do this to her? She turned to go, then hesitated. Surely someone was moving inside!

Margaret stood before the little house, her stomach clenched in fear. The primitive forest stood about her, silent, dreamlike. She heard nothing, neither horse nor human. If Jed had had a dog that's what she might have heard inside. But Jed had no dog. Surely even the wild pipe-smoking towhead would have answered her.

Her horse was in a sorry state, breathing in great snorts. She listened carefully for movement in the forest. She could no longer hear the mysterious rider, so she seized a wooden bucket from the yard and headed off to where she judged the spring to be. Returning, she heard a horse approaching. She stopped short, pressing a hand to her lips to suppress a gasp. Her horse craned his neck to drink from the bucket as she hastily dropped it. She looked wildly about, wondering where to flee.

But this unseen rider was coming from the direction of Memphis!

"Jed! Jed!" she called, running forward through the trees to the road, wild with relief. She halted in confusion. The man riding towards her was not Jed Sawyer but Edmund Blair!

Margaret hesitated but an instant, then ran back to her horse and climbed into her saddle, jerking the horse's head from the bucket. She dug her heels into the chestnut sides and headed in the direction of Athena Hall. She raced breathlessly almost half a mile with Blair directly behind her when a figure leading a horse stepped from the woods.

"Mose!" she said, halting in confusion. So he had followed her!

But Blair was immediately upon her. One hand held a flintlock pistol laid across his saddle.

"So." He reigned up. "I have found you without your lover. But perhaps this is another one?" There was a little smile on his face.

"Oh, my God, Blair, what are you up to now?" She felt cold with fear. She had wondered what vengeance he would exact for Jed's blow.

Mose stood, awkward, uncertain, watching the two of them. His hands moved nervously on the reins of his horse.

"I am almost through with Athena Hall," Blair said.

207

"But not quite yet." He rode towards her. Dropping his reins, he seized hers. His unnatural smile disappeared.

"Let go," she demanded, tugging to free her horse and praying that his pistol would not go off. The mare snorted and stamped. Margaret grabbed its mane to steady herself, cursing her undependable sidesaddle. At any moment she might be pitched on her face in the dust.

Mose let go of his own horse and crept a couple of steps closer.

"I could kill you, or take you right here in the road, and no one would ever be the wiser," Blair said, ignoring the black man.

"You wouldn't dare."

"You think not?" Blair laughed without humor. He stared at her as though she must understand his dark and twisted thoughts. In fact, he would dare anything. He was mad. Margaret knew she must get away from him any way she could. Quickly she slipped from her horse, half falling as her foot caught in the stirrup. She ran for the woods. Out of the corner of her eye she had just time to see Blair lift his pistol and level it. She froze in her tracks as the blur of Mose's heavy body passed her. Appalled, she turned to see the black man striking upwards at Blair's pistol arm. Blair dug his heels into his mount to recover from the attack. He rode back a few paces, then turned to face them again.

Mose stood rooted as though turned to stone in the midst of the roughly cleared path, one arm still upraised. A look of mortal terror crossed his face.

Smiling grimly, Blair rasied his pistol. He waited several long moments so that they might savor their fear of him. Then he fired a single shot. His victim nodded as though the attack was what he had expected all his life long. Clutching his belly, while blood oozed onto his ragged shirt, Mose sank slowly into the wilderness road.

"Oh, my God!" Margaret cried.

Blair sat unmoving in his saddle, watching the black

man die. Before he could load again, Margaret, blind with rage, rushed at her adversary, crying, "I'll kill you for this, Blair!"

"No you won't, my dear. A white man always has the right to kill a nigger who attacks him. And this will show you plainly how I feel about Athena Hall—and what's to come."

"You can't go on terrorizing us!"

"You can't stop me, my dear."

"Jed will, then."

"Oh? Where is he?"

Margaret stepped back from him. Where on earth was Jed? Fearfully she took another step backwards. There was a snap as she stepped upon a fallen branch. With sudden inspiration she snatched it up and with a swish began lashing at the horse's withers. Blair had released his reins in order to pack ball and powder into his pistol, a sensitive operation. The horse snorted, reared, and started off with a jolt. Startled, Blair reached for the reins with such haste that the heavy pistol slipped from his relaxed grasp and slid to the ground. He tried to rein up the horse, but Margaret, all flashing skirts, upraised branch, and rage, screamed after him. Showing the whites of his eyes, the horse bolted for the trees.

The ride and the loss of his pistol should take some of the wind out of his sails, Margaret thought. She picked up the pistol and returned to Mose's side. His face was twisted in pain.

"Oh, Mose. I am so sorry." She felt that she was responsible for his suffering. "Can you stand?"

He shook his head. "No, Missus. I be dyin'. I just want to know, Missus, that you keep Athena Hall—whatever—whatever Mistah Henry—I got to see so I know you stay."

"Hush, Mose. We would protect you all as best we could. Is that why you rode out after me before?" She bent to raise his heavy head from the ground to see if she could offer him some relief.

"Jason say—" There was a bubble of blood at the side of his mouth. He coughed painfully. "Jason say everything still be all right if *you* want it. Jason say—"

"Yes?" Margaret had a sudden urgent need to know what Jason had said.

Mose's eyes began to dull. There was a rattle deep within his throat and he breathed no more. Gently Margaret lay his head back upon the ground. Sadly she stared down at him. He had been a fearful man, and his fear in the end had killed him. Yet despite all his inadequacies he had tried to save her. Blair must be punished for this. With a cry of grief and anger she picked up the pistol and rose to her feet to fling it as far as she was able into the brush.

Henry's anger knew no bounds.

"Why on earth did you go riding off like that without telling anyone? Now we've lost one of our most valuable men. Don't you think we've had enough by now?"

"I told Mose I was going." Margaret bowed her head. Her impulse to ride out to Jed had led to this. But how she longed for him! No matter how madly he might behave at times, he knew what to do in a crisis. She was not so afraid when he was around.

"I fear we have not heard the last of Blair yet, Henry. He threatened as much. He should be locked away somewhere rather than allowed to roam at will with his madness. Do you suppose he killed Jason in the same way?" And Elena, she thought.

Henry did not answer. His thin mouth tightened into a grim line. His linen shirt hung loosely on his skeletal frame.

"There seems no end to it," he said finally, his voice breaking.

They stood in the hall. Through the open door she could see two men riding off on Mose's horse and the other farm horse. She had been unable to lift the heavy body, instead dragging it off the road out of sight, but marking the location well.

It was late afternoon before they brought Mose back. They all gnawed hastily at some dried corn bread before attending one more burial. To please them, Henry spoke a few words and even quoted Scripture. Margaret stood dry-eyed and shaking with unspent emotions.

"Go up and rest now," Henry said, relenting. "It has been very difficult for you."

She nodded thankfully and went to her room. She took Phillip's letter out of her reticule and smoothed it and set it on the table. She tossed restlessly for a while, finally dropping into an uneasy sleep.

She was awakened by a voice calling her name.

Margaret sat bolt upright. She knew that voice well. It was Maria's!

Chapter Thirteen

"Maria!" Margaret cried. "Thank God you are safe!"

"On the contrary," the black woman answered in her melodious voice. "We are all in the gravest danger."

The room was dark because the moon was on the wane. Margaret started up from her bed, her thoughts suddenly very clear.

"Blair. I knew he'd do something."

"I don't know whether Blair is with them or not. But there is a great crowd gathered on the road, singing and preaching and carrying torches. They're carrying on about devilish slave lovers."

"Is Brad there, too?"

"I think he is the one doing the preaching."

Margaret hurriedly skimmed off her bed gown and slipped into her homespun. She would dearly love to ask Maria where she had been, but for now it was enough that she was here.

"Where is Henry?" Margaret asked.

"Downstairs. I came up past him."

That was odd, Margaret thought. Why had she not spoken to Henry?

"We must tell him at once."

The two women entered the sitting room, blinking in the sudden light of the candles.

Henry rose to his feet as though stunned. His slate clattered to the floor.

"Maria! Thank God you are unharmed."

"But I have grave news," she said. Quickly she described the situation to him. Margaret studied her. She seemed to be wearing the same clothes as when she left, only much washed and mended. She was quite obviously pregnant by now.

Her news greatly agitated Henry. The blacks had risen with their faces showing terror, since they knew three among them had died so far, besides Elena.

Maria spoke quickly to her fellow slaves and began giving orders.

"Take the horses out and tie them in the woods by the dead oak," she said.

"Do you think that wise?" Henry began falteringly, his hands fluttering nervously as he picked up his slate. "It may be that we should consider a better plan."

"—And bring all the weapons you can find," Maria continued, brushing Henry's objections aside.

Margaret began to see why Maria had come to her first. She would have no time to talk Henry into practical sense. Margaret would back her to the hilt in this dangerous situation. Maria was obviously very collected.

"Margaret, we must gather some food and some cooking things and take the women and children out into the woods. I only pray the mob does not know we have had warning. They are taking a lot of time working themselves up along the road. How many guns do you have?"

"Two. A rifle and a musket," Henry said.

"It is not much to hold off a mob. Who will stand with you?"

"I will," Margaret said. "It was Elena's house."

"Can you shoot?" Maria looked at her with her mockingly dubious expression.

Margaret shook her head.

"Then you would be of far greater use with the women. For that matter, I am not sure it is a good idea at all to try to hold the house."

Margaret flushed. She had been guilty of making a foolishly grand gesture. Without further ado she took a candle and went to the kitchen to gather some kettles, buckets and other utensils. She seized a sack of unground corn off a shelf along with the corn grater, then dragged everything she thought they would need out the door. She did not forget the flint and steel, but stacked everything near the woodpile. She could hear the horses being led away and the frightened voices of the women and children.

Maria came to join her.

"If they can't find us for a while they may lose interest and go home. And if Brad holds them long enough with his preaching and singing we may have time to escape. It is such a long way from Memphis some of them may drop by the wayside."

As they stood near the woodpile they saw men scurrying here and there and flashes of light from the torches they carried. Others with buckets were dousing cooking fires and wetting down straw piles and dangerous areas in case they tried to burn them out. But there was no time to do it thoroughly. The Ibo was brought forth, his head hanging between his shoulders dejectedly, his hands tied. They were cutting the ropes that bound him.

"Who is that?" Maria said.

"An Ibo that Blair forced upon us. His fellow hanged himself."

215

"If he speaks no English he will be a danger to us."
Maria hurried towards him, then took him by the arm
and tried to communicate with him. Margaret wondered
if Jason had started thus.

One of the men ran into the kitchen and began to
mould bullets for the long Kentucky rifle and the musket. Another brought the two axes, and a third collected whatever knives he could find. But these weapons would be of little use if a full scale war descended
upon them.

In the front hall two men with the rifle and musket
watched. Henry was placing axes close against the wall
where they could be picked up quickly if needed. Margaret felt a thrill of fear. One of the axes had already
killed Jason, its bloody handle wiped clean so it could
return to ordinary use. She looked at Henry and bit her
lip. Something bothered her about him. She had the
strange feeling that she had forgotten something—
something important. The nagging thought lay just below her consciousness.

Then she turned, shielding her candle carefully, and
went upstairs for her riding boots. Her dainty slippers
would be cut to ribbons in no time in the woods. Sitting
on the bed, she pulled on her boots. The candlelight fell
upon the little room where her sister had died. The
bloodstains might never be erased . . .

She straightened suddenly and gazed towards the
window into the darkness. Images rushed into her mind
with the clarity of a prophetic dream: the bloodstains in
this room, the gold-handled dagger, Jed and herself
bending over the buried cloth that looked to be a shirt
of some kind, the bloody axe handle, Jason's crushed
skull, Henry's hand on the axe, his pallor when she first
asked about the workman's smock, and now his white
linen shirt!

Slowly she picked up her candle and walked towards
the bloodstains. There had been so much blood!

Why had Henry stopped wearing the workman's

smocks of which he had been so fond? She remembered his sick look when he told her that Elena had made two for him—just two. No other mention of Elena had seemed to affect him so deeply. Was he remembering all that blood on his favorite clothing?

She felt stricken with horror, gazing out into the forest where disaster threatened them. Henry. It was slim evidence, but Margaret had an uneasy feeling, a dawning comprehension, that the emotions Henry had revealed hinted at the truth. Could Henry really have killed them?

"Oh, Elena," Margaret whispered under her breath. "What happened to you here?"

They had always trusted Henry, never questioning his loyalty to the family. Now she thought of it, he was behaving strangely here. She would have noticed it before had they not always taken him so much for granted. Their very blindness to him must have cut him deeply.

She remembered his rage at her opening his chest. Was it merely the banknotes—or something more? Softly she opened his door and went to the chest. Had the rage been greater than the provocation?

In the rush to fortify the house he had left the chest open. The gold and banknotes were taken to a safe place. Margaret saw several of the fine shirts he had worn as a clergyman in England, but no rough smocks. Could this one be buried in his horror of blood as the other had been? There was only a narrow chance that she would find it. Yet his attitude about the chest puzzled her.

Quickly she pored over the contents. There seemed to be nothing unusual until the last corner where, tucked away, she found a small bundle wrapped in old linen. As Margaret opened it, flakes of burnt cloth fell out and floated to the floor. But he must have been interrupted as he tried to burn it, for there was a lot of blood still on it. Sick at heart she stood looking at the mess in her hands, until she heard a step on the stairs.

217

She made no attempt to hide the packet as Henry came into the room, carrying a candle. Their eyes met and there was perfect understanding between them. It was as though she should always have known, and for a moment she was not even afraid.

"Why did you do it, Henry?" she whispered.

His mouth quivered. It was some time before he could force his words out. They were too loud, like the words of an idiot child learning to speak:

"The child. Blair told me she was to have a child. Elena—and I loved her—" His voice broke.

Could this be Henry? Emotions seemed unnatural and bizarre in him.

From the distance came shouts and the sounds of a shot. She dropped the debris in her hands, moving convulsively away from him.

Henry continued speaking as though from a dream.

"She was so selfless, so dedicated, or so I thought—and then she played the whore. She would have thrown away all that Athena Hall means for a moment of passion."

"She had no intention of abandoning Athena Hall, Henry." Margaret once more heard voices in the distance. I must wake from this nightmare, she thought. Find Maria. Looking out the window, she shuddered.

"Perhaps." Henry still saw that scene of long ago. "I lost my head. She was so very fragile, it seems, and bled so much."

There was a scream from outside. Panicked, Margaret stepped towards the door, then stopped and turned back to him in confusion.

"But everyone swears that you were gone, that you left on the *Criterion*."

"And so I did," Henry said grimly. "I left and then I doubled back. Blair had just told me about Elena as a parting shot. After—it—was over, I thought I would never catch the *Criterion*, but she ran aground and turned back. As it turned out I had more time than I needed."

"Yes." What good would it do her now to know her sister's killer? God knew what would happen to any of them after this night. "Come, Henry, we must hurry."

He seemed not to hear her and did not move.

"Jason knew. He was content to be silent until you came. Then he knew there was someone else to carry on. He had quite a sense of justice for a man treated so badly." Henry looked over his candle at her with feverish eyes. His thin body trembled.

Margaret went to take his arm, though to touch him chilled her.

"But in killing them you killed every chance of success for Athena Hall. Don't you see that, Henry?" They had known him for so long. So long. He had been part of their family.

Henry began to shake as though the fever was upon him.

"He would have destroyed me. I was in the end more valuable than he. I needed him for the farm, it's true, but the education meant nothing to him. To get his way, since he discovered that you would have continued the work of Athena Hall, he would have told you or the sheriff."

Then what would I have done? Margaret thought. She could not live under the same roof with Henry, a man who killed from reforming zeal, who killed those he loved.

"Please, Henry," she said urgently. "We must go. We must help the others."

"Mose knew something. Jason must have told him something."

"Please, Henry." Margaret's voice rose in strained anguish. She gripped his arm more tightly.

He shook her off and raised a trembling hand from his side. Margaret felt her eyes widen with fear. He held the gold-handled dagger.

"Henry," she said. "For God's sake. The mob is coming. This may be the end of Athena Hall."

"Oh, I am not going to kill you, Margaret," he said with a thin-lipped smile. "It is too late for that. And I cannot surprise you as I did the others."

"You mean you will save my death for later."

He looked at her, considering, but she was at the door in a moment.

"Perhaps it would be better to spare me to fight on for your dream of Athena Hall," she said bitterly as she ran down the stairs. He followed her closely.

They heard several shots fired from close by. It was too late, indeed. Margaret looked out the window to see torches appearing. The two of them had been standing there too long. Some men from Athena Hall had been shoving logs from the bridge into the river. They doused their torch and ran across the fields. Maria was with them, looking awkward and ungraceful with the burden of her pregnancy. The bridge was partially destroyed and that would slow the attackers.

But the river was much lower than when she crossed in the spring. Just as they went into the sitting room, Henry grabbed her arm.

"Margaret," he said. "What do you think your father would have thought?"

"Oh, God, Henry. This is no time to think of that!"

The candles were all extinguished, but they could see the first members of the crowd cross over. A few had horses, but most were on foot. It must have been a tremendous walk, but then frontier people were used to hardship. Margaret recognized one or two of them from the camp meeting. But they must have picked up other settlers and townspeople along the way. Some of them were drunk, others fanatically sober.

Those first across on horseback stopped uncertainly, looking up at the house. Others splashed across awkwardly on the submerged logs, torches raised high over their heads. There looked to be twenty-five or thirty of them in all. Only two were women. A good half of the men carried firearms. The rest were armed with sticks and rocks and hoes. A kind of silence fell over Athena Hall as the attackers consolidated.

The defenders of Athena Hall were seventeen, including four children and one half-grown girl. Margaret only prayed most of them were safe in the woods by now and Maria among them. Those still in the house might draw attention away from the rest in the woods. The weapons were primed and cocked, the two muscular black men who held them flattened against the wall out of sight. The long barrels of the guns poked ominously through the windows, revealing themselves to the crowd. Bullets, powderhorns, and bullet patches lay about on the floor.

Maria drifted quietly into the sitting room just as the first rock shattered a window.

"Maria," Margaret cried. "I thought you were safe by now."

"I came to see what was keeping you."

"It may be too late," Margaret said sadly.

Again there was no sound but the chirping insects. Here and there fireflies lit the night. A thin man dressed in linen shirt and black trousers touched his torch to a dried, dead bush near the river and it blazed brightly.

"I kin git one of em now," a black rifleman said grimly.

"No—wait," Maria said. "They have many more weapons. We may unleash a hurricane."

In the light that came through the windows, the two shirtless riflemen glistened with sweat. Margaret felt her own body wringing wet.

A skinny black-clad figure walked towards the center of the clearing. Margaret had half been waiting for this moment. Now they would know what Brad was about. Halting dramatically, the preacher raised his arms to heaven.

221

"Henry Stanley, are you ready to be tried here before your Maker?"

Henry's hands shook in agitation and he seemed about to say something, but Maria touched his arm in warning.

"Margaret Havershill, are you here?" Brad's voice pealed like a death knell.

A cold chill gripped Margaret's stomach.

"We want to know if you've been teaching niggers t'read, Stanley," a harsh voice carried across the clearing.

"Are you for abolition?" another called.

"Tell 'em. Tell 'em, Preacher Brad," a skinny grey-haired woman screamed.

Another rock came crashing through the window. A burly man stepped forward and uncoiled an enormous whip.

"For teaching slaves to read the penalty is one hundred lashes, Stanley. Unless you can prove yourself innocent."

Henry stiffened. He looked about wildly.

"Get 'em! Get 'em!" the woman yelled.

Brad raised both his hands again to heaven. "Oh Lord," he intoned in his high whine. "Thou sees before you these wretched and awful sinners who have gone against Thy will, spat upon Thy holy word, raised the niggers beyond their place, embraced the sons of Ham . . ."

With a hoarse cry Henry sprang to the window and grasped the rifle.

"Give it to me," he cried as the black man's grasp automatically tightened on the stock. The man fell back uncertainly and released the rifle. Henry trained it shakily on Brad.

"No, Henry, wait!" Margaret called.

There was a sudden report. When the smoke cleared they could see Brad lying headlong on the ground, a stain of blood on his chest. There was another report,

222

this time from near the river, and Henry fell back among the watchers. They could not see his expression in the dark, but he seemed to be dead.

There was a howl from the crowd.

"Murder! Murder!" the woman cried. "The preacher is dead!"

"There will be no holding them now," Maria cried.

The black man hesitated not an instant, but began reloading, ramming the bullet and patch into the barrel.

The crowd surged forward, torching another bush. Fire crept dangerously close to the house.

"Y' hadn't outa have done that!" someone called. Several men raised their rifles, rifles almost as tall as themselves. The two black men fired the instant they heard the crack of rifles from the other side. Three bullets hit the house with sharp blows. It was amazingly poor marksmanship for Western men, but they had fired on the run and maybe they were too drunk to aim.

A fourth rifle misfired and its owner ran to one side and began to clean the flash pan.

The black men's bullets managed to nick one rifleman, who retired splashing through the river.

"Where is my old friend, Preacher Brad?" an oily voice uttered loudly from the clearing.

Margaret peered cautiously through the window to see Edmund Blair walk forth from the shadows. It seemed he had been careful to keep himself covered up to this point.

But it was as though Brad's derangement had found a new mouth. Blair came to stand over his friend's body. Looking down, his already large body seemed to swell.

"Oh Lord, wilt Thou let let this attack upon one of Thy servants go unavenged?" His voice carried plainly. He raised one arm with finger pointed towards Athena Hall. The hot night winds blew his wisps of hair about his bald spot.

"They got the white man," someone called to him.

"Stanley?" Blair asked. "Well, well."

The smell of smoke was in the air. The brush was still burning wherever it was dry enough and the clearing was clearly lit.

"I don't know if we can make it to the woods," Maria whispered.

They were trapped here in the house like animals, Margaret thought, her brow growing damp with fear. She broke loose from Maria's restraining hands and showed herself at the window.

"Please!" she screamed. "All of you! People have been killed. In the name of God stop this!"

For answer a bullet came through the window, narrowly missing her head. She ducked down.

"Margaret Havershill, come forth and take your punishment," Blair called. "I warned you not to stand against me. Be judged by decent folk. We've heard of the wanton behavior of you Havershill women. England was too small for you. You must befoul our land, teach our niggers—skinny Henry Stanley will never go against me, bitch. We have you at last."

"Come on out!" One of the attackers leveled his rifle.

My God, Margaret thought. It was a scene from hell. They would very likely never survive this. She turned cold and emotionless as she watched the scene unfold.

There was a blaze and sudden report in the darkened room. Outside the last speaker fell, blood staining his shoulder, his rifle useless on the ground. But it was picked up by another who had been carrying a hoe.

Several of the crowd moved back warily to take shelter among the trees.

"Whore! Whore!" The skinny woman danced about wildly, loosening her bun until her hair slipped free and blew wildly about. In the light from the dancing flames she looked like a witch.

The slave rifleman was reloading. Margaret saw Blair, feet planted firmly, raise his pistol, holding it with both hands.

"Look out," Margaret called. But it was too late. Blair had aimed carefully at an angle. A bullet came crashing through the glass. The black man pitched forward onto the floor. The back of his head was blown away.

Margaret acted swiftly. As the second slave shot the musket, she picked up the dead man's rifle and took aim, leaning across his body and bracing the stock against her shoulder the way she had seen the men do it. The black's musket bullet had creased the fat man's skull. Blood began to ooze down the side of Blair's face. He let out a cry of pain, then wandered forward.

"I told you we would get you," Blair yelled wildly. "I know what it is you women hide under your skirts! Do not think you can evade me—like Mother—she tried to hide what she was—"

Swollen, gasping, mad eyed, he came within a few feet of the veranda. He was mad, they were all mad, she thought.

For a moment Margaret's fingers felt too large and too stiff to move. She hesitated for what seemed an eternity, then pulled the trigger, feeling the pressure on her shoulder as the gun went off. She ducked down, then carefully raised her head.

She could not believe what she saw; Edmund Blair with half his face blown away, lying on his back on the ground. The witch woman was screaming and running towards the stream. Gagging, Margaret pressed her fingers over her mouth.

"It is just as well you were not trained to shoot," Maria said wryly, "or there is no telling what you might do." She took the rifle and began to reload.

Margaret had no time to consider the awfulness of her deed. There was a crash as another rock heaved through the window, then an arc of light as someone threw a burning brand. It landed on the veranda.

"Oh, my God," Maria cried hoarsely. "There is only

one bucket of water in the house." She ran towards the kitchen.

The black musket man fired again. There was a groan of pain. Margaret picked up the rifle in shaking hands and fired again, but the shot went wild.

Suddenly there was an unearthly cry, half groan, half shriek, from the forest behind the house. A grotesque, insane figure burst into the clearing uttering words no one could understand.

"It's the Ibo!" Margaret said.

The half-naked figure ran forward crazily, past the house, towards the torch-carrying men like a moth towards a flame.

Maria came in with her bucket just as the fire on the veranda began to take hold.

"Now it is your chance," the black man said. "Quickly while they are watching the Ibo. Run!"

"But what about you?" Margaret said.

"They won't take me alive," he said grimly.

Maria grabbed Margaret by the hand and pulled her through the door. Margaret cast one glance back into the room at the portrait of her father lit by the lurid light of the fire.

As the two women ran they heard a shot and the Ibo gave a great groan. One more death to the credit of Edmund Blair, Margaret thought. The two women ran silently. Maria, encumbered by her heavy belly, began to lag behind. Margaret prayed that she would be able to keep running, but dared not speak to her. Her own desperate breaths seemed to tear at her lungs.

The trees were only a few yards away when a hail of bullets descended upon them from unseen marksmen creeping around the back through the brush. Moaning sounds and cries of children came from deep within the woods. Margaret could hear crackling branches as the survivors of Athena Hall moved deeper and deeper into the sheltering trees.

Margaret and Maria pushed on. Maria seemed to

have a sure sense of where she was going. Suddenly Maria stumbled.

"What is it?" Margaret asked in fear.

"I'm bleeding. My arm. Those shots."

Margaret reached out to touch her. Maria had said nothing at the time the bullet must have struck. Her arm was sticky with blood. Maria winced with pain. Margaret reached down quickly and tore at her petticoat impatiently until she managed to rip it and tear off a strip. Quickly Margaret bound the ugly wound. Maria shuddered under her touch.

"Can you go on?" Margaret whispered.

"Yes. The horses are over that way—unless they have taken them."

But all three horses still stood by the ruined oak. The others had fled without them. Margaret untied her chestnut mare.

"Can you ride?"

"If you lead me."

Margaret freed another horse and helped Maria into the saddle. Maria lay forward, her good arm over the horse's neck. Margaret's horse wore the sidesaddle. It would be a precarious ride.

"Maria?"

"Yes?"

"Can we get to Jed's from here?"

"If we are careful we can try the deep ford and avoid the road."

Margaret dug her heels into the chestnut mare. The horse started and Margaret soothed her until she moved off at a slow but steady pace, picking her way through the heavy vegetation.

When they got to the stream bank they could clearly see the flames at Athena Hall. They halted in a grove of cottonwood trees. Dimly Margaret saw several figures retreating across the stream at the shallow ford. What, after all, was left for the mob to do? But there must still be some searchers in the woods.

"How are you, Maria?" she called softly.

"I think the bleeding has stopped, but I am light-headed."

"Is it safe to cross?"

"We must. We will have to swim across the middle. Drop the reins. My horse will follow you."

Margaret let go and concentrated on keeping her seat as the horse plunged into the stream. Thank God the water level was down with the summer. Margaret looked nervously downstream where tremendous flames were licking the sky. Some of the brush near Athena Hall was smouldering and some of the outbuildings afire. She could hear men's voices, and she thought she heard the squealing of Henry's pig. Maria's horse followed close behind her, twitching her ears nervously as though sensing danger. It seemed an age before they struck solid ground again, but in fact they had crossed very quickly. Margaret scooped up Maria's reins and soon they were sheltered in the trees once more.

"We are crossed," she said with satisfaction.

"I am still with you," Maria answered. Her voice was so faint that Margaret could barely hear her. Margaret halted and dismounted. She put her arms about the other woman. She felt cold to the touch and seemed almost unconscious.

"Perhaps you should lie down," she whispered.

"No. No," Maria said. "We must get away from here."

Once they heard a horse pounding by. Later shadowy figures moved in the direction of Memphis. Still later five or six horsemen rode silently. Margaret looked back as Maria groaned, but the riders seemed not to hear.

It seemed hours before they reached Jed's house in the darkest hours of the morning. The two women halted, reluctant after all they had been through to leave the protection of the trees. What would she do if she again beat on Jed's door and no one admitted her?

Margaret wondered. Lay Maria down in the woods, she supposed, until they could get help somewhere. Perhaps Jed's friend near Memphis. Then she would write to Phillip in Manchester.

"We must get you inside." Maria must have a rest. If there was anyone there at all they must be forced to let them in. A night like this could bring the black woman to childbed. It was still too soon for the baby to live. Jason's child must live.

Though the night had never really cooled, Margaret shivered. Her emotions were still numb. It would only be later, she judged, that the full horror of the history of Athena Hall would strike her. But the immediate problem was survival.

"Margaret!" Reviving, Maria whispered hoarsely.

"What is it?"

"Listen! Wagon wheels!"

Both exhausted women listened silently, soothing and quieting their horses. Margaret strained to hear. The sounds were coming up the road from the direction of Memphis, yet there had been no light nor sign of fire from the cabin since they had arrived. Jed had no wagon, she knew.

Finally the horse broke free of the trees. In the dark of the night they could indistinctly see two figures, a man and a woman. The man reined in the horses. The woman reached over to embrace him and plant a kiss on his cheek. The man turned to her and they were lost in each other's arms.

The embrace would have to be interrupted, Margaret thought grimly, her heart sinking. Maria must have immediate care. Margaret urged her chestnut out into the clearing.

The wagon horse picked up its head, then moved forward, disturbing the occupants of the wagon.

"Whoa, there," a familiar voice called.

Hearing it, Margaret broke into laughter, laughter that in her exhausted state was difficult to stop.

229

Chapter Fourteen

"Hello! Hello!" Margaret called, riding out from the trees.

"Why, Margaret," a voice answered. It was a voice far too light and young to be Jed's. It was the boy from the keelboat. The fragile orphan girl, for it was she, released him and they climbed down from the wagon. Margaret could see them more plainly now. She stifled her nervous laughter.

"Jed said someone would be here," the boy said.

"Oh?" Margaret drew back. Deep fatigue swept over her.

"Jed told me to bring all your things out, so I borrowed a wagon. I was gonna start out sooner, but me and Sara got to talkin' and all, and—well—and then there were a lot of strange-lookin' people comin' on the road, so we pulled aside for a while."

"Most the night," the girl put in.

"Some of them looked to be the ones from the camp meetin' and we didn't want no trouble. Sara don't want to go back to her stepfather."

Margaret knew she must not tarry. She dismounted, tied her horse to a tree. Then, while the two young people stretched and began unloading, she walked back to Maria's horse. There was no word of recognition from her. Margaret hurried to lay a hand on Maria's bowed head.

"Maria!" she said urgently. The black woman was unconscious. Margaret led the horse to the cabin door, then called to the boy.

"She's shot," he said with surprise.

"Some of our friends from the camp meeting," Margaret explained.

"I don't hold with that, even if she is a nigger," the boy said.

Together they lowered Maria from the saddle and carried her in to lay on Jed's blanket. The sky was just beginning to lighten so that Margaret could see that her friend's bandage had slipped and that she was still oozing blood.

"Oh, my God, I should have laid her down in the woods."

Sara, the orphan girl, came to look down at Maria.

"That nigger sure is bleeding," she said.

Margaret looked at her angrily, but it was no time to instruct them of the niceties of speech or the realities of race. Margaret tore off the remaining shreds of her petticoat to make a better bandage.

The girl stood looking thoughtful.

"What you need is a plantain poultice," she said, then wandered out the door. She came back shortly with a pile of leaves which she crushed in a wooden trencher, then handed to Margaret.

Margaret took off the soaked bandage, then bound the wound more tightly, including the poultice. Maria's body felt cold to the touch. Margaret spread the blanket over her as best she could. Then she sat by her side on the floor, laying her head on the crude bed.

Maria's groan woke her. Margaret prayed that it was

232

not the child come. The black woman opened her eyes.

"I'm so thirsty," she whispered.

Quickly Margaret took one of Jed's mugs and filled it from the water bucket. Maria drank rapidly and then lay back. Margaret looked out the door and by the early morning light saw the young couple curled up in the wagon.

She sat down at Maria's side again to find her patient opening her eyes. The stain on the bandage no longer spread.

"How are you?" Margaret asked.

"We—the child and I—will live."

"We carried you into the house just in time. I was so afraid Jed would have a woman here who would latch the door against us."

Maria laughed.

"But Jed did have a woman here. For a while he had two of them. One of them was me."

"You?" Margaret looked at her with surprise. Of course. That's why there had been smoke coming from the chimney. "But you could have answered when I knocked."

"I was not ready to reveal myself to you. I did not know how things stood between you and Henry."

"But you let me run out right into the arms of Edmund Blair."

"Blair? Blair was here?"

"And Mose. Blair shot him."

"Oh Margaret, I should have had more trust in you." Maria's high rounded forehead wrinkled in sorrow.

"But there were so many deaths, Maria!" Margaret buried her face in the crook of her arm and spoke without looking at her friend. "We meant to make things better. Did you know, then, that Henry killed Elena and Jason?"

"I had no way of really knowing, but I feared as much. I knew Jason knew something, and I knew he talked to Henry about it the night he was killed. But

Henry was so dedicated to Athena Hall it made no sense at all that he would kill his most valuable man."

"You are right. It made no sense. It seems as though some madness has swept the area—a mood of insane violence. I have heard stories of such things, but never in all my tame life expected to play some role myself. I never expected to kill a man."

"Who knew that your sister's dreams of freedom at Athena Hall would come to this?" Maria turned her head to one side tiredly.

"Now we must think what to do next," Margaret said as Maria's eyes closed.

"Margaret," her friend murmured drowsily. "Do not worry about your lover."

Margaret flushed. But it seemed there were no secrets from Maria.

"But who was that woman?" Margaret said.

"It is only his cousin. Jed has taken her back to her husband to see if he can patch up their quarrel."

So that's what it was, Margaret thought.

Maria's voice was tired and faint.

"Do not worry about how things will work out. Life will take care of the details."

Margaret stroked her friend's forehead, then rested her own head against the bed. Soon both were asleep.

Margaret was awakened by someone touching her gently.

"Sweetheart, your face is pretty smudgy for a lady," Jed said.

All the horrors of the past twenty-four hours swept into her mind.

"Oh, Jed!" she cried.

"What is it?" His hands tightened on her arms as he sensed her agitation.

"They have burned Athena Hall and killed—killed—so many! And Maria was hurt."

He jerked his head back to look out through the open door.

"Who? That low crawling bastard, Blair, and his leech Brad?"

She nodded, without looking up at him.

He leaned his cheek atop her curly head and spoke bitterly.

"I saw those pious psalm singers sneaking back through town—those men from the camp meeting. But if I'd had one idea what they were up to, I'd have filled their breeches full of lead. When I get my hands on Edmund Blair—"

"Oh, Jed." She began to sob. "I killed him! I killed Edmund Blair!"

Startled, he raised his head to look down at her.

"You did, little Englishwoman?"

"Oh, yes, Jed. How am I to bear it? Killing is against all I believe in."

"Bear it? Why, Margaret, I'm proud of you."

"But was this why we came here, Elena and I? And Henry—Henry killed, too. First Elena and then Jason. And now he is dead, too."

"And you've been up at the house with him all this time? What a fool I've been. But let me tell you, my sweet, Edmund Blair is lucky to be dead. For whatever you did to him is nothing to what I would have done." Jed grasped her chin so that she was forced to look up at him. "Are you all right, Margaret?"

"Oh, Jed," she said, tears streaming down her face. "I shall never forget this past night. It will haunt me always."

"You will forget." He helped her to her feet, coaxing her like a child. Then he lifted her into his arms and carried her bodily up to the loft. There on his pile of blankets he petted her and soothed her until she fell asleep again.

When she awoke hours later he was looking down at

235

her, worry creasing his brow.

"Honey sweet. I should never have let you out of my sight while those two poisonous cottonmouths were around."

"Oh, darling." She threw her arms about his neck. "I'm so glad you're here now."

The muscles of his arms tightened and he held her close as though he was afraid someone would take her away again. Then they kissed and loved far into the night, closer than they had ever been before.

The three of them stood near the burnt ruins of Athena Hall. Maria's arm was bandaged, but she was as strong again as her two friends.

"I think they may not hang you, sweet, if you are lucky," Jed said.

"Oh, I never thought of that." Margaret was horrified.

"No one alive knows who shot Blair—except us," Jed said.

"But even so, he was attacking us. He could just as easily have killed me."

"It's best to let the matter die," Jed said. "The courts can be strange at times. But a lot of the men who were drunk on liquor or religion are ashamed now and won't be pushing for the law to come out here."

Margaret felt the injustice of it. Surely in civilized England such horrifying events could not be so easily covered up.

"So many have died. It is hard to leave it at that."

No one said anything for a while. Jays and parakeets flew back and forth across the clearing. Margaret could see a few vegetables left growing in the trampled garden. The sun was hot and the day drowsy and sweet. It seemed impossible that so much blood had been shed on the spot.

Maria stirred as though from a dream. "I heard

strange noises in the forest last night. Time and time again I think I see faces staring out at me."

"If some of them are still alive, then we must do something for them," Margaret said.

"Freedom is what they need. But it will be a while yet before we can be free here. It may be we can take them to Haiti. It is a black-governed island since the revolt."

"I could sell my land for the cost of transporting them. I shall not have all that much left, but it is more than they have."

"Yes," Maria said thoughtfully.

"But to leave all the work Henry and my sister began undone . . ."

Jed cut her short, pulling so hard on a curl that it hurt.

"Well, we might take a trip to New Orleans after the crops are in—see what the trustees or whatever you call them have to say. We might find a preacher down there—if none comes by any sooner."

"It was too early—the work at Athena Hall," Maria said in a low voice. "But the time is coming. I know it."

Jed smiled at her. "The work at Athena Hall was like the name they gave the place—grander in design than the real building."

"That's a very fine speech for a frontier drifter," Margaret said.

"Do you know, he has actually read that Shakespeare, Margaret?" Maria laughed. "Though he does not admit it to his friends."

"Oh, you never know what drifts by here along the river," Jed said. "English ladies, French countesses— once I even saw a Frenchman who went out early every morning to paint pictures of the birds in the woods. Crazy Audubon, some people called him, but he was a fine hunter. You see a lot of things, drifting."

"But once you've begun to drift, can you stop?" Margaret spoke the words shyly.

"Well, if a lady like you doesn't drift back to England, I suppose a fellow like me could sit for a spell."

"I suspect I could." Margaret stood on her toes to kiss his cheek. She thought of Phillip's letter, burned in the fire. Poor Phillip would never understand what had happened to her.

"What about you, Maria? Could you sit a spell here with us?" Margaret asked.

Maria smiled. "I expect so. Especially if I thought you would free me and my child."

"It would be small return in exchange for instruction in the mysteries of housekeeping. The trustees must agree. Although you know I shall probably regret it, Jed, the way this woman bullies me."

"Good, then, it's settled," Jed said. "If Maria takes you in hand, it'll spare me teaching you to cook. But that means we have to build a bigger house next year."

"And if I find I don't have a very great fortune left, at least I still have a good deal of claret," Margaret said.

LOVE'S RAGING TIDE

by Patricia Matthews

This is the eighth novel in the phenomenal, best-selling series of historical romances by Patricia Matthews. Once again, she weaves a compelling, magical tale of love, intrigue, and suspense. Millions of readers have acclaimed her as their favorite story-teller. In fact, she is the very first woman writer in history to publish three national bestsellers in one year!

Patricia Matthews' first novel, *Love's Avenging Heart*, was published in early 1977, followed by *Love's Wildest Dream*, *Love, Forever More*, *Love's Daring Dream*, *Love's Pagan Heart*, *Love's Magic Moment*, and *Love's Golden Destiny*. Now that you've finished reading *Bitter Honey*, we're sure you'll want to read *Love's Raging Tide*. The following is a brief excerpt from the first chapter.*

It was one of those late Spring days that only Mississippi can produce—a day so soft and balmy that the air felt like flower petals against the skin, a day full of awakening and promise—and the sight of it made Melissa Huntoon want to weep.

She stood on the spacious, pillared porch of her ancestral home, looking out over the broad acres that had belonged to her family for two generations, and her eyes burned with the effort to remain dry.

She swallowed past the hard lump in her throat and gripped the handle of the pink parasol that her granddaddy had brought her from Paris the year before he died.

The day should be gray, she thought; the clouds full of rain like unshed tears. Today, Great Oaks would ring to the auctioneer's hammer. The plantation itself—two thousand acres of Mississippi bottomland, some of the finest cotton land in the South—had already been taken over by the bank. Today, everything in the house would go to the highest bidder.

Melissa smoothed the full skirt of her dress with her hand. From a distance, she knew, she would appear well-dressed. Only close inspection would show the neat patches and darns that held the now-fragile cloth together. The dress, she thought, was like Great Oaks itself—impressive enough on general inspection, but badly flawed. In the case of Great Oaks, it was debts, endless debts, incurred against the property before and after her father's death. When the day was over, Melissa would be left with little more than the clothing she wore, and a few personal trinkets. It was not much to show for twenty-one years of life, not much with which to start a new life.

Bitterly, she watched the stream of horses, buggies, and carriages coming up the driveway. Like vultures, she thought; except that they couldn't even wait until their prey was dead!

Melissa knew very well that all of them weren't here to bid. Many of them were here simply to gloat on the downfall of the high and mighty Huntoons. Jean Paul, her father, would have greeted them with a round of buckshot; and she sorely wished that she might do the same.

However, she had no choice. Amalie, her personal maid, and the only one of the servants left beside Henry, had advised her to stay inside, out of sight until it was over; but Melissa could not bear the thought of hiding inside, as if she was afraid of these usurpers. She was the mistress of Great Oaks until the day was over, and until then she would appear before them as she and her family always had, proud, with her head held high. Let them stare, these nouveaux riches, these Johnny-come-latelies. Let them see what a Huntoon looked like. It might be their last chance to see real quality!

She heard soft footsteps behind her, and did not need to turn around to know that Amalie had come out on the veranda to join her. The knowledge lifted her spirits. Amalie had been with her as long as Melissa could remember. The older woman had been her nurse, her mother, her friend, and her confidante. And Amalie, at least, Melissa would be able to take with her when she left.

A shabby carriage drove by the veranda, and a woman's pinched, tight-mouthed face turned in her direction. The woman's eyes were bright with avid curiosity, and Melissa stared haughtily back as the carriage passed, going to the stable area where the horses of the prospective buyers were being tended.

Another of the sightseers, Melissa thought. In these Reconstruction times, there were not many in the South with the wherewithal to buy property and furnishings, even at auction prices, and obviously this woman was not one of the fortunate ones.

The traffic was increasing now, as more and more people arrived, and Melissa felt Amalie draw close to her side. "Are you all right, little one?"

Melissa nodded and reached for the older woman's hand. Not trusting herself to speak, she squeezed it fiercely.

Melissa's mother had died some years back, of a fever, and her father, wounded in the war, had come home to cough his life away. The war years had been difficult for Melissa, but not nearly so difficult as watching her beloved father, the man who had been so proud and strong, growing weaker every day, and seeing his face as he was slowly forced to relinquish his dream of once again seeing Great Oaks as it had been—a busy, thriving plantation.

Melissa, with the help of Henry and Amalie, had struggled to run the plantation on her own; but it was not to be. With the slaves freed, and the family fortune given freely to the Confederate cause, only the house and the land were left when the war was over. There had been no choice but to mortgage the property to the bank in town.

If the bank had remained in Southern hands, she probably would have been granted loan extensions, but the bank itself failed and was taken over, along with a stack of overdue mortgages, by a man named Simon Crouse—better known to the local populace as the Carpetbagger.

The Carpetbagger was a smallish man, who appeared taller because of the proportions of his body. He was, as some of the women were fond of remarking, "well set up," with small, neat hands and feet, and a large head with a thick growth of brown hair, which, if you didn't look too closely, gave him a noble air.

However, Melissa was one of those who *did* look closely. The war years had made her expert at judging human nature, and despite Crouse's façade of good manners and elegance, she had seen and taken note of the greedy flicker behind his dark eyes, and the unrestrained sensuality of his mouth, when he thought he wasn't under observation.

Always, from the first time they had met, Simon Crouse had made her uncomfortable. His dark eyes, moving cautiously over her body, made her feel violated, and she always felt a sort of dreadful *eagerness* in the man, a secretive greediness, that she was hard put to set into words, but which made her feel somehow threatened.

Melissa knew that many of the ladies around thought him attractive, even though he was a Yankee moneylender, a carpetbagger of the worst sort. If he kept on his way undeterred, he would soon have his greedy hands on most of Mississippi. She had to admit, in all fairness, that the fact he now owned Great Oaks had some bearing on the way she felt about him.

And speak of the Devil!

Coming toward her was a handsome carriage, drawn by a fine pair of matched horses, throwing up dust, and jouncing importantly up the great drive. She recognized the carriage as belonging to Simon Crouse.

But what drew Melissa's attention was the man on the large, black horse, riding alongside the carriage. The horse was magnificent, the trappings luxurious for these impoverished times, and the man himself was certainly imposing—young, well built, handsome, and expensively dressed. It was obvious that he was accompanying the carriage. What sinister connection could he possibly have with Simon Crouse?

The carriage moved around the curve in the driveway, and stopped at the bottom of the steps, in front of Melissa.

Melissa felt her heart begin to pound, and tried to compose herself. She must handle this confrontation with dignity. That was all she had left.

"Miss Huntoon!" Crouse had climbed down from the carriage, and stood awaiting her on the bottom step. He doffed his tall hat, and inclined his head.

He's like an actor, Melissa thought with distaste.

Crouse turned to the man on the black horse. "I would like to present my associate, Mr. Luke Devereaux. Mr. Devereaux, Miss Melissa Huntoon."

Luke Devereaux swept off his broad-brimmed hat. "It is my pleasure, ma'am," he said in a deep voice. His hair was rich brown in color, and his brown eyes had a slightly golden tint. His full mouth wore a slight smile.

Melissa returned his gaze coldly. "I am sorry that I cannot say the same, sir!" she said tartly. "The circumstances being what they are."

His smile remained in place. "I am in no way responsible for your circumstances, Miss Huntoon."

"Perhaps not," she directed a scathing glance at Crouse, "but you may be held responsible for the company you keep, and certainly Mister Crouse is responsible for my plight!"

"My dear Melissa, that is simply not true," Crouse said with a superior smile. "I have always deplored a lady involving herself in business matters. Not only is it demeaning, but the female mind simply has no grasp of the problems involved. Your plight is a prime example of that fact. The bank held the mortgage on this plantation, and the payments were sadly in arrears. My foreclosure is nothing more than sound business procedure."

"You may call it what you like, Mister Crouse, but that does not excuse this humiliating auction today!"

"That, Melissa, is not my doing. But you do have other creditors, my dear, and I suppose they believe they are entitled to due consideration."

"Daddy collected many fine art objects over the years,

paintings and the like. Many of them are priceless. Now, today, they will be sold off to people who have no idea of their true value!"

"Now there you are mistaken. I fully appreciate them," Crouse said with infuriating smugness. "And this is precisely why I am here today. There are several paintings that I fully intend to have for my very own."

"You?" Her voice was scornful. "What do you know of art, Mister Crouse?"

His smile grew strained, and Melissa knew that she had stung him. The thought gave her pleasure, but she was also a little intimidated by the suppressed fury in his eyes.

"I don't suppose that a young lady like yourself, isolated, as it were, in this charming backwater, has had a chance to learn much about the sophistications of the larger world," he said smoothly. "If you had, you would have learned not to judge people so quickly. The fact that I am a banker does not mean that I do not appreciate the artistic things of life. In truth, I already have an excellent and extensive collection of art, and I intend to add to it this day."

Melissa felt herself flush, and suddenly her bravado failed her, and depression took its place. "I don't suppose it really matters," she said dully. "After today, none of it will belong to the Huntoon family."

Crouse moved closer to her, turning his back on Luke Devereaux. Melissa stole a glance at the man on the horse, but he was apparently watching the parade of visitors as they came up the large, circular driveway.

As she looked back, Melissa saw that Crouse was now quite close to her. Too close! She could see the high color on his prominent cheekbones, and the hungry glitter of his dark eyes.

She wanted nothing so much as to draw back from him, but she did not wish him to think that she feared him.

"There *is* a way your lovely things can remain in your possession, Melissa."

She stared at him, as her heart leaped in sudden hope, then plummeted. She did not trust him. It had to be a trick of some kind. She whispered, "How?"

His voice was low. "Become my wife. Become Mrs. Simon Crouse."

Melissa felt as if her body had lost all heat. She could only stare at him in consternation, as he looked at her intently, his mouth slightly open, and his eyes bright with something that she could not put a name to.

Her mind was chaos. "Why?" she finally managed to whisper, although this was only one of the questions that tumbled pell-mell through her mind.

He smiled slightly. "I need a wife. I have spent years building up my fortune, and now I wish to enjoy it. I have chosen Great Oaks to be my permanent residence, and I would like you to share it with me."

He leaned even nearer, and his eyes burned into Melissa's with frightening force. "Be my wife, Melissa. I can make you happy. You will then not need to leave Great Oaks, nor the family possessions you hold so dear."

The stasis that had paralyzed Melissa broke, and she almost staggered backward, until she felt the stone of the steps behind her. The touch of it seemed to give her strength.

Again he moved toward her, and she swung her parasol around so that it formed a shield in front of her, the sharp point of it directed at Crouse's chest. His smile faded, and his mouth tightened.

"Mr. Crouse," Melissa said softly but clearly, "you presume too much! Whatever made you think. . . ?" She shook her head. "Simon Crouse, I would not marry you if I were starving and you had the last loaf of bread in the world! I look upon you as my enemy. I thought you knew that!"

Crouse's high color slowly faded, and his expression was blank with shock. Despite her own confusion, Melissa sensed that he really had no inkling of how she felt about him, impossible as it seemed.

"Take care, girl," he said, and his voice was as taut and sharp as the flick of a whip. "I am a dangerous man to cross. Perhaps you had better reconsider your words!"

Melissa, looking into those blank eyes, felt sudden fear. She shivered, as she thought of the water moccasin she had once stumbled upon, coiled by the side of a stream—Crouse's eyes now had that same deadly, mindless stare.

She conquered her fear. "I don't need to reconsider," she said, her voice as soft as his. "I spoke my mind. I hate you, Simon Crouse! You are everything that I find despicable in a man, and I could never, never become your wife. I would certainly much rather starve first!"

The corner of Crouse's mouth twitched, and he raised his hand as if to strike her, but paused as Luke Devereaux stepped between them.

"I think the auction is about to start." Devereaux's voice, speaking in a normal tone, seemed to break some kind of terrible spell, and Melissa found that she had been holding her breath.

Crouse turned away, and then, in a swift, lethal movement, wheeled back to face her.

"So be it," he said in an icy voice. "And what you said, about starving to death. That could very well happen, you know. In fact, I shall do everything in my power to see to it, and I have a great deal of power in Mississippi, far more than you know. Good day to you, Miss Huntoon."

There are love stories...
And there are *love* stories!

Over 1 million copies in print!

by William D. Wittliff & Sara Clark
☐ 40-406-9 $2.25

Set against the volatile circumstances of an innocent child's needs, a desperate woman's desires and a brave man's fears, this haunting, sensitive love story uncoils with the sudden urgency of a snapped spring to reveal passions, hatreds...and a choking, heart-wrenching secret whose impact lingers long after the last page has been turned.

Yes, there are love stories....And there are *love* stories! *Raggedy Man* is a story of love that you will never forget!